To Stue

THE WRONG KIND OF CLOUDS

With all best wishes,

Amanda

THE WRONG KIND OF CLOUDS

AMANDA FLEET

Matador
9 Priory Business Park,
Wistow Road, Kibworth Beauchamp,
Leicestershire. LE8 0RX
Tel: 0116 279 2299
Email: books@troubador.co.uk
Web: www.troubador.co.uk/matador
Twitter: @matadorbooks

ISBN 978 1785892 011

British Library Cataloguing in Publication Data.
A catalogue record for this book is available from the British Library.

Printed and bound in the UK by TJ International, Padstow, Cornwall
Typeset in 11pt Aldine401 BT by Troubador Publishing Ltd, Leicester, UK

Matador is an imprint of Troubador Publishing Ltd

For all those who believed in me

TUESDAY MORNING

There it was. The face of the boy he had been searching half the world for, popping out of the computer screen like a firework exploding. A wide smile; the rippled scars from falling into a fire coursing down the right side of his face; a missing left incisor. Patrick had been hunting him for weeks and there he was, in Chicago according to this blog.

Patrick ran a stubby-fingered hand through his thatch of blond hair, pushing it back from a long forehead – a gesture more suited to an Oxford don than a liar and a thief. He sucked his teeth, picked up a pen and added 'email Moyenda – tell him Limbani's in Kent and Mabvuto's in Chicago' to the growing list of things to do that perched at the side of his laptop. He wondered how Moyenda would take the news.

He glanced at his watch, closed down his laptop and picked up his dirty coffee cup. Crossing his flat in three steps he reached the tiny kitchen that led straight off the lounge: too small to swing a rat in. Even his slight frame filled the place, making it feel claustrophobic. The empty walls of the flat depressed him, but it was just stuff that had gone and maybe life was too full of stuff. One day he might have dreamed of a bigger place, full of the trappings of consumerism, but for now this poky, ground-floor cupboard would do. It wasn't as if he had a choice.

He peered through the grimy window as he filled the kettle,

1

staring out at grubby communal bins and the desolate industrial buildings beyond the road. His brain was still on the little boy in the blog and how the hell a street kid had got from Africa to America. He scraped the last few grains out of a coffee jar and lobbed it into an overflowing yellow crate. The jar bounced back out. Patrick sighed, retrieved it and shoved it into a cranny between several beer bottles, and then picked up the whole crate, perching it against his hip as he manipulated the door. He tottered towards the chest-high recycling bins, glancing up at leaden skies between Edinburgh's crowded buildings, his brain whirring. How had Mabvuto got to Chicago? Not under his own steam, that was sure. He opened the lid of the bin and started tossing in the bottles, the enclosed yard amplifying the cacophony as the glass splintered, the sound riding over the rat-tat-rat-tat of a long goods train heading slowly out of the city. As Patrick reached the bottom of the crate, he hefted it upwards to tip in the last few shards and his shoulder deflected something solid just before a searing pain ricocheted around the back of his head.

He sprawled to the ground, yelling out, trying to look behind and see his attacker.

'I can get the money,' he cried. 'I really can this time!'

The man had raised his arm again, a club silhouetted against the monochrome sky. Patrick scrabbled forwards. Using one hand to propel himself, he groped in his pocket with the other, feeling for his mobile. A blow landed on his ankles. The man grabbed at them. Patrick kicked back, his heel connecting with his attacker's chin; the grip on his leg died. He scrambled away, his feet slipping on broken glass, bringing him crashing down heavily on his hand and almost knocking the phone from his grip. He could see the gate to the street and it was open. If only he could reach it. The tinny sound of ringing distracted him briefly as he scuttled behind one of the bins.

'Patrick? Jesus, this had better be good!'

His eyes widened. How had he called *her*?

Movement in the corner of his eye made him turn. The thug was getting up. He stared at his phone.

'Summer? Please. You have to help me!'

His voice rode over hers, urgent and panicky. He crabbed sideways, keeping the bin between him and the man, his eyes flitting between freedom and his approaching assailant.

'There's no escape, you little *fuck*,' said the heavy, his face a sneer.

'Patrick? What the—'

'Help me!'

The man had reached him. He kicked the phone out of his hand and stamped down, crushing it into splinters of plastic and electronics. Patrick's stomach tightened and fear curdled as he saw a thin smile twist the edge of the brute's lip. The man brought his arm down, his weapon arcing perfectly to connect with Patrick's skull.

'You stupid bastard!' he spat as Patrick slumped against the fence, a stream of blood trickling over his face and dripping steadily on to his shirt.

Patrick stared dully, willing his body to move, but he felt like he was made of string. Crippled, he watched his attacker glance around briskly; then he was heaved on to his shoulder like a sack of coal. The man snorted and grunted with the effort. Patrick could smell the man's sweat, feel the scratch of his shirt against his face. He opened his mouth to yell for help but all that he could manage was a faint croak.

The man carried him through the open gate to a van backed up close with its rear door ajar. He hooked his knee into the door to open it, dropped Patrick on the floor of the van and swiftly bound his wrists behind his back with a cable tie, tightening it viciously before repeating the manoeuvre on his ankles. He rolled Patrick into the centre of the van and slammed the doors shut.

It had all taken less than five minutes.

***

Summer Morris stared at the phone, blinking, rain dribbling off her hat and down her neck. For some time now, she wouldn't have pissed on Patrick if he was on fire. Why the hell had he called her?

She tipped her head back, glared at the clouds and sighed heavily. Her short nails clicked over the keys on her phone to call him back as her emotions kaleidoscoped with colours she hadn't felt for months, before fracturing into the hue of a day-old bruise. She recognised the colour as apprehension.

'Hello! You have reached the mobile for Patrick Forrester. I am either already on a call or unavailable right now, so please leave me a message and I'll get back to you as soon as I can.'

She sucked in a quick, impatient breath.

'Patrick? What the hell's happening? Are you okay? It's Summer. Call me back.'

She hung up and clutched the phone in one hand, wrapping her other arm around herself as she sat on the waterproof rug, drawing her knees up to her chin.

'Call me back, you bastard. This had better be some kind of prank.'

It hadn't sounded like a prank. It had sounded horribly like something violent had just happened to Patrick. Summer stared at the rolling hills and glittering loch arranged before her, drumming her fingertips against her knee, for once oblivious to the beauty of her surroundings. She uncoiled long, muscular legs, rearranging them impatiently next to her tripod and camera. The mizzle wormed its way under her collar; the clammy grass was starting to breach the edges of the square she was sitting on.

'I really don't have time for your games, Patrick,' she muttered, shrugging her shoulders to dislodge the damp.

Her thoughts ran back over the phone call. Was it a game? Was it real? If it was real, what the hell was she expected to do? Why call her? Why not call the police?

Why call *her*?

Summer scrabbled in her camera bag to retrieve the notebook

she kept there. She balanced it on her knee, pulled the top off a pen with her teeth, and started to transcribe what she had heard, working quickly. A muffled voice. Speaking English or a foreign language? Not sure. She closed her eyes, screwing her face up as she concentrated. A train in the background? Traffic noises? A train. Yes, definitely a train. The other voice... male, deep, no more than one? What were Patrick's words, his tone, his emotions? What had happened? Had he been hit? Was that last sound his phone being destroyed or was it something horrible happening to Patrick? She wrote as swiftly as she could, trying to capture everything while it was fresh and raw, and then leaned back and reviewed the notes. Should she call the police? Her guts twisted at the thought. What could she tell them if she did? Where was Patrick when he made the call? She closed her eyes, listening to it again in her head. His flat was near a train line. The noise had kept her awake at nights. A million places were by a train line. He could be anywhere.

Why had he called *her*?

The signal strength on her mobile flickered between two bars and none. It was amazing he'd even managed to reach her. She clicked keys again on her phone, finding the number for the police, a slick of sweat forming on her skin despite the cold April air. She didn't want to talk to the police, certainly not over a shit like Patrick. Too many bad experiences. Too much brainwashing from her parents. She stared at the number, not even starting to rehearse words for a call she wasn't sure she could make, but a sickening uneasiness suffused her with the colour of marigolds and would not go away, keeping her from tossing the phone back into her bag. She wondered how people without synaesthesia knew when to trust their feelings.

She dialled slowly, the notebook open on her knee, her insides churning, hanging up twice before finally allowing the call to connect.

'Fife Constabulary.'

She swallowed, her mouth dry.

'Oh, hello. Er, my name is Summer Morris and I don't really know who I should talk to, but I think something bad has happened to someone.'

'Just one moment please.'

She waited. How should she describe Patrick? Could she in all honesty describe him as a friend? It's not how he would describe her. Why had he called her and not someone else? When they put her name and his into the system, would their history flash up on the screen?

She almost hung up, but the line clicked.

'PC Mark Collins. How can I help?'

'Oh hello. I had a very peculiar phone call from someone just now and it sounded like he was being attacked.'

'Just now?'

'Yes.'

'Right. Could you tell me what happened?'

She explained the mysterious call, giving PC Collins Patrick's mobile number and all the details she could remember.

'Do you know where he was when he made the call?' Collins asked.

Summer could hear the impatience in his voice. Her mind ran back over the background sounds and she glanced at the notes she had made.

'Not for sure, but it could well have been his flat. Or near his flat.'

'Which is where?'

'Edinburgh.'

She gave him the address.

'That's not our jurisdiction,' he said, and she could hear relief flood his voice. 'But I will pass all this information on to them. Thank you for calling.'

'Er... is there a case number?' she asked, recognising a brush-off. 'If I wanted to call and ask about this, what reference would I give, please?'

There was an audible sigh on the line before the officer gave her a number.

'But in all likelihood, Ms Morris, it will be nothing.'

'It didn't sound like nothing. I'd appreciate it if you could keep me up to date, please.'

Another sigh on the line.

'It's not our jurisdiction but we'll do our best. Thank you for calling.'

He hung up, leaving Summer with dead air. She dialled Patrick's mobile again, ending the call as soon as his voicemail message started, and then called his home number, only to hear his answerphone message. She clicked on end call.

Turning her collar against the persistent drizzle, she stared at her scuffed boots. The police would be able to do something. That was their job. Surely she had done everything she could? What more could Patrick reasonably expect?

Especially of her.

She started to stow her camera and tripod, preparing to hack back down the hillside to her beaten-up Land Rover, parked below at the end of a stony track. The green of the hillside was so intense it almost hurt to look at it, but uniform grey clouds had rolled in and looked settled for the day, and anyway, her mood was shattered. She would take no pictures worth a damn now.

She tucked her notebook into the top of the bag, frustration flooding her head with ochre.

'Jesus!' she exclaimed, tugging the zip shut. 'What more could I have done?'

Her cries disturbed some small birds in the grass and she watched them fly upwards. Her call to the police had been utterly futile.

***

The van turned a corner, rolling him on to a bruised rib and making him groan. Patrick lifted his head, groggy and disorientated. His left eye wouldn't open but through his right he peered at his surroundings. A crack of light invaded through the edge of the door; he was still in the back of the transit. The hard floor was cold under his shoulders and his arms ached. Wriggling slightly, he realised his hands were tied behind his back with what felt like plastic. A cable tie? Squinting at his feet confirmed his suspicion; a narrow black strip of plastic bit into his flesh above his ankle bone. He licked his lips and tasted the metallic tang of blood. What the hell had happened to him?

His head pounded, retaliating against his efforts to remember. He had been taking out the recycling. Glass in the yellow crate. Someone had been behind the bins.

He lurched sideways again, banging the side of his head on the wheel arch as the van cornered sharply.

'Vuck!'

His voice was thick and blunt, his mouth too bruised to aspirate. Where was he going? He listened. Busy road? Quiet road? Was it worth trying to shout for help? Probably not.

He manoeuvred himself painfully until he was sitting up and able to brace his legs against the movements of the van.

Who had it been by the bins? Someone he knew? Some thug back to give him another reminder? They had hit him. Knocked him to the ground, saying something. What?

Phone. His phone had been in his hand. He'd wanted to call the police but he must have hit speed-dial when he fell. Who had he phoned?

Christ on a bike, it was Summer.

Well, could have been worse, could have been Kate. Could have been better, could have been Helen, but he wasn't stupid enough to have either of them on speed-dial. Sheer laziness that Summer still was.

She didn't hang up. Would she help?

How can she help, stupid? How can she know where you are? You don't even know where you are.

We're slowing. We're stopping.

'Help! Help! Help! Help!'

The van door swung open.

'Shut the fuck up! No one can hear you anyway!'

Patrick squinted at the brightness, trying to see the man's features against the sudden light.

'Who are you?'

'Someone you'll wish you'd never met. Where the fuck's your shoe?'

The man climbed into the back of the van and kicked Patrick's foot. Patrick gazed greedily at the freedom through the van door and thought he caught sight of someone walking a dog.

'Help! Help! Aagh!'

The man swung his boot into Patrick's face, cutting off his cries.

'I *said*, shut the fuck up. No one will help you.'

He jumped back down and slammed the door shut. Patrick reeled backwards, blinking away stars and spitting blood.

The man walking his dog would have seen and heard nothing.

TUESDAY AFTERNOON

Moyenda Mkumba swung off the bicycle as he reached Masala Primary School in Bangwe, on the outskirts of Blantyre. The school was like a thousand others in Malawi – orange-brown mud bricks, a dusty yard with a few trees to offer respite from the blazing sun in the hot season; too many kids and not enough teachers. He didn't need the shade today. He liked late April. In a couple of months, the heat would be building and by October they would be desperate for the rains to come and quench the land, but right now, it was warm enough and dry enough. He smiled. Goldilocks weather.

He propped the bike against the wall, unstrapped his satchel, and ducked out of the sun to read his notes ready for his weekly meeting with the headmistress. Through the open door, the sounds of lessons vied with one another and Chichewa mingled with English. He glanced up and smiled at Chotsani Banda who ushered him into her office.

'Moyenda! Come in. Come in.'

'Chotsani. It is good to see you. You look very well.'

Chotsani waved at the wicker chair opposite her desk, her smile wide. Moyenda grinned broadly and sat, resting his empty satchel against her wooden desk. A light breeze filtered through the window behind her. As ever, her desk was neat and ordered with a single pile of files right in the centre. Old wooden filing cabinets stood like sentries along the wall, their brass bindings glowing in the light.

'How are the boys doing?' Moyenda asked, shuffling though his sheaf of papers. 'Is Justin still preferring to hang out at the airport, looking for rich tourists to carry their bags, rather than come to school?'

Chotsani laughed, her long earrings jangling as she did so.

'Yes, although I have explained to him that he will get more money if he can speak English to them and that he should think about the long term. He could learn how to drive and get work bringing them into Blantyre as well as carrying their bags. He will be all right. He is a clever boy, but maybe he was on the streets for too long. He does not seem to like being enclosed by walls. Or rules.'

Moyenda nodded, smiling wryly, and jotted some notes on his papers.

'And Henry? Have you seen him recently?'

Chotsani shook her head, her face suddenly serious. She folded her hands carefully.

'Not for weeks. Nor Tendai. And they were so good – they were always here and doing well in class. They seemed so happy to come to school. I don't understand. Have they gone back to their families?'

'They have no family. Both of them lost their fathers to AIDS so long ago they can hardly remember them and then last year their mothers too. Is Tendai's sister Joyce still coming to school?'

'Yes, but she says she has not seen Tendai for weeks. She thinks he has run away, but she does not know why.'

Moyenda's brow furrowed. There was no reason for Tendai to run away. Or Henry for that matter. They had both been living at one of the few orphanages that Moyenda rated highly and had been overjoyed to be registered with a school for the first time and get their brand new, bright green uniforms so they could attend classes. At eight and nine, they were too young to be on the streets but their plight was hardly unique in Malawi where there were over a million orphans. Moyenda had found them nearly two years ago, begging on a street corner, scared to go home if they hadn't collected much and unable to go to school because their mothers could not afford it. He had talked to them, talked to their mothers, and persuaded the women that if his charity, Samala, bought the boys their uniforms and books then they could afford to send them to school. He had watched them flourish and do well, proud to be at school and determined to show 'Uncle Moyenda' that he was right to have helped them. They still begged at weekends and Moyenda had been dismayed to see Henry carrying heavy bags for people in the market for a few kwacha, but at least they were getting an education during the week.

Then three months ago first one of them had vanished, then the other. Henry had disappeared first, not returning after a weekend. A few weeks later, the same thing happened with Tendai. The boys in the project often did come and go, but they usually showed up in their community again at some point. Tendai and Henry were both from Bangwe but no one had seen even their shadow since their disappearance. Moyenda was worried. They were the sixth and seventh boys to have vanished in the past eight months and they were also the youngest.

He shook his head. There were thirty-two other children enrolled with Samala and however worried he was about Henry and Tendai there were plenty of other children who also needed his attention. He noted the two were still absent from school and was about to move on to the next child on his list. At Masala there were six other boys he needed to check on before travelling on to two more schools. It would be a long day.

'You are fretful, Moyenda,' said Chotsani, breaking into his thoughts. 'You think something bad has happened?'

Moyenda looked up.

'I do not know. But yes. Yes, that is what I fear.'

***

12

The bench in the park was cold and damp. Kate Hampton perched carefully, glancing around her, her fingers fidgeting on the handles of the large leather handbag grasped in her fists. No one recognised her. No one decided that they absolutely had to come and talk to her about manifesto pledges or waiting lists. A young man stared at her and her palms became slick before she realised he was staring because she was acting weirdly. She fingered the handles of the bag again then brushed a stray lock of dark hair back from her face. She tried to relax. Tried to look like she was just an ordinary woman taking a few minutes to sit down on a bench. It was hard to look natural when her heart was hammering in her chest and her anxiety levels were soaring. She clung on to the bag like a lifebuoy, suddenly terrified by the thought of a mugger snatching it from her and finding an unexpected bonus in the envelope in the side pocket.

He was late. What if he didn't come at all? Where would that leave her? A few thousand better off but with a sword of Damocles still hanging over her. Could he afford not to come?

She glanced around, trying to spot him in the smattering of people coming and going around her. The park was a small oasis of green in the city, full of squabbling seagulls and scabby pigeons scrounging for scraps. Office workers from the surrounding buildings came here to eat their lunch, grasping at the oxygen here, kicking dispassionately at the begging birds when they came too close. Two young women were laughing, sitting on the next bench down, feeding the remnants of their lunch to some of the pigeons. Across from her were two businessmen, each clinging to the far edge of the bench to maximise their personal space, each reading the same broadsheet. All witnesses, she suddenly realised with a sick feeling.

She wished she'd brought a paper or a book to read – maybe she'd feel more natural and less like there was an enormous arrow above her head, screaming 'Suspicious! Look! Look!!'

It was a huge sum of money. Yes she could afford it financially, but it was a life-changing, career-ending meeting if anyone found out. She checked her watch. He was very late. She would have to go soon. She fished her mobile out of her bag, wondering where the hell he was. Would it be incriminating to call him? She stared at the phone for a moment then put it back into her bag, unused. Her temper was rising. It had taken a huge effort to squeeze this time into her packed schedule and she couldn't afford to be late back. There was only so long you could claim to have a screaming headache and need some air. She didn't want to think what it would mean if she didn't pay on time. Not this of all weeks.

She lifted her bag on to her lap and tugged open the zip on the side pocket to peek at the edge of the envelope. Satisfied that her savings hadn't gone anywhere, she re-zipped the pocket and bounced the bag on her knees for a moment. Her eyes did one last sweep around the rendezvous point then she swallowed and started walking briskly back to her office, her brain churning.

She didn't have a Plan B.

***

'Rob? Rob, are you home?'

Helen Wright pushed the door to her flat closed, juggling two plastic shopping bags and her handbag and tipped her head to listen for sounds of her brother. There was no answer. Taking the bags through to the lounge she sighed at the mess there. This was supposed to be a showcase for her blossoming interior design business; somewhere she could bring clients and impress them. It wouldn't impress them like this. The sleeping bag her brother was using lay like a shed skin, rumpled and wrinkled. And still on the sofa. On the floor were dirty socks and shorts, a mug with scummy dregs of coffee in it, a used cereal bowl and spoon and a T-shirt.

She rubbed her eyes, groaning. She had just wanted to come home and relax.

'Your sergeant would have had your guts if you'd been this slobby in the army,' Helen muttered, starting to pick up.

But the army wasn't something they talked about any more.

Helen straightened the room up, smoothing her hand over the velvet cushions and rich, silk curtains. It was usually her favourite room – lavish and opulent yet still managing to be cosy and relaxing – but since Rob had moved in it was a constant source of stress. Maybe if he managed a few more jobs for her he'd get back on his feet and be able to move out. Mind you, she'd been hoping that since Christmas, four months ago.

She crumpled into a seat and hauled her organiser out of her capacious handbag. She read over the bookings.

'Did you make it to the McKays',' she wondered aloud, 'or did something *happen*?'

Her mouth twisted on the last word as she remembered the last time he'd got into a tailspin. Yes, it was hard for him after what he'd gone through, but her patience was running out. She sighed, closing her eyes and feeling guilty again, but she ran a business, not a charity. Money wasn't abundant enough for him to skip off and leave clients in the lurch but what could she say? The two occasions when she'd tentatively suggested he see about getting help he'd gone ballistic. According to Rob, hard work and lots of exercise was all that was needed. Him and his damned macho pride.

She unpacked one of her bags, crooning over the fabric samples in it and trying to work out the best way to display them. She laid them aside, still unsure, and carried the other bag through to the kitchen. It too was a showcase; part of the image. It too bore traces of Rob's stay. She bit down her irritation and unpacked the bag which contained the makings of dinner.

'Am I eating alone again?' she muttered, picking up her phone.

He answered on the third ring.

'Hey Robbie. You going to be back for dinner?'

'Hi sis. Er, no. I'm going to be away for a couple of days. Sorry. I should have left a note.'

The line sounded crackly. Helen scrunched her face up.

'Did you go to the McKays' today?' she asked, ready to flinch.

'I did. They said that they wanted me to go back next week because they hadn't finished clearing the space. Is that okay?'

'Of course.'

Helen pulled her organiser towards her, flipped to the diary and scanned through the days.

'Next week was pretty clear anyway,' she said. 'I'll tell them Tuesday, shall I? Week today?'

'Whatever suits them best. I'm just the decorator.'

She ignored the edge to his voice.

'So, where are you? Somewhere nice?' she asked, snapping the fastener closed on the Filofax and leaning back against the counter.

'I'm over in the west. After the McKays cancelled me, I called a mate from…' he tailed off for a moment. 'Called a mate, and we're doing a spot of fishing. Archie also called about the place in Skye. Do you need me back?'

Helen was secretly relieved to have the place to herself for a while.

'No. Not at all. The diary's empty. Have fun!'

They said their goodbyes and hung up. Helen stared at her mobile, spinning it round in a circle. She desperately wanted to call Patrick. Talk to him. Apologise. Work things out. Make things right between them again.

She knew he wouldn't answer if she called.

***

LB Stewart was bored and he knew it.

He should go out, do something, go somewhere; except he preferred company and everyone else was at work. He smoothed a hand over the back of his head, his cropped hair prickling his palm.

There were only so many times you could tidy an immaculate flat.

The catalogue in his hand stirred up a mixture of memories.

It had been tucked into the magazine rack that squatted by the side of the sofa. The rack was hers as well. LB picked it up and turned it upside down, allowing more of Anya's catalogues and magazines to slither out and flop on the floor like dead fish. He stepped over them to carry the rack through to the hall. Next time he was out he would take it to Oxfam.

Did he have any regrets? He walked back to the lounge and stared at the pile on the floor. No. Not really. Anya could never have been described as high maintenance, but she'd needed more time and effort than LB could muster and she wasn't one to accept second place. However, it was galling to be reminded, yet again, that he couldn't find anyone who commanded more commitment from him than his job.

He flipped through the catalogue. It was for a company that made expensive leather briefcases and personal organisers. Some of the pages had their corners turned down and he looked to see what she had been marking. A turquoise laptop bag on one page and on another a notebook, similarly coloured, but to his mind just mismatched enough to be infuriating. He tossed the catalogue on the heap then scooped the whole lot up and threw them into the recycling crate in the hall.

A final legacy of Anya hung above him and he straightened up and gazed at it. It was an abstract by an up-and-coming Fife artist. Anya, who knew about these things, had talked to LB about the artist and taken him to an exhibition of his work. He had seen the abstract and fallen in love with it, only at ease once it was in his possession. Every time he looked at it, he felt a new emotion and marvelled at the artist's skill. He had toyed with hanging it in the lounge but feared he'd get too used to seeing it and that it would lose its freshness. Here in the hall he could see it several times a day but not have it constantly in his vision.

Having drunk his fill of its glory, he breathed deeply, returned to the open plan area and headed for the kitchen end to make coffee. While it brewed, he flicked idly through his collection of cookbooks, leafing through each one then replacing it precisely in its original place on the crammed shelf. He settled on his favourite – a book given to him by his mother and one which instantly made him think of warm summers, fresh bread from the boulangerie and greaseproof-paper-wrapped packets from the charcuterie. He turned the pages slowly, ever amused to see the stains and grease-marks on the pages he referred to the most. He checked through the fridge, the book cradled in the crook of his arm like a child, occasionally cross-checking with the recipe book as he chose what to prepare for dinner.

He should have gone to France after all.

It was his week off. In fact, it was his first week off in months. Yet it was only Tuesday and already he was fed up. He and Anya had planned to visit his parents for the weekend and then go on to Paris for a few days. Of course, he had cancelled that when he'd cancelled their relationship, but with hindsight he should have just gone on his own. He might have managed to unwind, clear his mind, stop thinking about work. His own fault for being stubborn.

He poured a mug of coffee to take through to the lounge, tucking the recipe book under his arm. Eschewing the sofa, he sank down into a beaten leather club chair, its decrepitude making it stand out in the otherwise pristine flat. The dark wood of the simple furniture was silhouetted crisp and clean against the pale walls. A square table stood guard in the window and a low side table nestled between the cream sofa and the battered chair. A crimson cushion, a scarlet vase and a print on the wall broke the monochrome, like splashes of blood around the flat. Apart from the chair, the place could have stood in for an advert for IKEA. Only tidier. The chair, however, was for holidays; somewhere to lounge, somewhere to drink too much whisky. Somewhere to allow the laissez-faire French side to escape from the Calvinist Scots.

LB drew one knee up to support the book in his lap, his arm hanging down over the side of the chair, his fingers tapping lightly on the leather. His tall, bulky frame filled the chair and its leather hugged his body. He read through the recipes, sipping his coffee, trying to tame his restlessness. A wry smile flitted across his face as he thought he should work harder at relaxing. It took him at least a week to move out of work mode and into holiday mode, by which time he was back at his desk.

Time off came so rarely with his work. He knew he should use it more profitably but was blowed if he knew what to do. The last time he'd been single with time on his hands, he'd redecorated the flat but it scarcely needed doing again so soon. He needed a project.

Coffee finished, he returned to the kitchen and propped the book he'd been reading on to a stand, open at his chosen dish. LB leaned over to the end of the breakfast bar that divided the kitchen from the lounge and set his iPod to play on shuffle. To an eclectic compilation, LB rolled his sleeves up and donned a large green apron. He worked steadily, humming or singing along to the music, tasting the meal as he went. Only when all the preparation was complete and the dish was in the oven did his ennui return.

'*Merde*,' he muttered, pulling his apron off and folding it neatly.

He turned the music volume to low and picked up his mobile, dialling his partner at work.

'Ben! No surprise. You bored?'

LB chuckled.

'Hi, Sandy. Yes. How's work going?'

'Miraculously, we are holding up without you.'

LB listened to the bedlam in the background, picturing the chaos that was Sandy's home life. He heard Sandy's wife Isobel ask who was calling and the voices muffle as Sandy put his hand over the receiver to answer before the line cleared again.

'Sorry, Ben. Izzy was just asking me who it was. What's up?'

'Nothing, nothing. Just as you say, bored.'

'Ben, it's your holiday! Enjoy it! Christ, I wish I was having a week off!'

The sounds of three small children screeching in the background drowned out Sandy's words and LB glanced around his spotless, empty flat.

'Are you going to the pub later?' he asked, despite knowing that once Sandy had gone home he never made it back out again in the evening.

'Oh, no, sorry. Probably not. Some of the others might be there though.'

Again the line went muffled as Sandy called out to one of the kids. LB waited, rubbing the back of his head. It was a few moments before Sandy returned.

'Was there anything you really wanted?' he started before LB's growling laugh interrupted.

'I mean, it's time for the kids to go to bed,' Sandy added, 'but if you needed to talk or something...'

'No... Go! Go! I was just bored and needing inspiration. Go enjoy your family. I should have thought and looked at the time before I called you. I'll pop down to the pub later, see if anyone's there. See you next week.'

Sandy laughed.

'Ten quid you're in the station before then!'

LB chuckled.

'See you next week. Go sort the kids out.'

He rang off and poured himself a large glass of red wine before switching on the TV to catch the end of the news. A chilly-looking young reporter was standing in the street near a strip club in Edinburgh, waving her hand towards a cordoned off skip, explaining the discovery of a second body earlier that day. LB watched the report, wondering who was heading up the inquiry in Edinburgh. He sipped his wine as the programme moved on to cover the elections, showing the shadow education minister smiling through gritted teeth as she helped out with some finger painting at a primary school, followed by a glimpse of the health minister as she opened the new wing of a maternity unit.

If LB had realised how much the health minister was going to feature in his forthcoming week he'd have paid a bit more attention.

TUESDAY EVENING

Summer leaned back into the corner of the sofa, nursing a glass of wine, wriggling her toes. She too was watching the local news, wondering if there would be any mention of Patrick's disappearance. There wasn't. Summer shook her head, fed up of hearing about the forthcoming Scottish elections and the various politicians as they annoyed people around the country pretending to be hugely interested in the artwork of primary school children while in reality looking for any popularity-boosting photo opportunity. Once the weather forecast had finished, Summer switched the television off. She wanted to read but her brain was too flittery over the call from Patrick and the serried rows of books lining the room mocked her. Should she call the police again? She chewed her thumbnail, staring at her mobile, old encounters staying her hand. Finally she picked up her phone and dialled, trying to quell her unease.

'Good evening. Fife Constabulary. How can I help?'

'Oh, good evening. My name is Summer Morris. I called earlier today to report an incident and I wondered if there was any update on it. I have a case number if that's any help.'

'Yes, Ms Morris. Could I get that number from you, please?'

She reeled it off and waited.

'One moment. I'll just put you through to someone who was dealing with it.'

The line went quiet, and then just as Summer was contemplating hanging up, a man spoke.

'Hello.'

'Oh, hello. Is that PC Collins?'

'No, he's off duty now. This is DC Andrew McGinty. How can I help?'

Summer wondered why the desk sergeant had asked for all the details if he wasn't going to pass them on. She bit down her irritation – it wasn't this man's fault – and repeated them all.

'One moment. Oh yes. That was passed on to Edinburgh. That's about as much as I can tell you, I'm afraid.'

'Who's dealing with it in Edinburgh, please?'

'Er… doesn't say. It does say to contact you with any updates though.'

'Right.'

'Okay. Sorry I couldn't be more help. Thanks for calling. Bye.'

He rang off, his chipper voice annoying Summer and dusting the edges of her feelings with brimstone. She sighed and looked up the number for the Lothian police. Her call to them yielded even less information than the one to Fife. Yes, the information had been logged. No, they couldn't tell her any more. Summer thanked the woman and hung up, feeling frustrated and helpless. Maybe if she talked to someone face-to-face she might get somewhere. It was going to be too rainy for good photos tomorrow anyway. She smiled thinly. There would be the wrong kind of clouds, as Patrick had always said to tease her.

Of course, the downside of talking to someone in person involved stepping inside a police station – something Summer had sworn she would never do again.

***

Kate worked slowly, polishing the cutlery with a tea towel, setting the table carefully. Dinner was simmering away nicely on the range cooker in the kitchen, the house was neat and tidy and her BlackBerry was set to take messages. She needed no disturbances tonight if she was going to mend things. The dining room set, she went upstairs to shower and change, sweeping her long dark hair up into a twist and choosing subtly scented, luxurious products for the shower. Twenty minutes later, wrapped in a fluffy robe, she contemplated her clothes, standing in front of her lingerie drawer, trying to remember if any of the pieces could potentially bring disaster down on the evening. Kate picked through the lace and silk. What had she never worn for Patrick?

Suddenly she felt dragged down into a swirling murk and sank on to the end of the bed, shoulders hunched, head bowed. How could she have done all that? Made such a mess of everything? Because he was a charmer, a rake, a bit of fun, where Paul was always so serious. She had been flattered by the attention. It had started with silly flirting and then all of a sudden she'd found herself in a hotel in the middle of the afternoon discovering how good he was in bed. After that… well, after that Kate seemed to have entered a parallel world where none of it seemed quite real or to have any consequences. It had been so liberating to shake off the shackles of her upbringing; so invigorating to step outside the cage of her life and be who she craved to be. And then like an addict chasing a high she had gone back for more. And like an addict, the highs were never high enough and she was never quite satisfied.

She cradled her head in her hands. How could she expect forgiveness? How could she have been so naïve as to think there'd be no consequences? Or so vain as to think Patrick had actually found her attractive as a woman and not just groomed her to be a meal ticket? She scowled at her reflection. The empty side of the marriage bed behind her mocked her. Paul hadn't left, just moved into the spare. He hasn't left *yet*, she corrected herself and flopped backwards on to the satin bedspread, rehearsing lines in her head, trying to get the wording just right. She needed the evening to go well or she would be sunk.

After dithering for an age over her clothes, she finally dressed, dabbed perfume behind her ears and in her cleavage, put on enough make-up to look attractive but not overdone and clicked her way over the polished wooden floors to the lounge to wait.

She was fidgety, nervous. Really, she should be doing a million other things right now, ready for next Thursday's vote. For a start she should probably be on the phone to her party leader to tell him what had happened and offer her resignation but she was still hoping that none of it would come out. If Paul could just stay until the votes were counted and if Patrick could keep his mouth shut, maybe she could get back in, and then in the inevitable reshuffle that would follow, manage to step down without everything coming out. She had tonight to work on Paul. She still hadn't managed to reach Patrick. The little shit was probably screening his calls, and leaving a message that would cover what she needed to say would be akin to writing a political suicide note. She was not about to give him more ammunition to kill her with.

She jiggled her foot and started to flick listlessly through a magazine although her brain was still running through phrases. She tossed the paper down and paced the room. She daren't call to see what time he would be back, in case this triggered another row and he left without her managing to talk to him. Dinner had been planned accordingly – something that could simmer and simmer half the night and not ruin. It couldn't do to burn the food when she needed the night to go swimmingly.

At last she heard the front door open and she turned, trying to get her smile just right. Paul came in, looking suspicious.

'Didn't expect you to be home,' he said, holding up a bag. 'I got a takeaway on the way back. Assumed you'd be working late. As usual.'

'Oh. Well, I thought we could have an evening together. I cooked.'

He didn't advance any further into the room.

'I can smell it. Smells nice,' he said grudgingly. 'But won't the party need you for something?'

'Not tonight. I've said no calls. We need to talk.'

No, no, no. It was not how she had rehearsed things. He wasn't supposed to have bought a Chinese on the way home and none of the lines were coming out right. And now he was scowling.

'Do we? I thought we'd pretty much covered everything already.'

She crossed the room to take his hands but he stepped back, leaving her stranded in empty space.

'Paul. Please? I really want to try and work things out with you.'

'Isn't that all a bit late?'

'I hope not. I had a mad few months; we have years of marriage and two children. I was wrong, utterly, utterly wrong to do what I did and I really want to try and mend things with you. Please, can we have dinner together and talk?'

Paul studied her, the bag of takeaway clutched in front of him like a barrier.

'What about trust? I can't trust you any more. How can we mend things if I can't trust you?'

She swallowed, focusing on her expression.

'I know and I understand that, but can't we at least try?'

'What, with you busy all the time and working late so much? How would I ever manage to believe you were genuinely at work and not shagging some toy boy in a hotel?'

Kate breathed steadily, garnering phrases, trying to wrest control of the conversation again.

'Please, can we sit down at least?'

She sat, even though this ceded physical equality, and looked up at him. He stood for a moment and she held her breath. He would either walk out right now, or he would sit. If he sat, she would manage to talk to him and sort things out. Paul looked down at the bag in his hand, his jaw hard, and then looked at her before finally putting the bag on the coffee table and perching on the edge of a chair. She smiled. She hadn't been a politician for twenty years for nothing.

'Paul, I know you won't believe me when I say that I love you, but I do, and I am appalled at what I've done to you and to us. Even discounting what happened with Patrick, and I know that that's impossible,' she said hurriedly, seeing the expression on his face, 'I was damaging our marriage with work. The balance was all wrong. I was hardly home and always distracted.'

She paused, monitoring every aspect of him. How was he breathing? How tense was he? How angry was he? How was this playing?

'And assuming that I get re-elected next Thursday,' she continued, 'I'm going to resign as minister. So I can spend more time with you. If you want that.'

'Are you really resigning for me or because that bastard you were shagging was going to tell the press and you'd have to fall on your sword anyway?'

'I'm really resigning for you. What's happened… it made me take a good, hard look at my life and sort out my priorities and my priority is you. I would do anything to save what we have.'

'Anything? Including keeping your knickers on when some strapping young man wants to rip them off?'

Kate lowered her eyes and looked at her hands, calming herself.

'Anything,' she said, her gaze sweeping back up over her husband.

'I don't know, Kate. I think I want some time away from you. I need some space to think about things.'

He started to rise. Panic rippled through Kate.

'At least stay until next weekend?'

He turned, fury and abhorrence in his face.

'Anything, huh? Except lose your seat in parliament. I'm going.'

The rehearsed words abandoned her leaving her with pure desperation.

'Paul, please! I need you to stay. I'd hoped you might help me sort all this out. If you go, Patrick wins and I have nothing! *We* are ruined!'

He paused, looking at her with complete loathing.

'You should have thought about that before you shagged a bastard like him. It's not my fault that you messed up. God, you really are a piece of work, Kate. I might have sorted things out for you in the past but why should I make this go away?'

'For our marriage? For the kids?'

'For your career?' he spat back.

'I've already said that I'll step down.'

'Step? I think Patrick's going to push you, isn't he?'

Kate tightened her grip on her emotions and tried to recapture control. She had played it badly and she needed Paul to stay.

'That's all over. Behind me. I want to make it work with you. I know I haven't spent enough time and energy on you and that I've been too focused on work. Please? I want to try and make it work with us.'

He stared at her, his gaze levelling.

'When would you have told me? If he hadn't written to me? If I hadn't read your emails?'

She paused, fiddling with her nails.

'Probably the weekend you found out. It was all over with him; I realised what a fool I'd been and what I would be throwing away.'

'Your career,' he repeated, his lip curled.

'Yes. But more than that. You. Us. Everything.'

'I can't stay, Kate. I'm too hurt. But I'll get Patrick Forrester off your back.' He shook his head. 'How could you have been so stupid?' he muttered.

She chewed her lip, her eyes pleading with him.

'Please stay?' she said.

'No. I can't be sure if you want me to stay so that you get re-elected or because you want to be with me. I'm going to pack.'

He turned on his heel and she listened to his footsteps on the stairs, a lead weight in her guts. She had lost. She felt as if she was sitting inside a house of cards that was slowly collapsing around her, card by card, and she was powerless to stop it. A few minutes later Paul returned, an overnight bag in his hand. He stood in the doorway.

'I'll come and get more things tomorrow, when you're out. I'll be at a hotel. I'll let you know which one.'

She nodded, her tears only just in check.

'Good luck with the election,' he sneered.

She smiled bitterly and looked away. Paul leaned over and picked up the bag of takeaway.

'Don't worry about Patrick. I'll sort it out. I always do, don't I?'

'But you won't stay?'

He shook his head. A moment later the front door banged and Kate sank down into a chair, her head in her hands.

'Patrick, you fucking shit.'

WEDNESDAY MORNING

A cloud of paparazzi thronged the route to the car. When had they arrived? Had they camped there all night? It was only 7 a.m. *Why* had they arrived? Kate's mind raced. She didn't believe in coincidence. Someone had told them to be there. She swallowed. Going out the back wouldn't help as in the end she would have to run the gauntlet past them. She watched them as they lounged by the gate, smoking, chatting among themselves like it was all a lark for them. It probably was. The thought made her seethe. Her life was falling apart and they were enjoying not only watching, but participating in its downfall.

Kate stepped back from the window, shoulders bowed, and glanced at her image in the mirror. She looked tired and haggard despite the careful application of make-up. A strand of her hair had fallen loose from her chignon but she left it hanging free. Her bag was ready by the door and she checked through it, taking her time. To have to make a return journey through the crowd of them because she'd forgotten something would be beyond bearable. Her phone still had no new messages from Paul. She tucked it back into a pocket and ran her eye over her diary, groaning at the itinerary ahead. Straightening up, she grasped the door handle, fixed a smile to her face and prepared to face the onslaught.

The second she opened the door, the clamour started.

'Mrs Hampton? Mrs Hampton? Where's your husband, Mrs Hampton? Has he left you?'

Kate fought hard to keep the thin smile plastered to her face and marched past them, trying to keep her head high despite being jostled from every side.

'Mrs Hampton? Was your husband having an affair? Have you thrown him out?'

Oh dear God, they really don't know yet. She kept her lips clamped firmly together and struggled to her car. A feeling of security flowed over her once she was inside and the doors were locked. She turned the engine over and started to creep through the journalists, wishing that they'd get out of the way, knowing that she really couldn't clip any of them with the car. Eventually they peeled away and she put her foot down.

At the party offices she was relieved to be able to park near the back entrance and so escape the scattering of journalists hanging around the front. She headed straight for her office, glad to see that her stalwart PA, Penny, was already there. With a quick gesture she beckoned Penny into her office, waiting until she'd closed the door behind her before speaking.

'Penny. Do you want to sit down? Before we get on to today's things there's something I need to tell you.' Kate waited until Penny was seated, her elegant legs crossed at the ankle, her face alert. 'Last night, Paul and I had a huge row… it doesn't matter what about… and… well… he's moved into a hotel for a few days.'

Penny's eyes widened but she said nothing. Kate carried on briskly.

'I have no idea how the press found out, but this morning there were some journalists sniffing around, looking for a story that isn't really there. The phone will no doubt be jammed with them wanting some kind of interview or comment, but really, it's a storm in a teacup. The official line will of course be "no comment".'

Penny nodded, her pen still hovering over her notebook.

'Shall I get Douglas on the line for you? Or have you already spoken to him?'

Kate's heart sank.

'Yes, please could you get him for me? That would be very helpful. I haven't managed to speak to him yet.'

Again Penny nodded.

'Anything else?' she asked.

'Er. No, not right now. Let me brief Douglas and then we can run through what's happening today.'

Penny rose to go. At the door she turned back.

'I'm sure he'll come back, Kate,' she said, smiling sympathetically.

Her kindness almost brought tears to Kate's eyes. She nodded in return.

'Oh, I bloody hope so,' she said, trying to laugh, but unable to believe her own reassurances.

'I'll get Douglas for you.'

Kate collapsed back in her chair once Penny had gone, fighting her tears and trying to compose what she would say to Douglas Rae, the party leader who had built his reputation on decency and moral probity. She hadn't had time to form coherent sentences before Penny told her that Douglas was on line one.

She swallowed, pressed the button on her phone and tried to sound bright and honest.

'Douglas. Good morning.'

'Good morning, Kate. What did you need to talk to me about?'

She coughed. His soft highland burr was low and soothing. A voice that had wooed the public into voting for him. One that oozed honesty and uprightness. Would Paul come back? If Paul came back, she wouldn't have to tell Douglas that she'd had an affair. At least, not until after the election results were in. Then he could reshuffle her quietly out of the Cabinet and on to the back benches and everything would be fine.

'Kate?'

A tinge of impatience was creeping into his voice.

'Sorry, Douglas. I'm sorry. It's a difficult morning. I have to tell you that Paul and I had a row last night… and that Paul has moved into a hotel for a few days, just while we sort things out. The papers have got hold of it, though goodness knows how, and have been doorstepping me this morning. I hope it won't affect the election coverage.'

'What was the row about?'

'Something and nothing. It's nothing.'

'Kate, husbands don't move out to hotels over nothing. Did he leave or did you throw him out?'

'He left.'

Her mouth was dry. Could she really keep her affair from Douglas for another week?

'So what have you done? To make him move out?'

'Worked too hard. Not spent enough time on him or our marriage.'

'I see. And that's all, Kate? Nothing else? You've not had an affair?'

He sounded like a kindly priest who, once she confessed, would absolve her of her sins. If only it were that easy. She took a deep breath.

'No. No, I haven't. I just haven't spent enough time and attention on Paul and he felt that he didn't want to be with me any more. The electioneering hasn't helped – brought it to a head, I guess.'

Once she started down this line, the words seemed to flow easily. Yes – blame it on work, getting home late, not having enough energy to focus on Paul. The lies and the half-lies slid out effortlessly and by the time she'd finished speaking she'd almost convinced herself. There was a pause on the other end of the line.

'Please be honest with me, Kate. If you have had an affair or done something foolish, it would be better to have it managed than for it to be revealed by the press.'

Kate swallowed.

'Paul thinks that I have, but he's wrong. When would I have the time?' she trilled.

'Well, let's try and keep you out of the headlines, shall we? It's only eight days until the election. Can we keep this under wraps until then? Are there skeletons hiding in closets that could leap out at the last minute and derail us?'

'I don't think so,' she said, screwing her face up.

'Good. Then keep saying "no comment" until you can sort things out with Paul. What's your schedule for today?'

Kate glanced down at her diary.

'I'm canvassing in Edinburgh this morning then over to Glasgow for the afternoon, taking in Stirling and Perth on the way back.'

'No wonder Paul thinks he doesn't see enough of you. Give me a few minutes and let's see if we can lift a bit of that schedule for you. I'll call you again in a few minutes.'

He rang off. Kate placed the phone back in its cradle and shook her head slowly. Penny popped her head around the door.

'How did it go?'

Kate didn't respond, still deep in her musings over what she hadn't said. Would it backfire spectacularly on her?

'Shall we get on with our meeting?' asked Penny, hovering by the chair.

Kate looked up finally.

'Er, Douglas is going to get back to me. He's going to try and lighten my load for today so that I can try and patch things up with Paul. Let's wait until he calls back? Penny, I could murder a good cup of tea.'

Penny nodded and retreated, leaving Kate to think. What had she done? She should have confessed all. Douglas would have been furious but nowhere near as irate as he would be if everything came out and he realised she'd lied to him. He would have managed the situation, had a chance to employ damage limitation. If everything came out now, the shit would really hit the fan.

If only Paul would come back. Maybe if Douglas could lighten her load, she and Paul would manage to talk and patch things up tonight? Then the paparazzi would back off, there wouldn't be a story and even if everything about Patrick came out, she would still manage to weather the storm politically. Could she manage to talk Paul round?

Penny disturbed her thoughts by returning with a cuppa. She smiled kind-heartedly at Kate and looked as if she was about to speak when Kate's phone rang. It was Douglas. Kate waved Penny out of the room.

'Douglas, thanks for getting back to me so quickly.'

'Good news, Kate. I've managed to shift the Stirling and Perth meet-and-greets to Phil, so you'll have to be nice to him for a few weeks, but you should be able to get back from Glasgow at a reasonable time now.'

'Thank you. That's enormously kind and helpful of you.'

'It's fine. I know how tough on a marriage this job can be. You get things sorted out with Paul tonight and then the story dies.'

Beneath the kindness in his voice was a current. Kate swallowed, recognising instructions when she heard them.

'Absolutely, Douglas. Thank you again for being so understanding.'

'Sort things out with Paul. Marriage is a blessing.'

He ended the call and Kate breathed deeply. She glanced up as Penny re-entered.

'Perth and Stirling are off the agenda today,' Kate said, smiling thinly.

'Oh excellent. The day was bloody awful with that much crammed in!'

She sat down opposite Kate, her notebook still in hand.

'Good on Douglas. I know he can be a bit…' she hunted for the right word, '*traditional* at times, but he will always back his team.'

Kate's smile thinned even further and she felt like a complete Judas.

Penny worked briskly, briefing Kate on the remains of the schedule – who she was meeting, a short biography and key points on each of them, where they'd each be and so on. Kate nodded, although little of it was sinking in. With a sigh, Penny handed Kate her briefing notes.

'Here. You can read them in the car. The team's all here now so we can debrief yesterday and then I'll call your driver and we can be off.'

Kate smiled and followed Penny through to the outer office where her team was gathered. Her press officer oiled his way to the front of the group and Kate shuddered over the thought of having to tell him about her affair. She stood back while he went over the previous day.

'Right everyone, gather round. Okay, the opening of the hospital went well. Kate, you did a great job talking to the patients and taking time to talk to the nurses rather than just the consultants. Showed a personal touch – that the party has commonality with Joe Public. Good stuff. Not so great in the afternoon with that old lady haranguing you about not being able to get an appointment with an NHS dentist. People, come on. We need to have answers for when this happens.'

Kate zoned out. There would always be old ladies with a personal hobby-horse who needed the limelight. There were no solutions for them. You smiled nicely and pretended to listen and escaped as fast as you could. No one was happy and the press made a meal of it. Move on. She glanced at Penny and indicated she'd had enough. Penny nodded, waited for a break in the flow and swiftly ended the team talk.

'Must move on, everyone. Busy day ahead. Thank you, Thomas, for your debrief, excellent as ever.'

She shepherded Kate out of the room and down to the car. Kate was surprised to find Thomas at her heels.

'Are you coming too?' Kate asked.

'Yes. Douglas called and said there might be some adverse press today. You can brief me in the car.'

Kate sucked in a long, deep breath. How the hell had she ever, *ever* got herself into this? Today was going to be hell.

***

Had she done everything she could?

The call sounded like it had been made at his flat.

She could go and see for herself.

Summer downed the rest of her coffee and headed for the cluttered room upstairs which she called her study, even though it was little more than a glorified spare room. The room overflowed with stuff even more than the rest of her house, with shoeboxes full of receipts perched on reams of printing paper, folders of orders rubbing shoulders with bundles of packing materials and her laptop clinging to a scrap of clear desk. The only pristine spot was the area around an expensive printer that could print photographic pictures up to A2 size. The top drawer of her desk was her 'miscellaneous' drawer, full of bits of string, labels for the printer, scissors and other odds and sods. Where better to keep the keys to the flat of an ex-lover? She yanked the drawer open and rummaged around, picking through the junk until she found them, and then sat back in her chair, keys in her palm, staring at them. Could she really go to his flat? What if there was someone there? Someone new in his life?

There had only been his name on the answerphone message.

She rolled the keys back and forth in her fingers. What if the police were there?

Good. Then she *would* have done everything she could and could go to that new camera shop she'd seen advertised.

What if they weren't?

He had called her. He had asked her for help. She breathed deeply, flicking her index and middle fingers across the knuckles of her other hand, her thumb through the key ring. The call with Patrick reverberated through her, burning orange flames and making up her mind. She closed her hand around the keys and picked up her notebook. At the threshold of the study she hesitated for a moment, and then picked up her camera bag too. Who knew what she'd find when she got there.

The drive to Edinburgh gave her mind time to run wild. Would whoever had attacked Patrick still be there? Would the place be crawling with police? What had Patrick got himself into?

By the time she turned into Patrick's road, tangerine orange was percolating through her and her palms were slick from fear. She turned off the engine, grabbed her camera bag and let herself into the block, still wondering what she would say if someone challenged her.

She'd hoped to see police tape at the very least but there was nothing to indicate that there was any investigation going on. Patrick's flat was on the ground floor, the last door on the right. Her nerves taut, she padded softly past the first flat, her eyes scanning the floor for anything untoward. Nothing. She reached Patrick's door and tapped on it, her heart pounding. No answer. No sound from inside. She tapped again then eased the key into the lock, her hands trembling. The door squeaked loudly as she pushed it open but the flat was empty. Very empty. She pushed the door closed behind her, flinching at the noise, and tiptoed around the flat. As she headed towards the kitchen, something ginger leaped down and scampered past her to batter through the cat-flap. Oscar. Patrick's hostile, semi-feral cat who treated the place like a hotel. She breathed out, shaking her head at herself, her heart hammering, orange fear colliding with damson apprehension.

Summer frowned as she looked around. Maybe she was used to her own place too much with the floor-to-ceiling books and clutter, but this place looked monastic. She pulled a pair of thin rubber gloves from her bag, put them on and started to make a thorough, methodical survey of the room. She scanned the walls, doing a mental check of the African masks hanging there but couldn't remember clearly how many he'd had and so whether any were missing. His beautifully carved bao board was still there, as were other cheap carvings that had been bought from the flea-market in Blantyre, Malawi, but very little else. Cautiously, she retrieved her camera and took pictures of everything, trying to cast her mind back to when she and Patrick were together. Surely he'd owned more things than this? Maybe he'd been burgled? But then, where was he? Burglars stole things, not people. And although it was empty, it hadn't been ransacked. Her photos complete, she walked over to the small desk with the phone on it. The answerphone had a flashing light to indicate new calls and a '6' in the message count window. Next to the phone was a piece of scrap paper covered in figures; some numbers crossed out, question marks next to some numbers, circles around others. Next to that was a to-do list. Summer photographed both of them before heading through to the bedroom. She nosed through the wardrobe and drawers. It didn't look as if he'd packed to go away anywhere and a quick glance into the bathroom confirmed it. Patrick was vain and meticulous about shaving but both his personalised silver razor and his shaving oil were there, along with his toothbrush, designer cleanser and moisturiser. Summer smiled weakly. The sight of them was not reassuring.

She walked back to the kitchen and rummaged about. Unwashed dishes next to the sink, a half-made cup of coffee next to the kettle, new milk in the fridge – it certainly didn't seem as if he'd planned on being away. She glanced at the back door, her heart skipping a beat when she realised it was unlocked. She opened it gingerly. It led to a small backyard where the recycling bins for the flats were. She stood on the threshold, her eyes scanning. Three things caught her eye and she returned to the kitchen quickly. Patrick kept old plastic bags under the kitchen sink and she pulled out two – a supermarket carrier and a clear, flimsy bag that had probably held fruit or vegetables. Back in the yard, she photographed the three items from every conceivable angle and then used the bags to pick up two – the carrier bag to collect a shoe and the see-through bag for a smashed phone. She felt sick. Although she couldn't swear to the shoe, she was sure that the phone was Patrick's. She hoped that the horrible crunching sound she'd heard when he called had been the phone and not him. She looked at the third item – a yellow crate next to the bin for glass – but couldn't be sure it was Patrick's and left it where it was. She had several photos of it and no room in her bag to take it away.

Back in the flat, she locked the back door, placed the wrapped shoe and smashed phone in her bag and packed away her camera. She looked at Oscar's empty bowl but couldn't tell if he'd been fed recently or ten weeks ago. She shook dried food out of the box, half filling the bowl, and then after pondering for a moment and realising she had no idea how much cats ate, filling the bowl to the brim. It would hopefully last several days, just in case.

She turned her attention to the desk, pulling open the top drawer and using a pencil to poke through the papers there. Towards the bottom, under some letters, was a bundle of leaflets for abortion clinics. Summer's eyebrows shot up but she left them where they were. Using the pencil, she pushed the letters around, looking at the postmarks – Edinburgh – and eventually decided that it was an invasion of privacy too far to read them and closed the drawer. She pulled a tape recorder out of her bag. She set it to record and then used the end of the pencil to press play on the answerphone.

'You have one, new message,' an electronically synthesised voice said. 'New message…'

The message was in fact silent.

'Tuesday: 1.29 p.m.,' broke in the electronic voice.

Summer thought for a moment then realised it must have been the call she'd made after she'd phoned the police. She scrolled to the caller log on the phone and confirmed her suspicion. The answerphone had stopped blinking, but still had '6' glowing in the message count. She pressed the play button again.

'You have six, old messages… Hi. I can get away tonight if you can. Text me? … Tuesday: 4.35 p.m.'

Summer jotted down the day and time and that the caller was a woman. The next message started automatically. Another female voice, not the same woman as the first.

'Hey, it's me. I don't suppose you want to come, but maybe it might change your mind. The appointment's at eleven on the twenty-sixth. I hope you'll be there. ... Thursday: 9.21 a.m.'

The next two callers were male.

'I've not been joking, Patrick. Full amount, plus what you owe from last time. No excuses. ... Monday: 3.15 p.m.'

'You leave us alone or I will fucking kill you! Do you hear me!? ... Saturday: 10.05 p.m.'

Summer's eyes widened but there were still another two messages to go. The first was a woman and sounded like the voice on the very first message.

'Patrick, you little shit*! How could you do that? How could you* do *that to me? God, I will* kill *you! ... Sunday: 7.01 a.m.'*

The last message was her call from the day before, and then the machine clicked off. With shaking hands, Summer switched off her recorder. She looked at Patrick's phone again, but only the ID of the last caller was stored. She put it back in its cradle and swallowed. Patrick had certainly been mixed up in something. Maybe lots of things. She had vaguely recognised the first caller's voice but couldn't place her with any certainty. She hadn't recognised any of the others.

She wondered how old the messages were. When she'd been with Patrick, he'd tended to screen all his calls and keep messages until the memory was almost full, so 'Tuesday' could refer to this week or to several weeks ago. She wished his machine was like hers and would record the date as well as the day and time.

She glanced down at his laptop next to the phone, debating whether she should look at it there or take it away with her. Taking it away would be easier, but could it be removing evidence from a crime scene? But since there was no tape up, was it actually a crime scene officially? She hesitated for a moment, staring at it, and then unplugged it and put it in her bag. Behind her, someone cleared their throat, startling her out of her skin and she whirled around, realising she hadn't shut the front door properly. She shoved her hands into her pockets to hide her gloves.

'Hello?' said a skinny man in his late forties who stood in the doorway, frowning at her.

'Hello,' said Summer, citrus scything through her as her heart pounded.

'What are you doing here?'

'I'm a friend of Patrick's. I… er… he called me… I've come to feed Oscar. The cat.'

She sized him up. Surely this guy was too scrawny to be able to take out Patrick? But maybe there had been more than one? Her mind raced. If she ran to the back door would she get it open in time? And what was beyond the recycling bins? How did you get out of the yard? Did it back on to the train line? Or was it just a road?

Her attention snapped back to the man and to her relief, he nodded.

'I'm Cameron – I live next door. I saw that the door was open.'

Summer sighed, her heart rate steadying. She wanted to ask him if he had heard anything odd or seen anything strange but stopped herself. She was just here to feed the cat. She forced herself to smile and nod.

'Pleased to meet you, and I'm glad that Patrick's neighbours are so careful. I'm just going. No doubt I'll see you again.'

'How long is Patrick away for?'

'I don't know. You know Patrick – never one for plans!'

'I don't really know him that well. Just to nod to. Pass the time of day and all.'

He smiled and left her alone. She picked up the list and the scrap of paper with numbers on and slid them into her bag, her hands still shaking, before she pulled her gloves off, dropped them into her bag and stepped through the open doorway. Cameron was waiting in the communal hall and he watched her while she locked Patrick's door before nodding to her and returning to his flat. Summer breathed deeply, her nerves shot to pieces. What the hell had happened to Patrick?

***

Back at her house, she brewed a pot of coffee and settled down in her study to look over the prints of all the pictures she had taken. It barely looked like Patrick's flat, it was so sparse. She read down the to-do list: 1. check out the blogs. 2. look at the accounts. 3. email Moyenda – tell him Limbani's in Kent and Mabvuto's in Chicago (Where are Henry and Tendai and when did they disappear?)

She remembered Moyenda from the previous autumn when she had been in Malawi with Patrick. An earnest, intense man, about thirty and slightly built, he was the project manager at Samala, a Malawian charity that worked with orphaned children. He was passionate about the work the charity did, always doing his utmost for the children there. She remembered going to photograph the children playing football and being mobbed by them all, all of them desperate to be in the pictures, all of them shouting 'Aunty Summer, Aunty Summer!' She'd found it so old-fashioned for the children to refer to all older men and women as if they were related. It was not a notion her parents had entertained even when she was small. What had been lovely was that the Malawian children had all happily accepted that she was named after a season. Certainly alongside Happiness, Freedom and Godknows, her name was utterly unremarkable and not something for her to be teased or beaten up over.

Something about Malawi had captured Patrick's heart and he became passionate about the country and determined to help the children as much as he could, this enthusiasm shining through in the articles he wrote for the Malawi–Scotland Alliance – the MSA – and in the fund-raising talks he gave about Samala.

She leaned back in her chair, her brows crumpling. What the

hell was he mixed up in? What had happened to leave his phone smashed on the ground and his shoe ripped off like that? Patrick was a communications manager for the MSA, he was a bit of a playboy and he enjoyed a drink. How did any of that lead to him going missing? Had he stolen something bigger than a bank card this time?

She plugged in his laptop and switched it on, hoping that Patrick wouldn't have been sensible or secretive enough to have password-protected it. She was in luck.

She clicked on 'My Documents' and started to look through the files. There were a few spreadsheets which seemed to outline household expenses but they were badly laid out and Summer couldn't make sense of them so she closed them again. The main folder contained files related to work or to Samala – articles or talks. He also had a series of electronic notebooks full of jottings and clippings – one for each article he'd written. There was work for a new piece but it seemed very preliminary and consisted largely of reminders to himself to email people in Malawi. She ran her eye over the list, recognising some of the people – Moses Chizuna, the government minister who'd helped to process the paperwork when Moyenda had been setting up Samala; Bradley Collinson, the minister of the local church; and Mzondi Malilo, another official at the government and board member of Samala – and wondered what the article was about. It didn't seem as though he'd started writing it yet.

There was another folder on Samala. Inside were a series of letters applying for funding, a number of spreadsheets and some stories about the children and about the history of the project. The accounts showed that the finances for Samala were healthy, with large deposits coming in at irregular intervals. Many of them were labelled – Unicef, Rotary, book sale etc. – but the larger ones weren't and some of these had electronic highlighter around them. They were shown in kwacha rather than having been converted from pounds, so she assumed they were funds raised in Malawi rather than transferred from the UK. Maybe

Patrick didn't have the full details about them. Maybe that was what he'd have been checking with Moyenda. The last file in the folder comprised a series of family trees drawn for seven of the children in the project. Summer remembered some of the boys, recalling the sadness she'd felt when they explained that most of their families were dead. She looked at the lists. Some of the family members were boxed in red – generally grandparents or distant relatives. Patrick had helped to draw up family trees like this when they'd both been out in Malawi last autumn, saying that it was important to find out who the remaining members of the family were. Moyenda would work with them to allow the child to stay with their community, adopted by these distant relatives. Orphanages could be appalling and Samala was keen for the children to remain with their family, however distant, as long as it was safe. She closed the file down, depressed by her memories and thoughts of these children's lives.

She hesitated over opening Patrick's email client and tipped her head back. Was this an invasion of privacy too far, like reading letters? Would it help to work out what had happened? She clicked the icon. The inbox opened, but prompted her for a password to check for new mail. She clicked on cancel, and then scrolled through the existing messages. Unlike her email where the inbox could run to hundreds of messages, Patrick's was almost empty. There were a couple of emails from Moyenda, some from a local Rotary club promising money for Samala, and a few from work. She opened the sent messages folder but it was as empty as the inbox – just a reply to the secretary of the Rotary club, a few emails to Moyenda asking if he'd seen various children and saying he was worried about them, and one message to a John Saunders asking if they could meet up. She didn't find a reply. She checked the deleted messages folder but it was completely empty.

Summer closed the machine down, disappointed not to have learned more, and leaned back in her seat, considering everything. It turned out she knew almost nothing about her ex-lover. There were few clues in the flat, there was nothing out of the ordinary on his laptop, yet there was something happening in his life that was serious enough for someone to have made him disappear.

She produced the two scraps of paper she'd retrieved and stared at them. The numbers still made no sense – they weren't long enough to be phone numbers and they didn't appear to add up in any way to be accounts. She put the paper aside and looked at the to-do list. Check out the blogs; look at the accounts; email Moyenda about some of the boys. All three items had also been in the jottings for the article. She opened her own laptop and started to compose an email.

'Dear Moyenda, How are you? How is your wife? I hope that the rains have stopped and the grain is ripening well in Malawi.'

Summer gritted her teeth over all the pleasantries that were needed. She would far rather just get to the point but that wasn't the Malawian way and she didn't want to offend Moyenda.

'I hope that you remember me. I'm the photographer who came out to Blantyre last October with Patrick – Summer Morris. How is Samala going? How are all the children? I hope they're all well and enjoying school.

'I'm emailing you because I'm worried about Patrick. I had a very strange call from him and I wondered if he was in trouble. He's disappeared. When I went to his flat, there was a note to contact you about the boys and he seems to have been very worried about some of them according to other notes I found. There was a to-do list that said, 'check out the blogs; look at the accounts; email Moyenda – tell him Limbani's in Kent and Mabvuto's in Chicago (Where are Henry and Tendai and when did they disappear?)' Do you know what any of this means? You're the person who I thought he'd talk to the most and I wondered whether you knew if he was in trouble?

'If you can think of anything, please let me know? I'm very worried about him. Many thanks, Summer.'

She clicked on send and closed her laptop down. The tape

recorder she'd taken to Patrick's flat lay next to the computer and she switched it on, listening to the messages again. The first woman's voice was definitely familiar. She ran though all her female friends but came up blank.

She walked slowly to the kitchen and made a cafetière of coffee. While it steeped, she scrolled through the numbers on her own phone.

'Hi Sandra. How are you? … Yeah, fine thanks… Have you heard from Patrick recently? … I know… I know! Have you heard from him? … A month? Really? … Do you know if anyone else has seen him or heard from him recently? … Okay, I'll try them. Yes I know he won't want to talk to me… It's just… Hey, it doesn't matter. Thanks.'

She pushed the plunger on the cafetière, poured a mug of treacly coffee and dropped two lumps of sugar in. She tried four more mutual friends and got the same response from all of them. No one had seen Patrick for a while, they didn't think he would want to hear from her, maybe he was working out in Malawi again. She called his office number. It too went straight to an answerphone, but it did give another number to try. Summer called it.

'Grace Stephens.'

'Hi. Er, this is a friend of Patrick's. Patrick Forrester. I've been trying to get hold of him but with no success and I wondered if he was back in Malawi?'

'No, not at the moment. He was out there at the end of last month but isn't due there again for a while. Who's calling?'

'Sorry, Summer Morris. We met briefly last year I think, but you probably don't remember me.'

'The Summer Morris who went out to Malawi with Patrick to take photos?'

'How many people with as dumb a name as this can there be? Yes, the very same.'

Grace laughed. Summer imagined her sitting at her desk, her short grey hair curling around her face. Grace had the office just down the hall from Patrick. Summer wondered what Grace knew about her and Patrick.

'When did you last see him?' Summer asked, trying to keep the emotion out of her voice.

'Oh, er, two Fridays ago. He's on holiday at the moment but he should be back on Monday. Is there a problem?'

'Er… no. No. I just wanted to get hold of him but his mobile doesn't seem to be working. I'm sorry to have disturbed you.'

She desperately wanted to say, 'Actually yes, there is a problem. Patrick rang me in a panic and then it sounded like he was being beaten up.' Grace was a serious, sensible woman who would probably know exactly what to do, but something made Summer feel foolish and hesitant suddenly and she bit back the words.

'No problem, Summer. If he pops in, I'll tell him you were after him. Can I help with anything else?'

'No. No thank you. Hang on. Yes. If you see him, could you ask him to call me? He should have my number, but just in case, here it is.'

She trotted out the digits thinking that if her phone got stamped on she would have no idea what most people's numbers were. She made a mental note to back up her SIM card and rang off. Under the notes she'd scribbled after every call, she added the dates when each person had last seen Patrick. The most recent had been Grace, eleven days earlier.

She breathed deeply, the threatening phone messages replaying in an endless loop in her head. What was he mixed up in? And why weren't the police *doing* something?

WEDNESDAY AFTERNOON

'I'm sorry, Ms Morris, but I can't help you. The matter has been passed to Lothian Police who've been asked to keep you informed of any developments. Since you haven't been informed of any developments, presumably there's nothing to tell you.'

Summer could have screamed. It had taken her ten minutes of staring at the door to the police station before she had summoned the strength to cross the road and approach the reception desk and her anxiety was almost overwhelming her.

'But, as I've already told you, they aren't actually investigating it.'

'There are two murders to be solved there,' said the desk sergeant drily.

Summer watched as his expression switched from irritation to relief and glanced over her shoulder.

'Problems?' asked the newcomer.

'No, sir,' said the desk sergeant, just as Summer said, 'Yes.'

The man who had arrived glanced from one to the other, humour twitching in his lips. His close-cropped dark hair was just on the long side of severe and his bitter-chocolate eyes settled on Summer.

'What seems to be the matter?' he asked.

'What seems to be the matter is that I reported an incident yesterday and no one seems to be interested.'

'An incident?'

'A friend of mine called me and it sounded like he was being attacked and no one knows where he is.'

The dark eyes swung to the desk sergeant, brows raised.

'He's gone missing in Edinburgh, sir. Not our region.'

'And Edinburgh don't give a toss!' interjected Summer.

'You haven't exactly given them much to go on, and they do have two murders to investigate,' flashed back an exasperated sergeant.

'Are you his wife?' asked the newcomer, looking at her left hand.

'No, just a friend. But he called me and now he's missing and I'm worried something terrible has happened and no one seems in the least bit interested.'

He nodded, his eyes boring into her. She blinked away old memories of raised batons and shouting, her stomach knotting as she forced herself to hold her ground in the face of his penetrating stare. Finally his gaze swung away, allowing her some respite and for mauve to join the kaleidoscope of orange and black sweeping through her.

'I'll take this, sergeant,' he said.

The sergeant looked relieved. The newcomer held out his hand, his expression suddenly soft.

'Detective Sergeant LB Stewart.'

She hesitated, and then took his hand. His grip was firm but not aggressive.

'Summer Morris.'

His lips hesitated on the brink of a smile then stepped back.

'Shall we go and have coffee somewhere and you can tell me what's worrying you? Then if it seems as if I should be kicking Edinburgh up the arse about it all, we can come back here and make a full report. How does that sound?'

It wasn't really a question as he was already gesturing for her to accompany him out of the station. Summer shouldered her bag and followed him. He didn't speak to her until they were both seated in a quiet nearby cafe and had ordered two coffees, giving her time to study him. He was a big bear of a man, broad-shouldered, well over six feet tall and with stubble that if it were two millimetres longer would be classed as a beard. For some reason his bulk reassured her, rather than raised old ghosts.

'So, what's happened?' he said as the coffees arrived.

'Could you tell me again who I'm talking to please?'

'Detective Sergeant LB Stewart.'

'LB?'

She arched her eyebrows but there wasn't a flicker in his face.

'Is it okay for you to be out of the station, Detective Sergeant LB Stewart?'

He canted his head.

'I'm on holiday. I was only popping by to check on something, but if I need to, I'll give Lothian a shove for you. What's happened?'

'You're off duty?'

Summer sighed irritably and folded her arms, leaning on them and hunching her shoulders. She should have followed her instincts and left it all alone.

'Did you want to tell me what's happened or not?' he said, his voice steady. 'If you don't, you can buy your own coffee.'

His face remained neutral but his eyes spat out, *I'm on holiday. I'm doing you a favour. I don't have to.* Summer swallowed. Could he actually be willing to help her? Or was it lip-service as usual?

Only one way to find out.

'I'm sorry, I didn't mean to be rude. It's just that I've been given the brush-off by everyone and just when I think someone might listen to me, they say they're on holiday.'

She tore the top off a packet of sugar and poured the contents into her mug, repeating the action with a second sachet. DS Stewart watched her closely.

'Tell me what's happened,' he said, his voice soothing.

Summer flicked her eyes up to meet his. He nodded for her to talk. Maybe it wasn't just lip-service then.

'Yesterday, I got a phone call from a friend. All he said was "Summer, please, you have to help me." And then he cried out as if he'd been hurt and there was a horrible crunching sound and the line went dead. And I've been to his flat and he's not there, and it doesn't look like a burglary, and his phone was all smashed up outside the flat and there was a shoe on the floor too. I took pictures of it all.'

DS Stewart stirred his coffee slowly, his eyes on her.

'Let's take this more slowly. He's not your husband, but your lover? Boyfriend?'

'No. No. Neither of those. Not any more. In fact I'm surprised he called me.'

'Why?'

Summer paused.

'Er, well... we *were* lovers but not for a long time now. Er...'

'It didn't end well?' he said, shifting his mug so the handle was on the right.

'It could have ended better,' she acknowledged.

'But nonetheless, he called you and you think he was being attacked.'

'Mmm. And the background sounds – I thought it could have been in his flat, and I told the police that, but then when I called and asked for an update, nothing had happened so I went down to see if there was anything there.'

'How did you get in?'

'I still have keys.'

His eyes widened; his expression hardened.

'Does the phrase *crime scene* mean nothing to you?'

'There was no tape up,' she retorted. 'And Edinburgh certainly don't seem to be treating it as a crime.'

'They're busy.'

'With two murders, I know. They could have three soon!'

He said nothing, his brows creeping up. He paused before asking, 'And what exactly did you find at his flat?'

Summer told him, and then outlined what she'd found on Patrick's laptop. There was a long silence from him.

'Well?' prompted Summer.

'Well what?'

Summer sucked her teeth, shaking her head fractionally.

'Something has obviously happened to him!'

He was still staring at her, making her uncomfortable. She produced the pack of prints she had made.

'I took all these. Maybe they'll be helpful. And the phone and the shoe – they're still in the plastic bags in my car.'

He placed a long index finger on the prints, drawing them slowly towards him, his jaw hard. He cleared his throat before speaking.

'Let me get this straight – you think your friend was attacked at or near his flat, you go there, it looks as if your suspicions are right because you find the back door left open, a damaged phone and a single shoe, and instead of calling the police, you decide to photograph everything and remove these pieces of evidence from the scene? The only help that's been is to ruin the chance of any kind of conviction based on forensics, if indeed there has been a crime committed. Courts are quite picky about chain of evidence, you know.'

'Yeah, with hindsight, that wasn't the right thing to do. I wasn't thinking. But at least I photographed everything,' she flashed back, feeling sick and lime-green.

'Mmm. Why did you do that?'

'I thought it would be helpful.'

She sounded suspicious even to herself. His eyes drilled into her.

'But calling the police wouldn't be?'

'I'd already called them! They weren't doing anything. No one was taking me seriously.'

DS Stewart pinched his lips together as he breathed deeply.

'So why might your friend have been attacked?' he asked.

'I don't know. I can't think of any reason why he would be. I mean, he can seriously piss people off, but... no. I don't know why someone would attack him.'

'What's he like?'

'He's taller than me but not as tall as you, has blond, floppy hair, grey eyes, longish face, quite good-looking. He's er… thirty-four. Birthday was March.'

'And personality?'

She thought for a moment, staring out of the window, watching the pigeons while she marshalled her thoughts.

'He's a chameleon. He blends in, whatever circumstances he finds himself in, whether it's a posh dinner or playing with street kids in the dirt in Malawi.'

'Malawi?'

She looked back.

'He works for the Malawi–Scotland Alliance. He's a communications officer. He used to be a journalist. We went out to Malawi together last year to do some articles for them. I'm a photographer.'

'Ah.'

He looked down at the photographs as if they suddenly made sense. Just as he was about to ask another question, Summer grabbed the photos back and started rifling through them.

'The carving's not there,' she said, putting them back on the table.

DS Stewart watched her, unmoving. His stillness was making Summer's stress veer towards bolting-level. She blinked away the fracturing colours and tried to breathe freely.

'What carving?' he asked.

'The one of the chameleons. I hadn't realised until I described him as one. He bought it when we were at the Mua mission in Malawi. I remember the carvers were surprised, and glad to sell it.'

'Where? Why?'

'The Mua mission? It's a heritage centre we went to which also has craftsmen working there – they do some really beautiful things. Patrick saw this carving of two chameleons and just adored it.'

He still hadn't looked at the pictures. She slid them back towards him but he didn't even glance down at them.

'But the craftsmen were surprised by that and glad to sell it?' he asked.

'Mmm. Chameleons are thought of as unlucky in Malawi – they're thought to bring death.'

Her voice quavered and she snatched her gaze down to the muddy depths of her coffee. His eyes finally travelled over the pictures.

'And you're sure the carving is missing?'

She nodded rapidly, not trusting her voice to hold.

'When did you last see it?'

'Oh God, the end of January. When I was last there.'

He screwed his mouth up, straightening the pictures, carefully aligning their edges with the edge of the table.

'So it could have gone at any time between then and now?' he said evenly.

'Well, yes, except that Patrick wouldn't get rid of it. He loved it.'

DS Stewart nodded, pursing his lips.

'Why do Malawians carve them if they're considered unlucky?'

Summer looked up and smiled for the first time.

'Because stupid rich white people don't know the myths and buy them?'

His lips flickered into a smile and his expression softened for a moment.

'Is the carving valuable? Could it have been stolen?'

She shook her head.

'It probably is quite valuable although Patrick didn't pay a lot in real terms, I suppose, but I doubt if it was stolen. It's too quirky for high art.'

He drank his coffee, his face unreadable. Summer waited, trying to figure out whether he believed her or not. He drained his cup and placed it carefully on the table.

'Okay, I've heard enough,' he said. 'Let's go back to the station and I'll do a full report. Can I keep these photos? And can we have the things that you took from the flat, worthless as they will be as evidence now? I'll be sending it all down to Edinburgh as it's still their case but I'll try to push them on it.'

He fished in his wallet for money and his business card. She watched him scribble his mobile number on the back.

'I have absolutely no doubt that you will continue trying to find your friend, but you go back to the flat once more and I'll have you arrested for obstruction. Are we clear?' he said, handing the card to her, the look in his eyes leaving her with no doubts over his sincerity. 'Keep me up to date with anything you find out and I'll keep you posted about developments from our end.'

It wasn't a question. Summer nodded, handing him her business card. DS Stewart put it in his wallet without looking at it and then ushered Summer out of the coffee shop.

***

The office building was finally empty. Wilson, one of the volunteers, had taken the children to play football and although Moyenda was dismayed to be missing the match he was grateful to have some peace and quiet. He had plenty of paperwork to be getting on with and he always got side-tracked when the children or other volunteers were around. He sat at the rickety desk, pulled his satchel towards him and drew his notes out, piling them into a heap. Monday and Tuesday had been filled with school and community visits and he needed to file all his notes before he lost them.

It was cool in the office, the Malawian winter creeping in early. Moyenda rubbed his hands together briskly then sifted steadily through the sheaf, separating out school notes from community notes. He worked slowly and methodically through each section, adding comments or snippets of information as he recalled more detail than was included on the sheets. It took him over an hour to put the pages into order and file them. When he was finished, he stretched his neck and switched the computer on. It was old, slow and had an unreliable internet connection, but it had been free – a gift from a volunteer. It would be a good five minutes before he could log in, so to warm himself up, he made himself a tea, stirring in a spoonful of powdered milk. Fresh milk would have been nicer but Samala couldn't afford to run a fridge in the office and anyway, the electricity supply was unreliable.

When the computer was finally perky enough to work on, Moyenda logged in and opened his email. More work. Several emails from a local NGO Samala liaised with that needed replies, some meetings that needed to go into the diary and a number of requests for reports that he hoped he could pass to Joy since her skills with a word processor far exceeded his.

His eyes paused over a thinly familiar name – Summer Morris – and he clicked to open the message. His eyes widened as he read.

Good question, he thought as he finished, I wish I knew where those two waifs were. But what did she mean – Patrick might be in trouble? 'Check out the blogs; look at the accounts.' What blogs? Which accounts? Samala's accounts? No, surely not. He read the email from Summer again. No, she had copied a to-do list she'd found and only some of it was linked to him in all probability.

He tried to remember Summer Morris. The lady who had come to take the photographs. He left the desk and walked slowly along the wall, scanning the pictures hanging there. He finally found the one he was looking for – a bright picture of Patrick, this Summer Morris and himself, taken last October. Yes, the photographer lady. He smiled. She had been nice and spent time talking to the children when others would have shuddered at their rags and filth. He returned to the computer and read her email a third time. What did she mean, Limbani is in Kent and Mabvuto is in Chicago?

His brow crinkling with concentration, he opened some old

messages from Patrick. Patrick had been upset when Moyenda had told him about the boys disappearing and had asked lots of questions. He had asked for a full list of which boys were missing, and Moyenda had sent it. Then he said he thought that he had found some of them, but hadn't said where. Moyenda had asked him how he thought he had found them when he was in Scotland and the boys were missing in Malawi, but Patrick hadn't answered. Instead, he had asked about a series of dead people – distant relatives of the boys – asking where they were. Moyenda had written back to say that they were all with the Lord and had passed on many years ago and asked why he was interested. Again, Patrick hadn't answered.

Limbani is in Kent; Mabvuto is in Chicago. Did Patrick really think that he had found these two boys overseas? How was that possible? And why was Patrick now in trouble?

Moyenda sat back in the chair, trying to think rationally. If the boys really were overseas, how had they got there? Certainly not under their own steam – neither of them would have a passport or be able to get visas even if suddenly, miraculously they could have afforded to leave Malawi. It was surely impossible to stow away on a plane and the nearest port was in Mozambique, hundreds of kilometres away. So, if they did not get there by themselves the only other option was that someone had taken them there. So why did no one know where they were?

He stared at the screen, suddenly fearful. All of these emails were on the shared office computer and anyone could have read them. It was not set up with separate accounts because so many people needed to access all of the documents for Samala. He swallowed, his mouth dry, and took a gulp of his tea. He accessed the internet, hoping the connection at the office would stay up long enough for him to do what he needed to. He worked quickly, creating a new Yahoo account for himself and then forwarding all the emails from Patrick to it, along with his replies. He also forwarded the email from Summer. Once he was sure they were all safely in the new account he started deleting them from the account on the office computer. In the novels he read, spies always seemed to be able to retrieve deleted files from computers but he wasn't sure any of the volunteers had those kind of skills. Satisfied that he had done all he could, he closed down the machine. If he hurried, he would be able to catch the last of the football match. Maybe it would take his mind off things too?

He locked up the offices and started to walk towards the playing fields where the game was taking place, his brain churning over Summer's email and what everything might mean. Every now and then, he looked over his shoulder. Was he being followed?

He shook himself. Of course he wasn't being followed. He was just being paranoid. The emails had made him jittery. He would talk to Chifundo tonight and she would be able to reassure him he was making a mountain out of nothing.

Nonetheless, as he walked through the market he stopped at one of the stalls and bought three new SIM cards, just in case.

***

Summer flopped down in the corner of the sofa in her flat, exhausted. The police station had been everything she expected and hated – colourless, soulless, bureaucratic, rigid. It had taken an age to go through it all again while DS Stewart made copious notes and the pitiful room they'd been in with its hard wooden chair and melamine-topped table had left Summer feeling grey and grubby. She had left the shoe and the phone there, still in their plastic bags, along with the photos and a promise to bring Patrick's laptop in as soon as was convenient. As she had left, DS Stewart had repeated his assertion that she would continue to investigate Patrick's disappearance, a fact she was far less certain of.

She stared at his card, turning it over and over in her hands. She was way too busy to do anything. It wasn't her job to investigate. She was already behind with work. The police had everything they needed from her. She had done what she could; fulfilled his request.

Washed her hands of him?

She tipped her head back and closed her eyes, wishing that the crunching sound and the yells and the death-threats on the answerphone would stop playing in a non-stop loop in her head, and that the lime green feeling in the pit of her stomach would go away and that life could become indigo again.

It wouldn't.

She opened her eyes and dialled the number.

'LB Stewart.'

'Hi. It's Summer Morris.'

'Hi. What can I do for you?'

She hesitated and he waited.

'Edinburgh won't do anything, will they?' she said at last. 'They've got their hands full with those murders and he has to be missing for three days or something doesn't he? To become an official missing person?'

'It won't be a priority,' he replied, his tone careful. 'Not at the moment. But I will try and push them. He's lucky to have a friend like you, though.'

'Yeah. Thanks.'

She hung up and stared at the wall of books opposite her, the loop still playing incessantly through her mind. Why had he called her, of all people?

Because he knew she would help.

WEDNESDAY EVENING

'Well, not our best day out there, but it wasn't a complete disaster.'

Thomas looked pointedly at Kate as they walked across the office. Kate ignored him. She was exhausted to the bone and still trying to work out whether she'd be able to talk Paul round this evening. So much hung on her being able to get him to move back in. Their marriage, obviously, but also her entire political career. She rubbed a hand over her face.

'Thank you, Thomas. You did a great job today.'

'It's what I'm paid for,' he replied, unsmiling.

Kate nodded. Most other people's reflex would have been to say 'my pleasure' but he was just being honest. No one could take pleasure from diverting questions away from her private life the way he had today.

'Well, it's been a long day, with another ahead of us. Let's debrief in the morning,' she said, collecting her things together determinedly.

The others looked equally relieved to be leaving the office at a reasonable time. Penny shot Kate a look that said 'good luck' and smiled encouragingly as she packed her belongings together. Kate wished she hadn't – it just reminded her what a Herculean task lay ahead.

She walked out of the office with the others, leaving them

in the foyer while she sneaked out of the back entrance again to her car. On her way, she checked the messages on her phone – still no reply from Paul. She would call him again once she was home.

There was one solitary journalist hanging around her gate when she arrived home and she smiled through gritted teeth at him but didn't answer any of his questions as she passed. Inside the house, she quickly drew all the curtains even though it wasn't yet dark and poured herself a large gin and tonic. She kicked her shoes off and collapsed into the sofa, gulping down a mouthful of the gin. Her answerphone was blinking away, indicating a full memory of messages and she leaned over and clicked on play. The vast majority were journalists. She rubbed a tired hand across her head, loosening her hair and letting it tumble over her shoulders. How had they got her number? It wasn't listed. She supposed they always had ways. The messages chirruped on. Buried in the middle was one from Douglas telling her that he hoped things would be back on track soon and that he was counting on her. She groaned. The hoped-for message from Paul did not appear. Keeping one finger on the delete button to wipe the entire lot, she pulled her mobile out and dialled with her free hand. To her amazement, Paul answered.

'Paul? Oh, I'm glad you're there.'

'What do you want?'

'I was hoping that we might be able to talk? Over dinner?'

'Have you finished for the day? Already?'

'Yes. Douglas shifted some of my appointments to Phil.'

'Bet Phil was happy!'

'Don't know. I haven't seen him. But I'm probably going to have to be nice to him forever now.'

Paul laughed and Kate's heart leaped. They were talking like old times – like they had when she'd been on the campaign trail in the past and away from each other.

'So how come Douglas shifted your load to Phil?'

Kate stumbled.

'I had to tell him you'd moved out. I was being doorstepped this morning.'

The moment between them was gone. Kate could almost hear their connection snap as Paul remembered why he hated her.

'Oh. And I assume that Douglas cleared your schedule so you could have the time to talk me into moving back home. For the sake of the party.'

Every word was laced with sarcasm.

'Actually, Douglas was more concerned about our marriage. As am I.'

'Ha. That's what he'll *say*, but we both know this looks bad for the party. Did you tell him you were so concerned about our marriage that you had an affair?'

Kate swallowed.

'No.'

There was a long pause on the other end of the line as Paul digested the information.

'Job first. Kate second. Me last. As ever.'

He hung up. Kate closed her eyes, feeling defeated, took another swig of her drink, and pressed redial. His phone cut straight to messages. She clicked the end call button and let out a bellow of frustration. Shaking her head, she stared at her phone and finished her drink. This all needed careful thought. Brainstorming always helped her to clear her head. She crossed the room to the desk on the corner and retrieved a piece of paper then rummaged around in the drawer until she found a pencil with a sharp point. Her writing was shaky but neat. Was Paul's comment fair? Was it always work first? From the amount of time and energy spent on it, it would seem that way, but now she was facing the choice of career-but-no-Paul versus Paul-but-no-career, she realised she would choose Paul every time. What was almost unbearable was the no-Paul-and-no-career option that seemed to be looming. She drew out various alternatives, listing pros and cons against each of them, exploring the avenues as far as she could before realising her thoughts were crystallising around one particular decision.

She sucked down a deep breath, needing to be sure that what she was about to do was the right thing. She couldn't make the promise and then not follow through. She gathered up the papers, poured herself another drink, took the notes and the gin upstairs and ran a bath.

As the scented water lapped her shoulders, her brain sifted options; discarding, reviewing, amending and sifting again. She knew that she should probably sleep on this decision and look at it with clear eyes in the morning, but she also knew that time was of the essence with Paul. As soon as she finished her bath she texted him.

'You first. I promise. I love you. I'm resigning.'

***

Patrick stared at his surroundings, his head still muzzy and his body screaming with pain. His stomach ached and his mouth was parched and sticky. His lips were beginning to crack and sting. Since the man had unceremoniously dumped him down here yesterday, Patrick had seen neither hide nor hair of him and there was no food or water in the basement. Patrick wondered if he was being left here to die. He had no idea where he was. The journey in the back of the van was blurry and indistinct and he suspected he was suffering from concussion. Parts of that nightmarish trip had been smooth and fast, but most had been bumpy and tortuous. The last part of the journey had been even slower and rougher. He thought he'd rattled round in the back for more than an hour. Maybe much more. In the brief glimpse he'd had when the door had opened, he'd seen flashes of green. Grass? Trees? It had been so fleeting he couldn't be sure. The man who'd brought him here had thrown a sack over his head, tied it with a rope so tightly around Patrick's neck that he'd feared he would suffocate, and then carried him into this building slung over his shoulder as if he weighed nothing. He'd been taken down some stairs before the man threw him on the ground. The bindings around his wrists had been sliced off, taking some of Patrick's flesh with them, but the freedom had been short-lived because the man had wrenched Patrick's hands in front of him and re-tied them with another cable tie. Some more expletives and a kick to the head followed. When Patrick had come round, the place was quiet. He'd managed to pick the rope around his neck undone with dexterous fingers, despite the ties on his wrists, and yank the sack off. He'd been able to do nothing about his ankles which were still tightly bound with the original plastic cable tie. That had bitten into his flesh, leaving angry wounds he didn't like the look of.

His watch was smashed – broken in the assault no doubt – so he had no idea what time it was. There was no light on in the room but there was a tiny grille almost at ceiling height and Patrick had watched the light fade to black then reappear.

The place smelled fusty, but from a lack of use, not damp. In the gloaming, Patrick could see concrete stairs with no rail on the open side, leading up to a door. In the corner of the room was a bucket. When the man had re-tied Patrick's hands he'd informed him that the bucket was his toilet. It wasn't being emptied.

Patrick shuffled up the steps, his progress painfully slow as he sat on each cold step, balanced with his bound hands then pushed himself up to the next one, feeling like a small child who hadn't yet mastered walking. When he reached the top he was met with an inward-opening door. Patrick tried the handle with his bound hands but although it turned, it didn't open. Even if there was space for a run-up to batter the door down, his bound ankles made the idea ludicrous. Instead, Patrick inched his way back down to the floor again on his bottom.

The cold of the basement crept insidiously through his body and Patrick hunched his shoulders and shivered. For the hundredth time he wondered why on earth this was happening. What had he done? He acknowledged that although he was generally well liked, he did have a tendency to really piss people off. Particularly husbands. Like Kate's for example. Who, like Kate, had rung him up and threatened to kill him. But surely that was just an empty threat? When people said, 'I'll kill you,' they didn't mean it literally. No. Surely it was much more likely that Keir Bevan had decided Patrick would never be able to pay up. What had the man said when he'd grabbed Patrick? It was all pretty fuzzy. Too many knocks to the head since then, he supposed. Maybe it would come back to him. Then again, maybe not.

Patrick shivered again, scared. He would probably die here. No one would find him and he couldn't escape. He tried to remember what the survival time without water was. Days? A week? Was it that he couldn't remember or had he never known? He shook his head. It was beginning to get dark again so he'd been down here for at least a day. How many more would he have?

The bucket in the corner smelled. Patrick smelled. A day of fear had seeped into his clothes and festered.

The sound of a lock turning and bolts being drawn back made Patrick's head snap up and his body filled with apprehension. A chink of light turned into a wedge and the man who had attacked him trotted down the stairs towards him, a canvas bag over his shoulder. Patrick stared, unable to form words. The man said nothing. All Patrick could think of was that now he'd seen the man's face clearly he was sure to die, but he couldn't drag his eyes away. The man had short, light brown hair and a sturdy build. Ex-army, thought Patrick. His jeans were faded and grubby, his thick work-shirt stained and his canvas boots were scuffed and covered in mud. He was chewing something as he stared at Patrick and Patrick became transfixed, watching his jaws and trying to ignore the pains in his stomach. Eventually, the man sniffed, fished inside the bag and put a litre bottle of water on the floor in front of Patrick, along with a packet of sandwiches that looked as if they'd been bought from a petrol station. Neither furnished him with any clues as to where he was.

'Don't gulp the water. It'll make you boak. Sip it,' said the man.

Patrick nodded dumbly, wondering why the man cared if he was sick. Before his brain could summon an answer, the man sniffed again, turned and jogged lightly back up the stairs. Patrick peered vainly through the gap trying to see what was beyond but to no avail. His heart sank as the bolts and lock were re-engaged with a bleak finality and he stared disconsolately at the door.

Shaking himself, he leaned forward in his chair and grabbed the bottle of water. He unscrewed the top with difficulty and had to force himself to take it slowly. He swirled the first mouthful of water around his mouth, letting it trickle around the edge of his tongue and wet his gums and palate before swallowing. He did the same with the second one, relieved the sticky mucus in his mouth was loosening. By the third drink he could swallow easily. He persuaded himself to put the lid back on the water at that point and pick the sandwiches up. They were at least a day out of date and a combination he would never choose for himself, but he tore the wrapper off and bit down ravenously, unable to make himself take his time over the first sandwich. He wrenched back some self-control and forced himself to pause while eating the second, terrified he'd bring it all back up if he wolfed it down too fast.

He was sure he hadn't seen the man before this week. It wasn't the minion Keir Bevan had sent before. Maybe he had more than one.

Why bring him food if he was going to kill him?

Patrick finished the last of the sandwich and took another sip of water. He stared at the mottling wounds on his ankles, looked at the bottle for a moment and then poured a small amount of water over the cuts, praying this wasn't a waste. His skin burned briefly making his breath hiss between his teeth before the pain abated. He put the top back on the bottle and stowed it carefully next to the chair and put the sandwich wrapper in the corner near the bucket.

If the man wasn't going to kill him, what *was* he going to do?

THURSDAY MORNING

'That man has surely been behind me since I left my house.'

Moyenda caught himself muttering out loud, startling himself almost as much as the people around him. He glanced back again at the man then scolded himself.

'You are just being paranoid! No one is following you. There is a simple explanation.'

Except Chifundo, his level-headed, rational wife, hadn't been able to come up with a sensible suggestion that explained everything. Moyenda doubled back on himself abruptly, apologised to the woman he ran into and scurried down a side street. A moment later, he dared to peek behind him. The man he had thought was following him had gone.

The streets were crowded with men in shiny suits and women in bright clothes with babies slung in cloths across their backs. A man who had obviously suffered from polio, scooted himself along on a crate with wheels attached, his lower limbs withered and misshapen, his grizzled beard unkempt, his outstretched palm asking for money. Two fat men brushed past the beggar, gold chains glinting around their necks. They didn't toss him any coins. Moyenda slipped into another side street, avoiding the large holes in the road and dusty weeds growing in the cracks in the pavement, and cut past the small supermarket. The air was thick with the smell of frying from the guys selling chips and people chattered loudly to one another in Chichewa. He cut through the path between two modern, concrete buildings, avoiding the men selling counterfeit electronics and side-stepping a young boy carrying a basket containing small bags of peanuts. He reached the edge of the market where a dozen or more white mini-buses waited, their drivers yelling their destinations and helping passengers in. The mini-buses were meant to have a maximum number of passengers but the drivers always managed to jam a couple more in, the conductor frequently hanging out of the open door when there were no more seats available. Moyenda kept his head down. The mini-bus drivers all knew him. A left turn after the market took him back to the main road and he glanced carefully up and down the road before he joined it. He moved into the stream of people heading to work and glanced over his shoulder again. The man locked gazes with him. Moyenda's heart battered his ribs and he turned away abruptly. He was far too well known to be able to lose this man in Blantyre. If he did manage to slip away, all the man would have to do was ask the shoe-shine boys or the boys peddling maps to tourists or the bead-sellers where he had gone and they would point him out. They all knew Moyenda. He had worked with the homeless and the disadvantaged for over a decade.

He wove his way through the brightly dressed women carrying flat baskets of bananas and men in cheap, grey suits until he reached Samson's tailoring shop. Samson was one of the boys who had been supported by Samala and given an apprenticeship and a sewing machine. Moyenda had wanted to see how he was getting on for a while now and this seemed like the perfect opportunity. The stocky young man was sitting at his sewing machine in the shade of the awning above the shop and he greeted Moyenda cheerfully, finishing a seam before putting the piece he was working on to one side, his broad grin running from ear to ear. The two exchanged pleasantries and Moyenda stood just inside the doorway and asked how the business was going.

'Good! Business is very good, thank you. You know I will always be grateful for the belief you had in me!'

He waved his hand towards the interior of the shop at the clothes hanging on the walls. Moyenda smiled. Samson cocked his head to one side, peering closely at his former sponsor and mentor.

'Is everything okay, my friend? You look worried.'

Moyenda looked back, his smiles all gone.

'I think a man is trying to rob me. He has been watching me all morning.'

Samson looked horrified.

'How could anyone would want to do something to hurt you?!'

Moyenda swatted away his comment with a wave of his hand.

'I need to get away from him, but everyone will point me out,' he said.

'Go through the shop,' Samson said quickly. 'You can cut through from the backyard on to Henderson Street. If he comes and asks I will say you left and went east down Haile Salassie Avenue. What does he look like?'

Moyenda glanced around but could not spot the man in the crowds. He described him as fully as he could and Samson nodded.

'Look, there is a large group of people coming. Slip through the back while they pass the shop.'

Moyenda smiled, thanking his friend. He waited until the gaggle of people drew level with the shop and slipped into the dim interior and out into the yard at the back. He jogged to Henderson Street, before heading towards a quieter part of town where he knew there was an internet cafe. On the way, he checked behind him several times but saw no sign of the man. He offered up a prayer of thanks and good wishes for Samson and ducked through the wire-grilled door into the internet cafe.

Inside, he paid for half an hour of use and settled down at a grimy computer. He checked his new email address and opened up the message from Summer. He had been over and over her words since he first got it. How could the boys be overseas unless someone took them there? And if someone took them there, it could not have been done officially because no one was talking about it. Whenever he had asked whether anyone had seen them he had received no information, only sad looks from the other volunteers. Sad because they knew the boys had been taken abroad? He had always assumed sad because they feared they were dead, as did he. Was being taken abroad better? It depended on who had taken them and why, he thought.

He typed quickly, composing a reply to Miss Morris. He didn't want anyone else involved, especially if it was going to lead to them being in trouble. He hoped that she would automatically hit reply if she emailed back and any message she sent would come only to this new address but to be absolutely certain, he told her not to use the old one. When he read back through his reply, he thought it sounded melodramatic and sat back in his seat, contemplating changing what he had written. He decided against it. He hoped he was wrong about everything, but it would not hurt to be over-cautious, just in case. Before he could change his mind he sent the message, navigated to a new page, cleared the browser cache and closed down. Was that enough to cover his tracks if the man came in and looked at the computer? He did not know. He opened the web browser again and clicked on history, relieved to see it come up blank. He closed the browser, smiled at the man behind the counter and left.

***

The waiting room was soul-sapping. A low table in the middle of the room was covered in glossy magazines which were several months out of date and the chairs were vinyl-clad monsters that were uncomfortable, sweat-inducing and a pale green colour that reminded her of pus. It smelled of alcohol gel and plastic. She glanced around, wishing that she wasn't here on her own.

No one else seemed to be. She entertained a brief fantasy of him rushing in through the door, breathless and apologetic, dashing to her side and holding her hands.

'Is the father going to be joining you?'

A smiling nurse snapped out of her reverie with a jolt. Helen swallowed.

'Er, hopefully. He might get caught up in meetings though. He said not to wait.'

She folded her hands in her lap, jiggling her foot nervously. If she was being honest with herself, she knew he wasn't going to come. He had made it abundantly clear how he felt about the whole situation. She waited to be ushered through, staring at the floor, avoiding eye-contact with all the happy couples around her.

As expected, there was no last-minute dash to her side. The scan came and went and afterwards Helen sat on a bench, her shoulders hunched against a cold breeze, with a fuzzy black and white print-out of the baby clutched in her hand and a hollow feeling inside. She picked up her phone.

'Hi Robbie.'

'Hi, how did it go?'

'Fine. Fine. The baby's okay.'

'Did he bother to turn up?'

She hesitated, hoping that her answer wouldn't precipitate another of Rob's rages.

'No. I imagine he hasn't changed his mind about things,' she said, her insides clenching.

'He will. You'll see. He will.'

She relaxed, the ferocity of his reply surprising her, and sighed heavily.

'I wish I had your faith. How am I going to cope on my own with a baby?'

'He'll change his mind. And anyway, you've got me. We'll manage.'

Helen's gaze spun out over Princes Street Gardens. She didn't share her brother's confidence.

'Where are you? The line's shocking,' she said.

'Still out west. I have to go. I'll see you at the weekend.'

'Okay.'

'Chin up! He'll change his mind.'

She put her phone back in her pocket and stared again at the grainy picture.

'God, I hope you're right.'

***

Summer stepped off the train and threaded her way through the other passengers dawdling on the platform. She bought a copy of *The Scotsman* as she passed the newsagents, tucking it into the top of her bag, saving it to read on the journey back. Dodging taxis and meandering tourists, she headed left out of the station, along North Bridge and up towards the city chambers on the High Street.

Inside, the building was cool with a smell of polish and old carpets. Summer trotted up the stairs to the area occupied by the MSA to find Grace. She tapped lightly on the partly open door and popped her head in.

'Grace?'

'Summer! How lovely to see you! Are you working for us again?'

'No. Well, not that I know! I still haven't managed to get hold of Patrick and I'm a bit worried about him. He left me a bit of an odd message,' Summer said, not quite lying but not being honest. 'He seemed concerned about some of the kids in Samala and I wondered if he'd talked to you about it. He's doing an article about it. He wanted me to chase up some stuff with Moyenda, but he didn't leave me enough information to know quite what he wants me to chase up! I'd ask him but he's buggered off somewhere.'

If Grace could see through the holes in this, she wasn't letting on.

'Patrick certainly hasn't said anything to me about Samala. You'd probably be better off talking to Ed.'

72

'Ed?'

'One of the interns. He worked with Patrick on the last two articles on Samala.'

'Where can I find him?'

'Down the corridor, second on the right. It's a big room with a few people in there usually. Ed's got greasy brown hair which he sometimes ties back in an ill-advised ponytail and usually looks too scruffy to be allowed anywhere near front of house.'

Summer grinned at her bluntness and went in search. Her luck was in. Ed was at his desk and no one else was around.

'Ed?'

He looked up suspiciously and clicked something closed on his computer. Summer hoped his reaction times were faster when his bosses came in as there'd been no mistaking what he was browsing on the internet. Ed crossed his legs to hide his erection, chewing gum noisily.

'Hi. I'm Summer Morris. You work with a friend of mine, Patrick Forrester?'

'Yeah. He's on holiday at the mo. Can I help?'

'Er, he was working on an article about Samala and he seemed concerned about some things. I wondered if you knew what.'

'Why?'

'He asked me to do the pictures for it and chase up some stuff, but he didn't give me much to go on, so I don't know what kind of images he wants.'

Ed shrugged, the gum making a smacking sound in his open mouth. Summer rummaged in her bag, putting her newspaper on the table while she pulled out her notebook.

'Hey. I know her!'

Summer looked up, bemused. Ed pointed at the paper. Splashed across the front page was the news that Kate Hampton, minister for health in the Scottish Parliament, and her husband had separated. It didn't sound like the decision was mutual. Paparazzi had taken shots of her husband Paul leaving the house with packed bags and a look of absolute fury on his face.

Ed was pointing to the small, official-looking picture of Kate Hampton.

'She's the health minister. Of course you know of her.'

'No. *Know* her. Not know *of* her. Course I know *of* her. I'm not thick! I met her. I'm sure of it. She was at a party I went to. Few weeks back.'

Summer crumpled her brow in disbelief. Ed picked up the paper and squinted at the picture.

'Yeah. It was definitely her. And this is the least of her worries, frankly.'

He waved the paper before tossing it back down on the desk.

'Why?' asked Summer, still trying to comprehend that Kate Hampton could have met *Ed*.

'Cos she should hope that no one from the party wants to make a bit of money for themself.'

'The party? SNP? Or—'

'No, the party I saw her at,' cut in Ed, rolling his eyes. 'If it came out what she was up to there, her career would be in tatters!'

'Why? What happened?'

Ed clamped his lips together, still chewing. Something clicked in Summer's mind. The voice had been familiar from the television, not because she knew her personally.

'Did Patrick know Kate Hampton?'

'Well he knew her at that party! He brought her to it.'

'Were they together?'

Summer was trying to imagine the free-spirited Patrick with the tightly buttoned Kate Hampton. Ed paused theatrically, then his nonchalant veneer dropped away and he leaned forward, bursting to share the gossip.

'Well, that's one way of putting it. If he wasn't in her knickers by the end of the night I'm fuckin' blind! In fact, I'm pretty sure he was in her knickers *during* the party. They certainly went off together for long enough and came back looking... fulfilled, shall we say?'

'Kate Hampton? You're sure? She seems a bit too…
conservative.'

'Huh? She's SNP!' Ed said. 'And it was definitely her, and
he was definitely shagging her. Looks like her bloke's found out.
Tarnished goods.'

He nodded at the paper again. Summer was still trying to
take the information in when Ed added, 'And she certainly *did*
inhale!'

'Inhale?'

'You know. Not like Clinton. You know, *"hey, I tried marijuana
once. I did not inhale,"*' he said, putting on a phoney American
accent.

Summer blinked, still finding the information difficult to
digest. Not that Patrick was taking dope or that he was screwing
around with someone else's wife. Just that the wife was Kate
Hampton. Was he stealing from *her* too?

She blinked away a surprising flash of pink tinted jealousy.
Christ, Patrick could shag whoever he wanted. It was none of her
business.

Had they overlapped?

'Hang on. You're absolutely sure *Kate Hampton* was there and
that she took drugs?' she said quickly.

'Yeah! I'm telling you!'

Summer was still sceptical. Ed bit his lips together.

'What was the party for?' asked Summer.

'For? What do you mean? It was just a party. Oh, hang on,
yeah, it was for Tiny. He was off to Oz.'

'Tiny?'

'Tiny Chris Jones. Huge guy. Works in finance here. Well.
Did. He's gone to Oz. And it was definitely her. I'm amazed
nothing's come out about it. She's got enough enemies wanting
to bring her down and she was pretty stupid to have gone. Anyone
could have snapped her with their phone. Guess we were all too
wasted to care.'

He smacked the gum round his mouth again. Summer's

mind raced, trying to join the dots between Kate's call, the headlines and this latest revelation.

'Anyway, what was it you came to ask me about?'

She dragged her mind back.

'Oh. Samala. Did Patrick talk about it much? As I said, he's asked me to chase up some stuff about the boys with Moyenda, the project manager, but I don't really know what he wants me to ask.'

Ed sniffed and chewed.

'Dunno. He said he was worried about some of the boys going missing, but then, they live on the streets, right? How d'you know they're missing?'

Summer remembered the long, hot day of outreach she had done, following Moyenda as he walked around Blantyre, looking for the kids, making sure they'd eaten, checking if new children had appeared. She remembered having to choke back tears when they found a boy of about seven who was crying; he'd been left abandoned on the steps of a bank by a mother who could no longer afford to keep him. Moyenda would know if *any* of the children were missing.

'Who else was Patrick working with recently?' she asked, too annoyed by Ed to want to stay in the room with him.

'Just me and Grace really.'

'Okay. Thanks for your help. I'll let you get back to whatever you were working on.' Summer smiled thinly. Ed didn't even blush.

Back at Grace's office, Summer asked if she could disturb her again for a few minutes.

'Of course. Was Ed any help?'

'Mmm. Sort of. I see what you mean about not being front of house though!'

Grace smiled, putting down her pen.

'Has Patrick seemed… odd… at all over the last few weeks?'

'Odd? In what way?'

'Has he seemed anxious? Upset? Distracted?'

'He got himself into a complete state about Malawi in general a couple of weeks ago, saying he was fed up of red tape and officials that were on the take and so on. Why?'

'He's been a bit strange with me for a while and I wondered whether it was me or whether it was something else,' she lied uneasily, wishing the colours would settle.

'Are you two back together? After… well, you know,' said Grace hesitantly, her eyes resting on Summer's.

'No. No. We're not back together,' Summer said, struggling to find an explanation that fitted all her lies.

Grace studied her silently. Summer cursed herself for not saying what was troubling her and why she was here, right at the start. It would have been easier.

'Patrick did come in a few weeks back, all battered and bruised,' Grace said slowly. 'He was obviously very sore and moving carefully. I asked him if he'd got into a fight, but he laughed and said he'd drunk too much and fallen down the stairs in his flat.'

'When was this?'

'Ooh. Maybe a month ago? Maybe a little more?'

Summer nodded. Patrick's flat was on the ground floor but maybe he'd slipped at someone else's. Kate Hampton's? Or had Paul Hampton come home early and given Patrick a beating? Was this linked with the leaflets in the desk? A wave of queasiness ran through her stomach. Election day was next Thursday and no politician could cope with the scandal of drugs, affairs and unplanned bastard children. Her mind ran back over other things.

'Patrick seem skint recently?' she queried.

Grace nodded, the creases around her mouth deepening.

'You think he's in trouble for that?'

'Don't know,' said Summer. 'I mean, Patrick's always skint… His flat's on the ground floor.'

'Oh.' Grace bunched her lips. 'I guess he could have been beaten up, not fallen, but he made very light of it.'

Summer nodded.

'I'm sorry,' said Grace, looking at the clock. 'I should get back to work. Can I help you with anything else?'

'No, thanks. Thanks for your time. Let me know if you think of anything else?'

Summer collected her things together quickly, waved and left, her mind in overdrive.

***

'Thought you were on holiday!'

Detective Sergeant LB Stewart smiled and shrugged at the desk sergeant, a pretty young woman who'd joined the force only recently and always seemed to be looking out for him.

'Yeah, yeah. You know how it is.'

He kept walking, not entirely sure himself why he was in, and cut through to his desk. The open-plan office was a sea of paperwork and files, with LB's desk presenting the only two square feet of clear surface in the room. Like the man, his work area was immaculately presented, with crisp, clean lines and a sense of order. He pulled out his chair and booted up his computer, his enamelled cuff-links clacking on the desk as he jotted notes on a fresh piece of paper while the computer warmed up.

'Hello Ben. What are you doing in?'

It was Sandy Davidson, LB's partner at work. He sat opposite, clearing a space on his own cluttered desk just big enough for a polystyrene cup of coffee and arched his eyebrows at LB pointedly. LB smiled, reached into his wallet and fished out a tenner, handing it across with mock resignation. Sandy smiled, pocketing the money rapidly.

'I'm not in. Not officially. My curiosity has been piqued.'

'Oh aye. Is she pretty?'

LB leaned back in his chair, considering.

'No. But she does her best with what she's got.'

Sandy laughed then sipped his coffee, waiting for his partner to elaborate. LB twirled a pencil around his fingers.

'Missing person. Friend of this woman, Summer Morris; gone missing in Edinburgh.'

'Summer Morris?'

'I know. Almost as shit a name as mine.'

'No. *The* Summer Morris? Photographer?'

LB blinked, straightening up.

'Er yes. Is she famous?'

'Not *famous* famous I guess. She won an award a few years ago for her photography of Scottish landscape and did a calendar of the pictures afterwards. Read an article about her just after she won the award. She's got synaesthesia. Sees emotions as colour or something like that. Not seen much from her recently but she's good. And fairly pretty.'

'If you like blondes.'

Sandy laughed. Anya had had long blonde hair.

'So how come you're involved if the chap's gone missing in Edinburgh?'

LB sighed and shook his head.

'Long story. She seemed genuinely concerned about something happening to this guy while she was on the phone to him and of course Lothian are running around like blue-arsed flies right now and not interested. Something about her doesn't quite add up though and I wanted to check a few things.'

His computer was blinking at him, waiting for a password. LB leaned forwards, jabbed his fingers over the keys and then sat back, scratching the back of his head with the blunt end of a pencil.

'What you checking?' asked Sandy, also logging in.

'Him. Her. See if there's anything in the system.'

'What's not adding up?'

LB typed again briefly, not answering, and then looked up.

'Your Isobel watches telly, right? How many police dramas are there on these days?'

'Hundreds. Why?'

'If she came across a crime scene, what would she do?'

'Call the police, not touch anything—'

'Exactly,' cut in LB. 'She wouldn't go through the place, taking photos and removing things she thought were suspicious and that indicated she was right to be worried. She would have pulled her mobile out of her pocket and called someone, right?'

'Yeah. Is that what this Summer Morris did? Photo everything and take things?'

'Yep. She went to the guy's flat after he went missing. If anything *has* happened to him, it'll probably be impossible to get any kind of conviction on forensics now… Oh, hello. That's very interesting.'

His eyes scanned the screen in front of him and he straightened up, reading rapidly. Sandy waited. LB jotted notes quickly then glanced across his desk to his partner.

'Patrick Forrester, the missing guy, had a complaint of theft against him this February. Never formally charged though.'

'Oh aye? Who made the complaint?'

'Summer Morris.'

Sandy's brows shot up. LB pulled up the case file and read, précising it out loud.

'Summer Morris and Patrick Forrester were in a relationship that, claims Morris, was sound. However, while she was away for a few days, over a thousand pounds was withdrawn from her account, using her card and PIN. The card had been left at Forrester's flat.'

'Any previous history of theft?'

'Just checking, but I don't think so. The only other thing on file about Forrester is that he reported a bike stolen a year ago. Never been recovered.'

'Insurance job?'

'Maybe.'

'What about Summer Morris?'

LB's fingers rattled over the keys.

'Nothing.'

He cupped his chin in his hand, his eyes flicking over his notes and back to the screen, the fingers of his right hand playing a pencil around his knuckles.

'Sandy, why do people disappear?'

'Sex… money…'

Sandy shrugged.

'Why call *her*?' asked LB looking over.

'She's still on speed-dial?'

LB acknowledged the idea with a tilt of his head.

'Does this all seem odd to you?'

'It all seems like Lothian's problem to me,' said Sandy. 'And that you should piss off and enjoy your holiday.'

'Yeah. Point taken.'

He printed off the information he had found, folded his page of notes crisply, logged out of the computer system and shut the machine down.

'Okay. See you when I'm back,' he said, waving his hand loosely over the top of his head.

Sandy grinned.

'Leave that to Lothian,' he said, pointing at the piece of paper in LB's hand. 'And enjoy your break!'

LB nodded, but his brain was fidgety. It all felt wrong.

THURSDAY AFTERNOON

Summer sipped her coffee, watching the passers-by on The Royal Mile. Still a little early in the year for the main tourist mobs, it was nonetheless busy. The wind was fresh and she was glad to be behind the plate-glass window inside the cafe. She flicked her notebook open and stared at her scribbles. Her eyes ran over the list of messages from Patrick's phone. Someone, possibly Kate Hampton, arranging a meeting; a different woman calling about an appointment; a threat about money it seemed; another angry man – Kate Hampton's husband? Last Saturday at the latest, according to the day and time stamp on the answerphone. Then another one from Kate Hampton, also now angry. Was she pregnant?

How did the bruises fit in? A month or so ago. Too early to be from Kate's husband? Loan shark? Certainly, Patrick could rarely balance the books. Could he have been blackmailing Kate? But that didn't fit in with when the party was, did it? Or was he blackmailing her about the affair? Did he sell all the stuff from his flat to pay off a loan shark or was it missing for another reason? Was it really just a break-in gone wrong? Were burglars that tidy?

Summer shook her head and dropped another cube of sugar into her coffee, stirring slowly, ignoring the hum and bustle of the crowded cafe. She was sure that Kate Hampton was involved somehow. Election day was exactly a week away and Kate

Hampton, minister for health, was having an affair, taking drugs and might need an abortion, and the person who could bring her down was Patrick, who sounded like he was being threatened by heavies. Had he threatened to tell her husband? Had he *told* her husband? Is that what her second message had been referring to? How much of all this should she tell the police? It was all supposition and gossip.

She tapped the spoon on the side of the cup, still undecided, and picked up her phone to check her emails. She dumped several spam messages into trash and skipped a couple from the shop on Skye that sold limited edition reprints of her photos, scrolling down to open a message from Moyenda. It had been sent from a personal email account and not the one at Samala where she'd emailed him. Her message was copied at the bottom – so he'd forwarded it on to this other account.

'Dear Summer, Of course I remember you. How are you? How is your business? Are you still taking pictures of mountains and water? My wife Chifundo sends her best wishes to you and hopes you are well. She is pleased that you remembered her!

'I am worried to hear your news. The boys and now Patrick. Bad things are happening. I cannot write about them. But you should be careful who you talk to. Do not look into the boys. Please. I do not want you to disappear too. I told Patrick not to but he is a headstrong man who does not listen. Please.

'I pray, my sister, that you will stay safe. I will try and phone you if I am able to, but I do not want to write things. Please do not use my old email address. I hope that Patrick returns safely. Your brother, Moyenda.'

Summer's eyes widened and her fingers clicked over the keys of her phone.

'Dear Moyenda, why do you think Patrick has disappeared? Where are Tendai and Henry? What about Mabvuto and Limbani? Please tell me what you know? I'm desperately worried.'

She signed off then caught the eye of the waitress and ordered another coffee, her mind spinning.

Just as she was finishing the second coffee her phone bleeped to indicate a new text message. It was a Malawian number, but not Moyenda's. Summer's brow creased. She didn't know anyone else in Malawi. She opened the message. There were just two words: *child trafficking*. The sugary coffee in her stomach turned to bile and her hand covered her mouth, flame-orange unease rippling through her.

'Shit. Shit, shit, shit, shit, shit.'

***

Helen had always prided herself on her organisational skills and time management. She might prefer an old-fashioned Filofax to a modern electronic organiser but she never missed an appointment, her to-do list was always cleared and the business was prospering. Right now though, she was sitting in her office at the shop, staring at the accounts with her mind on the grainy black and white image from the morning.

She had blocked the morning off for the scan and this afternoon she had written, in ink, that she would go through the accounts and make sure they were up to date. Writing things in ink usually made sure they got done but her method just wasn't working today.

She sighed and tried to focus, her fingers tracing along the creases in her brow as she stared at the screen. But the numbers were just symbols and she was making no progress whatsoever. She closed the files down, pulled her organiser towards her and looked for the next free slot when she could finish going through the accounts. She knew there wasn't one for a while, which was why she'd put it in for this afternoon, despite suspecting that her mind might not be on the task in hand. Eventually finding a free evening, she uncapped her fountain pen and wrote 'accounts' in the space and underlined it.

Resigned to the fact that she wasn't going to get anything done until she'd cleared her head, she called her oldest friend

Megan – a woman she could rely on for clear thinking and sensible advice.

Megan worked part-time at the library and Thursday was one of her days off.

'Hey, girl! How was the scan?' Megan asked as soon as she answered.

Helen heard the fears in her voice. Trust Megan to spot that things weren't okay.

'Fine. It was all fine. Meg, are you free this afternoon?'

'Of course. You okay?'

'No. Not really. I'm completely panicked about everything.'

'On my way. You at the shop?'

'Mmm. Sorry – I can't close up, just in case someone comes by.'

'No worries. Get the kettle on!'

Helen kept herself busy in the office at the back of the shop until she heard the bell above the shop door jingle. She popped her head out from the office and beamed to see the familiar, effortlessly chic, tiny form of her friend. Helen could never stop admiring how beautifully turned out Meg always was. She had once asked her how she managed it and Meg had said the key was to have everything in the wardrobe in one of three toning colours. Then you could pull out any combination and always look good. Her three colours were a dark grey, a silvery grey-blue and a cream, which offset her auburn hair and delicate colouring perfectly. However much the concept appealed to her, Helen had never had the guts to throw away all her mismatched clothes or the money to invest in a new wardrobe, but instead was trying to take the middle ground of only buying new things in her set of colours. She knew that as a consequence she looked smart on business days but somewhat uncoordinated off duty.

Helen made tea then perched in the office chair at her desk, leaving the comfortable sofa normally reserved for clients for her friend. She sighed heavily. Megan cocked her head.

'Come on, girl, talk. What are you panicking about?'

'The baby!' said Helen. 'What else?'

Megan waited and Helen smiled to herself, relieved to be able to rely on Megan to listen first and offer advice only later. She peeked into the shop, took a deep breath and started.

'Don't get me wrong – in many ways I'm delighted that I'm pregnant. I've always wanted to have children, but I'd imagined they would come after the part involving meeting the right guy and getting settled.'

She tailed off.

'Still nothing from Patrick?' Megan asked.

Helen shook her head.

'He didn't come to the scan this morning. I left a message for him telling him about it, but…'

Her words ran out again.

'Maybe he was busy?' offered Meg.

Helen cast her eyes up scornfully.

'No. He didn't come because he doesn't want me to keep the baby and he doesn't care about me. If he'd cared about me, he wouldn't have been two-timing me with *her!*'

She jutted her chin towards the paper. Meg bunched her lips sympathetically but kept quiet. Helen took a sip of her tea and sighed again, lost in her world.

'Do you think you two might ever get back together?' asked Meg.

'Much as it might offer some solutions, I doubt it. He's a liar and a cheat which makes it hard for me to trust him, and I've said and done things that can't be taken back.'

She fiddled with the paper, turning it over to hide the headlines before continuing.

'Last time I saw him, he'd gone and got some leaflets for an abortion clinic. And you know, some of me can see where he's coming from. I honestly don't know how I'm going to cope on my own – he's not going to support me, either financially or emotionally – so can I really bring this child into the world? I could force him to pay me child support, but the assessors would say he had nothing to give me! He's never got any money.'

'Ah, but is that because he spends it or because he actually just doesn't have any?' interjected Meg.

'Fair point. If I have the baby, I'll have to get him to support me financially.'

'If?' said Meg, looking up sharply, her curls bobbing as she did. 'I didn't think there was any question over that? Even if it might be easier.'

'No. No, there isn't really. Especially not now. This makes it all more real.'

Helen took the small black and white picture out and passed it across. Meg looked down at it.

'Boy or girl? Or didn't you ask?' said Meg, handing the picture back.

'Too early to be sure.'

Helen tucked the picture away safely into the back of her Filofax and fell silent, scratching her forehead.

'What the hell am I going to do, Meg? I can't still run the business when I'm waddling about, umpteen months pregnant and then with a baby in my arms, and I sure as hell can't afford to employ anyone to cover for me while I take time out!'

'Could Rob help?'

'Jesus, no. When he's okay, Rob's fine to help with the decorating and so on, but he couldn't run the business and he can't have the baby for me!'

'How is he at the moment?'

'He's out west. He's gone fishing with some mates. He's not been great recently so I'd rather he pissed off and regrouped than had a major wobble in front of the clients.'

She sipped her tea again, her eyes on Meg, her cue that this was now the time for advice. Meg screwed one side of her mouth up.

'I don't know what to suggest. I mean, the options are you have the baby and run the business, or you have the baby and someone else runs the business, or you don't have the baby.'

Helen shook her head rapidly at the final option and Meg nodded.

'Okay. You don't have the money to hand it on, even temporarily do you? So you've got to find a way of doing both. Hey, we'll work something out.'

She leaned forwards and rubbed Helen's shoulder. Helen smiled wanly.

'Yeah. I don't have any other choice, do I?'

Meg smiled.

'Why don't you come over to mine at the weekend and meet Annie and Bob. They have a four-year-old boy and a one-year-old little girl. I don't think they're intending to have any more kids so they'll probably be happy to pass on some of their stuff if you wanted it. That would help, yeah?'

Helen breathed out slowly, her face relaxing.

'Yeah. That would help. Thank you.'

Meg grinned.

'Little Miss Organised,' she chided gently. 'Normally, your day is planned so meticulously and you have weekly, monthly and yearly goals all mapped out too. This has really thrown your nice neat order, hasn't it?'

'You might well tease me about it, but it helped me build up a damn fine business!' Helen retorted good-naturedly.

'That you have, girl, that you have.'

The bell above the door jangled and Helen looked up.

'Oh, it's Mrs Evans. This will take a while.'

She looked apologetically at Meg. Mrs Evans was going to take up the rest of the afternoon in all likelihood, effectively ending their chat. Meg shrugged.

'No problem. I'll scoot off and leave you to it. I'll text you about the weekend.'

The two women headed out into the shop and Helen turned to her client.

'Hello there. I have a whole pile of new swatches for you to look at, Mrs Evans. Did you want to grab a seat and I'll bring them out.'

She smiled a goodbye to Meg and squared her shoulders. She had to believe that everything would work out or she would sink.

***

The meeting was spiralling out of her control. The night before, Kate had phoned Douglas to tell him that she was resigning. He'd told her to sleep on it and he'd discuss it with her today. She'd wanted to see him first thing, get it out of the way, but he'd been too busy to meet her and so she'd left her letter of resignation with his secretary. A morning of campaigning had followed during which she heard nothing from him. Now it was after lunch and they had finally managed to meet. Despite the comfort of the seats in his office, she was taut with stress. Douglas leaned forward across his old-fashioned mahogany desk and steepled his fingers.

'Let me talk to Paul,' he said, his voice soothing.

'No! No. It wouldn't help.'

God, the last thing she needed was for him to talk to Paul and find out what was really going on.

'No, Douglas, I've made my decision. I can't rescue my marriage *and* do justice to the job, and my marriage has to come first.'

'Kate, Kate, I understand that, but please, just wait until after the election? A Cabinet reshuffle's not unusual and I can let you move graciously to the back benches without you needing to resign right now.'

'I promised Paul that I would.'

'Let me talk to Paul. I'll tell him you offered your resignation but that I didn't accept it.'

'Douglas, you're not listening to me. I would like to resign as health minister. Now.'

His expression hardened.

'What aren't you telling me?'

'Nothing. Nothing. Please, Douglas? I need to keep my promise to Paul.'

'Kate, I have a packed afternoon ahead and I haven't the time to discuss this properly right now. I'll call Paul, tell him what you've said and that I'll accept your determination to step down once the election is over. He's a fair man. He'll understand that if you resign in the middle of the run-up to the election things could go badly for the party.'

There it was. The opening she should take. Things would go much worse for the party if he didn't accept her resignation now and her affair became public knowledge before election day. She had to say something.

'So, that's settled then,' said Douglas briskly, and the opportunity vanished. 'I'll call Paul tonight and then you can be reshuffled into a quieter role after next Thursday.'

Her eyes swam and she gripped the sides of the chair. Douglas was making her break her promise to Paul. It was all well and good for Douglas to want to keep it under wraps until after next Friday, but what if it all came out? What if Patrick made good on his threat and told the press?

She glanced up and realised that Douglas was waiting for her to leave.

'Douglas,' she started, her voice frail.

'Kate, it's settled. I'll call Paul tonight. Now, we both have busy afternoons.'

He stood and started to put his jacket on. Kate dragged herself to her feet, dizzy with emotion and nodded to him.

'Thank you, Douglas,' she said automatically, and hurried out of his office.

As soon as she was free, she called Paul. He didn't answer. She called his secretary who said he was in a meeting and couldn't be disturbed.

'Can I take a message, Mrs Hampton?'

'Er yes. Can you tell him I called? Thanks, Caroline.'

She rang off then texted quickly.

'I tried to resign. I really tried. Douglas won't accept until after Thursday. He's going to call you to explain. I love you. K.xx'

She hesitated before sending it. She really wanted to plead with him not to mention her affair, but knew that if she did it would only goad him into telling Douglas all the gory details and that really, really wouldn't do.

Could she be sure that Patrick wouldn't talk? The money that would have made certain of that was still burning a hole in the bottom of her bag.

THURSDAY, LATE AFTERNOON

Patrick was watching the light in the grille lose strength. He hadn't slept much again the night before – just fitful noddings-off interspersed with jerking awake in terror – and now exhaustion was adding to his pain and fear.

Why was he here? What was going to happen to him? When his captor had appeared this morning, Patrick had found the courage to ask him why he was being held and what the man wanted from him, only to have the shit kicked out of him again. His mouth was still scabbed from his follow-up question, asking the man if he was a hired thug or if he was doing all this for personal reasons. The man's terse reply had been that he shouldn't mess with other people's lives and that this had been coming to him for a long time, then he'd left abruptly. The trouble was, that hadn't specifically narrowed the options as to who was doing this to him. He wasn't even sure why it was important for him to know why he was here; it just was.

Patrick was sure he didn't know the man. He wished his head was less foggy so he could try and figure things out. Was he a friend of someone he knew? The man had a clinical brutality about him that suggested not. Patrick couldn't say that the man was enjoying hurting him; his attitude was aloof and disconnected unless Patrick tried to talk to him. Even when he turned violent, it was controlled and detached, as if it was something he did naturally. Maybe he was a boxer or a professional fighter, thought Patrick, or a bouncer or security guard or something. Ex-army? He had seen flashes of tattoos on the man's arms but lots of people had those.

He had no idea where he was being held. All he could see through the grille was a faint green blur – grass probably – and the changing light levels. Wherever he was, he was in the middle of nowhere; that much he could fathom. You can't hood a man and carry him into a house in suburbia and it was too damn quiet for there to be neighbours or even a road nearby. He hadn't heard another car since his arrival.

His head snapped up at the sound of drawing bolts and he waited. His captor trotted down the stairs with something in his hands. Patrick tried not to flinch as the man shoved it at him.

'Bacon butty. Enjoy,' the man snarled, thrusting it into Patrick's hands.

Patrick started to nibble on it warily. The man turned to go.

'Are you going to kill me?' Patrick said.

The man turned back slowly and Patrick's stomach started to knot in anticipation of pain. The man stared at him.

'Haven't decided yet. Probably. Unless I get convinced you're worth allowing to live. Morally and financially.'

'You'd really murder someone?' Patrick said, trying not to let his voice quaver.

The man snorted a laugh.

'Done worse,' he said and spun back to the door.

Patrick watched him leave, listening as the locks were refastened. He bit hungrily into the bacon roll.

Morally and financially. What did he mean? Had someone been sent a ransom note for him? He laughed hollowly at the absurdity, wondering if there was *anyone* who would pay to have him released. He certainly had no money. It always seemed to go through his fingers like water. Which brought him circling back to Bevan. If Bevan was behind this, was it to frighten him into paying up? All well and good except Patrick hadn't got the money yet. He would already have paid it if he had. He didn't want to think about the consequences of Bevan knowing that.

Morally opened a whole new basket of reasons. Kate? No, surely not. Neither Kate nor her husband would have the connections or the nerve to kidnap him. He shouldn't have threatened to tell the papers though. It had been a rash threat, a last-ditch attempt to get Bevan off his back and be rid of her, but maybe Kate had taken fright and was keeping him out of the way until after the election.

The thought cheered him mildly. If that was the case, surely once next Thursday passed he would be freed. His spirits sank immediately. No, that wouldn't work, because what would there be to stop him going to the press *then*? To have an affair revealed would be nothing in comparison to having held the lover hostage to protect your reputation until the votes were counted.

It must be Bevan. In which case, once he'd been stripped of anything financially viable, he would be dead.

***

Summer flared her toes and balanced her laptop on her knees, her feet on a wicker footstool. Spread out on the sofa next to her were all her notes and new copies of her photos of Patrick's flat; on the table next to her, a half-pint mug of coffee and Patrick's laptop. She started browsing the internet, frequently referring to Patrick's laptop, in particular his notebooks and his internet bookmarks, working her way through blogs and Facebook pages that seemed to make no sense whatsoever. Every now and then she lifted her head, stretched and shifted her focus to the crammed shelves of the floor-to-ceiling bookcases opposite her, trying to understand what thread Patrick had been unravelling.

Two hours later, she clicked on a link in one of Patrick's electronic notebooks that took her to a page of pictures in another blog. She skimmed through, glancing at the children shown at a birthday party. Suddenly a smile stood out and she caught her breath. She right-clicked on the picture, saved it and printed it. For the next half-hour, she followed links from the blog to a Facebook page, and then through various friends listed there, and then through friends of friends and their pictures, shaking her head at the way people forgot to sort their online privacy settings out. The smile she was chasing appeared several times and she saved and printed a copy of each incidence. Half a dozen pictures later, she shifted her laptop to the space next to her, balancing it on her notes, and scampered upstairs to retrieve the pictures from the printer in the study. Back in the lounge, she squatted in front of the bottom shelf of one of the myriad bookcases that encircled the room, pulling out photo albums and leafing through them. She found the vein of pictures she was after and slid them out of the acid-free sleeves. Sitting back on her heels, she compared the pictures she'd just printed off with the ones from the albums, her head tipped first to one side then the other as she stared. Her thoughts clouded with grey and black.

They were definitely the same child. Limbani. Now in Kent.

She returned to the laptop and pulled up the Facebook page again.

'Not savvy enough to block any old sod from seeing pictures of your children, adopted or otherwise, but savvy enough not to put your number on the contact details page, huh?' she muttered and accessed an online telephone directory.

She typed in 'Saunders', put Kent for the location and clicked on 'find'. A long list of names and numbers came up and she tried to cross-reference with other information from the web pages – where the party had been, what people had listed they were doing in their status box – eventually narrowing the list down to about a dozen numbers. She started calling.

She hit pay-dirt on the eighth number.

'Oh, good afternoon, I'm looking for John Saunders of Saunders and Preston.'

'This is his home number, not his office number. Can I give

you that? The office will open again at eight thirty tomorrow morning.'

'Actually, it was his home number I was after. I'm a journalist writing an article on adopting children in Malawi and I wondered if your husband or you would be prepared to talk to me?'

There was a pause on the end of the line. Flickers of damson apprehension danced around orange sparks of unease as Summer wondered if she had found the reason that Patrick was missing.

'I'll check with John.'

'Thank you. The article is a good news one – about how much benefit the children have gained now they've been adopted. It would be really good if you could give me a few minutes of your time.'

'I'll talk to John. I'm sorry, what did you say your name was?'

Summer thought quickly.

'Susan Morris.'

'Okay.'

The woman rang off abruptly. Summer circled the number several times in her notebook. Was she imagining things or had the woman been cagey?

She drew her notebook towards her and wrote 'Patrick' in the centre of a fresh page, enclosing it with a wavy line until it looked like his name was written in a cloud. She drew lines radiating out from the cloud, one for each aspect of Patrick's life that she'd discovered, adding notes along the lines and blocks of information at the ends. How much was true and how much just supposition, she wondered, and fished out a highlighter, marking up all of the facts she was sure about. When she finished, there was a lot of information on the sheet but precious little in yellow. Had any of the missing children been adopted? If so how? And by whom? Moyenda might know, or at least know how to find out. She emailed him quickly to ask.

The emptiness of Patrick's flat still bothered her. She twirled the pen around in her fingers, staring at the page, then on a whim she opened her laptop and accessed eBay. The most distinctive item that was missing was the chameleon carving and she searched completed listings for it. It took a couple of attempts for her to find it but once she had and could pull up what else the seller had listed she found that Patrick had been busy. She jotted down the long list of sold items in her notes. No wonder his flat had looked empty. None of it had fetched much, not even the chameleon carving he'd loved so much. He must be in serious trouble.

She checked the clock and grabbed her mobile.

***

Detective Sergeant LB Stewart answered on the fourth ring.

'Hi, Summer,' he said in a resigned voice, putting his folder down on the glass-topped table in front of him and lining it up with the article on Summer he'd printed from the internet.

'How did you know it was me?'

'Caller ID. Don't you dare tell me you've been back to the flat.'

'I haven't, but I did want to update you on things.'

'Can't you update Lothian?' he said gruffly.

'No.'

'Why?'

'Because it's mostly conjecture.'

'So why are you wanting to tell me?'

There was a pause at the other end and LB smiled to himself as he imagined her biting back her impatience. He leaned back in the battered leather seat, the most comfortable and lived-in looking thing in his flat.

'You showed an interest?' she said at last.

'Okay. What have you found out?'

LB reached for a pen and flipped the papers over in front of him until he got to a fresh sheet.

'It's too complicated to tell you over the phone.'

'So why are you phoning?' he said, leaning back and tossing the pen down.

Again there was a delay before she answered.

'To see if you wanted to have dinner. So I could tell you what I've found out.'

This time the delay was on his side. He rubbed his palm over his chin.

'Are you asking me out?' he said eventually.

Summer's laugh shot back.

'No I'm not. It's just that it's too late to meet for a coffee, so I'm offering to cook you dinner and tell you what I've found out about Patrick and Kate Hampton.'

'Kate Hampton? What about Kate Hampton?'

'Let me cook you dinner and I'll tell you. As I said, it's largely conjecture, which is why I'm reluctant to tell Lothian. The last thing Kate Hampton needs is another scandal, especially when it's built on the word of a ned.'

LB laughed, his curiosity piqued.

'Okay, I bite. Maybe. Can you cook?'

'Yes. I cook very well, thank you very much. Anything you don't eat?'

'Badly cooked food.'

He heard her laugh again on the other end. He hadn't actually been joking.

She gave him directions and rang off. LB tipped his head back and sighed.

'Curiosity killed the cat,' he said, placing his phone squarely on the table.

He re-read his notes, scratching his head with the end of a pen, one knee up, his toes pressed against the edge of the table. A copy of *The Scotsman* lay on the table and he glanced at the headline. Patrick Forrester and Kate Hampton, allegedly, and now her husband had left her and Patrick had disappeared. His eyes narrowed and he sucked his teeth, details of old cases and possible links crystallising in his brain. He added to his notes, his writing neat and succinct, and then gathered the pages together, carefully checking the order of them. Once satisfied, he slid them into a brown leather attaché case, slotted the pen into the holder and zipped the case up. Did he really want to get suckered into this? It wasn't his case; wasn't any of his business.

'*Merde*,' he muttered, checking the clock and calculating how long he had to shower and change.

Boredom would be the death of him.

***

The ringing phone shattered the silence of Patrick's flat. It rang four times before Patrick's recorded voice cut in.

'Hello! You've reached Patrick Forrester's number. Please leave your message after the bleep.'

'Patrick? Are you there? I know you're probably screening, but please, pick up? Please? … Okay, well, the scan went well… I'm sorry about what I said… I'm just scared. I would have helped you, but now with a baby coming… I can't. I'm sorry. I'm sorry for what I did. Please, Patrick, call me back? We really need to talk.'

The caller hesitated and then hung up, leaving dead air in the flat. The light on the machine blinked, next to a glowing eight.

THURSDAY EVENING

'It's not a formal dinner,' Summer said as she opened the door.

'I'm not dressed formally.'

He watched her eyes skip over his jacket and tie, the expensive white shirt and the polished-conker leather shoes. She raised her eyebrows. She was wearing jeans, a loose-fitting kaftan-top and no make-up. Her feet sported hiking socks. As he'd presumed, dinner really wasn't a date. Did she think he'd assumed it was? This *was* casual for him.

'Come in,' she said, standing back and letting him pass her. 'Let me take your jacket.'

He crossed the threshold and stood in the hallway next to a plastic tray of muddy walking boots while she hung his jacket up, his eyes drifting over the framed photograph that filled the wall opposite. The picture had been printed as a single sheet and took up the full width of the hallway.

'Wow.'

She followed his gaze.

'Thanks. It's not really the right space to hang it in and it was a vain folly to get it printed in the first place, but I like it.'

'How much does it weigh?'

'Oh, God, lots. The fixings for it are industrial! That's not the first thing people usually ask!'

He acknowledged the point with a flick of his brows and a shrug.

'Is that the one you won an award for?'

'One of them. I used some of the prize money to get that printed and hung. I'm surprised you know about that,' she said, her modesty fresh and genuine.

'My partner told me.'

He saw her glance flash to his hands.

'Work partner,' he added.

She nodded and ushered him through to the lounge. His gaze swept over the room. The room had floor-to-ceiling bookcases filling one wall entirely and most of another. What wall space wasn't taken up with shelving sported high quality framed photos.

'I take it you read a lot?'

He met her eye as he sat on the sofa.

'Yeah. You could say that. Can I get you a drink?'

'Just something soft please – I'm driving.'

'Okay. And what should I call you? DS Stewart? LB?'

Her mouth scrunched up as she tried out both names. LB smiled.

'LB is fine. My partner calls me Ben. Either will do.'

'Ben? Presumably the B of LB?'

'Almost. And would you prefer Summer or Ms Morris?'

'Christ. Ms Morris makes me sound like I'm seventy, living with my twelve cats and wearing a hairnet! Summer.'

He nodded, laughing. Summer disappeared to make drinks. Left alone, LB took in the room. The bottom shelves of all the bookcases held photo albums, with more laid sideways over the tops. The rest of the cases were filled with paperbacks apart from one shelf that held leather-bound notebooks. He wondered how anyone could read this many books in a hundred years, never mind at her age. A small, flat-screen TV huddled in the corner, its remote control on the top, the angle of the screen confirming that it wasn't regularly watched. The wooden table at the side of him was made from a slice through a tree-trunk, irregularly shaped but with a high polish on its surface. Three more books were on it, bookmarked at various levels of completion, together with two coasters, also made of wood and looking as if they were slivers through branches of the same tree as the table. On the more conventional, modern table in the window were more papers and clutter. The mantel above the open fire contained a few carvings and a painting hung on the wall above. LB walked over to look at the signature – P Morris 1971. Mother? Father?

He turned as Summer reappeared.

'Relative?' he asked, indicating the picture.

'Mum did it. Dad made the table.'

'Artistic family.'

She shrugged.

'Elderflower cordial okay?'

'Perfect. Thank you.'

He took the glass from her and moved back to the sofa, unsure as to how to play things. He didn't have any close female friends and was used to gathering evidence and taking statements in very different surroundings than over a home-cooked dinner. Summer made the decision for him.

'Dinner will be another half-hour or so. Perhaps I could tell you about what I've found out – well, what I think I've found out – about Patrick?'

He nodded. Summer retrieved a bundle of papers from the table in the window and settled back in a chair at the side of the sofa, placing her glass of wine carefully on a coaster on the table. LB waited while she shuffled through the sheets, watching her fidget and wondering why she was so anxious. She put half the stack on the floor for a moment, a mind-map on the top. LB read over it quickly while Summer found the sheet she was looking for, snatching his gaze away as she scooped the bundle up again.

'Okay,' she started. 'Shall I tell you my theory first, and then explain how I got to it?'

LB would have preferred evidence first, leading to a theory but he shrugged and nodded.

'Would you mind if I jotted notes while you talk?' he asked.

She shook her head and he picked up the attaché case and retrieved his notebook from it, tucking the case against the side of the sofa.

'Fire away.'

Summer settled herself in the chair and looked at the sheets in her lap, composing her thoughts. LB watched her carefully, part of him still questioning why he was there. He uncapped his fountain pen, a fresh page in front of him.

'Okay. Much of this is based on conjecture and something a complete ned told me,' she started.

LB hid his smile, his eyes twinkling.

'I think that Patrick and Kate Hampton were having an affair,' Summer carried on. 'Which is why her husband has walked out.'

She started to draw breath to continue, but LB jumped in.

'Whoa! Patrick was having an affair with Kate Hampton, minister for health?' he asked, eyebrows arched. 'Based on what evidence, other than that her husband has left her?'

'That's where the ned comes in. Guy at the Malawi–Scotland Alliance, the MSA. He was at a party and said Kate Hampton and Patrick arrived together and that they were obviously *together* at the party. Also said that Kate smoked dope.'

LB felt his eyes pop and forced himself to look more neutral.

'And his evidence would be…?'

'None. No one took pictures as far as I know and from his description of the party, everyone would have been too stoned or too drunk or both to be able to accurately verify any of it. Hence me telling you and not Lothian.'

'And what do you expect me to do with all this information?'

'I don't know but you asked me to keep you informed so I am.'

LB jotted notes, shaking his head slightly.

'And I think that Patrick might have been blackmailing Kate to get money, to pay off a loan shark.'

LB's gaze crawled back up, his head still lowered.

'What?'

'You heard. And before you ask, no, I have no evidence for that either. Patrick arrived at work one day about a month ago, beaten up, although he claims he fell down the stairs in his flat. His flat's on the ground floor but maybe he was at someone else's flat. But anyway, the messages on the phone…'

LB's head snapped up, his eyes locking on her.

'What messages? Whose phone?'

His words seemed to rock her backwards and her reply came back hesitantly.

'Patrick's. I recorded the messages on his answerphone. Anyway, one of them sounded like it was from a loan shark.'

'Wait! You did what?!'

'Made a copy of the messages on his answerphone. I haven't deleted them, they're still there. I thought I'd told you this.'

'No.'

LB breathed slowly to settle his frustration.

'Why would Patrick get involved with a loan shark?' he asked when he'd managed to compose himself.

Summer's mouth was sulky and he had to force himself not to snap at her.

'Don't know for sure, but he was always short of money and always full of grand schemes that'd make him rich. I know he needed money earlier this year. My guess is that he overstretched himself on one of these grand schemes and it didn't work out and so he went to a shark.'

'Why not go to a bank?'

'The banks wouldn't lend to Patrick. His credit rating is shit.'

LB stared at her, still trying to follow the thread from Kate Hampton. Summer opened her mouth as if to continue but LB held up his hand.

'Okay, stop. I want to start right at the beginning and have you outline what you know, how you know it and when you found it out. Let's start again at Tuesday, after you got the call. What happened next?'

Summer sighed, gathered all her papers together again and sorted them into a different order. Taking a deep breath, she started again, working her way chronologically through her week. She reached Ed's assertion that he'd met Kate at a party.

'So I thought, that's where I know the voice from and therefore Patrick and Kate must have been having an affair.'

'Don't,' cut in LB, his voice clipped. 'Don't tell me what your theories are. Just tell me what you did and what you found out. I just want the evidence.'

Summer stared at him, bunching her lips.

'Why? Why don't you want my reasoning?'

'As Sherlock Holmes said, "It is a capital mistake to theorise before one has data. It biases the judgement." I want to see if I come to the same conclusions as you, based on the same facts.'

'Stop talking to me as if I'm a child being told the school rules. Why wouldn't you reach the same conclusions?' she said, her brows flicking into a frown.

'Because your reasoning could be biased. As could your evidence.'

Summer raised her brows, her mouth set, her eyes like ice shards. LB rubbed his jaw, his stubble rasping against his palm. He was too used to interrogating witnesses. He needed to stay patient; remember that she wasn't a detective, even if she had been trying to find out why her friend was missing. He needed to stop treating her like an inept junior.

He held his hands up in peace.

'Sorry. I'm not explaining myself well. Some of your evidence is based on the words of a ned as you so delightfully called him. The rest all comes from you. It will all have inherent bias.'

She folded her arms challengingly, waiting for him to explain, no warmth in her demeanour.

'All witness statements have inherent bias,' he said carefully. 'Mine, yours, everyone's. Some witnesses are racist, some don't like women, some are religious, some aren't... What people are like, how they've been brought up... it flavours what they remember, how they describe things. How your ned describes that party will be very different from how I would describe that party.'

She nodded, her posture relaxing slightly, a smile tickling the edges of her mouth. LB ploughed on.

'You made a complaint against Patrick Forrester for stealing from you, less than three months ago. It makes your information biased.'

Summer blinked, looking as if she'd been slapped.

'I asked you here for dinner so I could tell you what I know. So you could help Patrick. Not so you could sit there and cast things up like that!' she spat.

LB fired back.

'You asked me here because I'm a cop. I'm just telling you how cops work. We have to take each piece of evidence and assess its value, its credibility. And frankly, you stretch my patience and you look wrong. All. Wrong.'

Her eyes were glacial but he went on, needing to clear the atmosphere.

'You report this guy for theft, yet it's you he calls when he's in trouble. I have to wonder why. Why are you involved at all? You go to his flat, you photograph everything, you take things away. Why? If he winds up dead in a ditch we have your word and your word alone as to what his flat looked like when he went missing. What was there… what has gone? How do I know that you didn't rearrange things before you photographed them? How do I know whether you found those bits and pieces in the yard at the back or somewhere else? Or made it all up? Is he even missing? Why has no one else reported him missing? You say you listened to the messages when you were there. Why? Why even go? Why not leave the police to do their job?'

'The police aren't *doing* anything! I asked you for help and you treat me like *I'm* the one who's behind all this!'

There were furious tears brightening her eyes.

'I went to his flat to see if anything was being done to find him. There was nothing. No tape, no cops. Nothing! Why would I rearrange things? Why would I make this up? Believe me, I have *never* wanted to be involved with the police.'

LB sighed, letting the air trickle slowly out of his nose. Arty parents? A name like Summer? He could almost smell the dope-filled house and feel the antipathy towards authority. No, she wouldn't want to get involved with the police.

'Summer, I'm just telling you what I see. Most people would not have acted the way you have. You contaminated a crime scene! You're asking me to help you because you say you're worried about this guy, yet your history with him is difficult, angry, complicated. Then you tell me that you think he's having an affair with a high-powered woman. Maybe you're jealous about that. Maybe there's more anger in there.'

He looked carefully at her, trying to make his expression soft. She was shaking, her mouth a hard line, her shoulders tight.

'I think you should leave.'

Summer's voice was brittle. LB drew a deep breath, his eyes measuring her. He nodded.

'I'll leave if you insist, but if you are genuinely worried about this guy disappearing, if something really has happened to him, if your assumptions are in any way valid, you need me to help you.'

Summer leaned back, her arms still tightly folded against her chest, her lips pressed so hard together they were almost invisible. He waited.

'Excuse me,' she said, getting up abruptly and stalking past him. 'I need to check something in the kitchen.'

LB's eyes followed her until she left the room and then he closed them, sighing heavily. He genuinely hadn't intended to upset her, but once he'd got started, it had all come tumbling out. He stretched his back, wishing he hadn't come, his eyes scanning the books and the pictures jostling for space on the walls. Presumably she had tidied up before he arrived but the sheer number of items in the room along with their complete lack of order made him feel agitated. His gaze fell on the mind-map again and he tilted his head to look at it. She'd only talked about half of what was on the page. He read over the other half. Child trafficking? Was Patrick involved with that? He frowned. Would that link in with his job? He tore his gaze away as Summer returned.

'Would you still like me to leave?' he asked politely.

She hesitated, and then forced the words out.

'No. You're right. I do look wrong as you put it. And I do need your help.'

LB nodded.

'Child trafficking? Did you want to tell me about that? Continue your narrative?'

'Just the evidence?'

She spoke as if the words tasted bitter.

'Mmm. Give me the analysis and supposition afterwards. But be prepared for me to challenge every assumption you make or conclusion you draw. I don't mean to offend you by doing that. I'm meaning to be objective; to drill down to facts and strip away as much bias as I can, to see what's really there. If even half of what you're thinking is true, then I'll need to talk to Lothian about it and I want my facts straight for that. You are casting aspersions about a very important politician with elections looming next week.'

'I know. It's why I wanted to talk to you before saying anything to them. I just wasn't prepared for your reaction.'

'I'm sorry if I ranted.'

She fixed him with an unwavering stare.

'Dinner's ready. Come through to the table?'

He stood and followed her. She waved him to a seat in a richly painted dining room. One entire wall was taken up with books and the others were decorated with more photographs. The walls were painted in a blood-red colour and red velvet curtains embroidered with gold filigree covered the window. He'd not been expecting it and stared. The darkness of the paint and furnishings should have made the room oppressive, but the minimalism of the single table and four chairs as the only furniture present made the depth and richness seem cosy instead. He sat at the place indicated and folded his hands in his lap. The table was decorated simply, with placemats, side plates, cutlery and no tablecloth, allowing the polished wooden table to glow in the low light. There was no candle on the table, but a single peony flower floated in a small glass bowl.

Summer returned with a tray bearing two bowls, a pottery butter dish and a basket of bread. LB smiled, leaning back to allow her to put the bowl in front of him. She positioned the bread and butter between them and slid into the seat opposite, smiling back, although LB could see the reservation ricocheting through her.

'Did you want me to carry on where I left off?' she said.

'Actually, no. I don't have my notes and anyway, it would be rude to write while we're eating. Why don't you go right back? To when you and Patrick met. Tell me more about him.'

LB lifted his spoon. Summer paused, selecting a piece of bread and buttering it slowly.

'I worked with him on an article. For the MSA. They needed a photographer. Patrick knew of my work and rang me up.'

'When was this?'

'Last autumn. October.'

LB's mind flickered. A lot had happened between them in very few months. He said nothing.

'So, we went out to Malawi together and he got the information for his piece and I took the pictures.'

'What was the piece on?'

'Some of the projects that are linked with members of the MSA. There's a project with health worker exchanges, which is where I imagine he ended up in contact with Kate Hampton.'

'No. Just the facts. In order. I'll find out what you imagine later.'

Summer looked away and pinched her nose.

'Okay,' she said and turned back. 'There was the health worker project, one on farming, one on tailoring and of course there was Samala.'

'Which is what?'

'It's a project that works with the homeless children in Blantyre. They end up on the streets because either their family has died or can't afford to look after them, and Samala works with the kids and any remaining family they have to help the kids get back to school. Often, just the fact that Samala can pay for their school uniforms and books is enough to allow their families to let them go to school rather than beg on the streets.'

'And if there's no family?'

'There's usually someone – there's a big extended family system in Malawi so the kids might end up with grandparents or aunts or uncles or cousins. Samala just has to be sure that the child will be safe and looked after properly. Moyenda ensures that the kids are okay and works with the schools and the communities to support them.'

'Who's Moyenda?'

'Moyenda Mkumba. He's the project manager out there.'

LB held her gaze, glad to hear more fluency creeping into her answers.

'You seem to know a lot about Samala.'

'Patrick got very interested and did a lot of fundraising for it when we came back. I donated some of my photographs to the fundraising effort.'

LB drank some soup and crumbled some bread into his bowl.

'This is very good,' he said, smiling.

'Thank you.'

'So, you went to Malawi with Patrick. What then?'

'Well, it's a long flight and Malawi is a very beautiful but very challenging place. Steals your heart and breaks it at the same time, you know?'

She looked up and LB nodded.

'And we got talking and so on.'

The barriers were rising again. LB weighed his words.

'And so on. Okay, that's how you met. What was your relationship like? Other than short if this was last autumn and by February things were more strained, shall we say?'

'It was good fun at the start. Patrick can be a laugh. He's very easy-going, free-spirited.'

'Too free-spirited?'

'Not for me. Probably for others.'

LB raised his brows, requesting clarification. Summer paused before answering.

'He's not big on monogamy. But as you appear to know already, that's not why we broke up. There are other kinds of trust that can get broken.'

She sipped from her soup and LB waited for her to continue. There was a long pause before she did.

'He stole from me.'

'Go on.'

'I went away for a few days. Up to the Highlands. Slept in a bothy. I was away for four days. When I came back, I went to get some money out of the bank and my card was refused. When I went in to see why, I found out I was completely broke. Apparently I had drawn out three hundred pounds from an ATM in Edinburgh on each of the days I was in the bothy, taking me up to my overdraft limit. Various other payments were scheduled to have been made that weekend, but there were insufficient funds and so I was stung with massive charges.'

Her eyes were hard and her mouth pinched fine lines around her lips.

'Where had your card been?'

'In my bag in Patrick's flat. There was no need to take it north. No ATMs where I was.'

'Did you tell him your PIN?'

'No. But then, I didn't make a big palaver about shielding it from him while I used the machines and he was with me. He could have seen it.'

'Did you ask him about it?'

'He denied all knowledge. And there was no evidence. My card was completely devoid of fingerprints. Even mine.'

LB stared at her. Then his face suddenly softened.

'Yeah. I'd be livid about that too. Did you ever get the money back?'

She shook her head.

'You don't get receipts from a bothy. Oh, it was all very tightly worked out. I couldn't prove I didn't draw the money out, nor could I prove that he did. And even if I could, he knew my PIN so I would have been liable anyway. Thank God there were some good pictures from the trip! The right kind of clouds, as Patrick would say.'

Her voice was light with sarcasm.

LB looked up, his spoon hovering above his bowl, seeking more information. Summer smiled, looking comfortable.

'Clear blue skies can be boring in a photograph. Small fluffy things aren't very good either. You need big dramatic clouds that have light and dark in them so that you have something to accentuate with filters and so on. I'll show you some pictures later. Actually, just above your head is precisely what I'm talking about. Top right. Look at the clouds.'

LB screwed himself round in his chair and peered at the pictures, staring at an image of sunlit hillside against ominous-looking clouds.

'Ah, I see. I've never thought about it before,' he said, turning back. 'So you made the money back off pictures from the trip?'

'Yes. But then I would have sold them anyway. I was still twelve hundred pounds out of pocket, and my credit record damaged.'

Her fluidity had gone. LB knew that politeness dictated he should change the subject but he still needed to ask something.

'Are you still upset about you and Patrick?'

Her eyes lifted to meet his.

'Not about us breaking up. I'm not really a keeper. I don't

want kids – I would probably fuck them up worse than my parents did me – and if I ever find Mr Right, then great. Until then, Mr Will Do For Now suits me just fine. We would have been over by now, even without him wiping me out of money. But yes, I'm still fucking furious about the money.'

She jutted her chin. LB smiled.

'Your parents can't have done you too much harm. You're a smart, artistically gifted woman who has a house, a business, respect and acclaim. What did they do so wrong? Apart from give you quite a stupid name.'

Summer shrugged, grinning suddenly.

'Could have been worse. I found out later they were seriously considering calling me Caraway, because my mum likes seed cake.'

LB laughed loudly. Summer rested her spoon and eyed him carefully.

'On the subject of names, what does LB stand for?'

He paused and then tipped his head briefly to the side.

'Ah. Maybe later. Were you just making soup for dinner or is this other cutlery going to have a purpose?'

Summer leaned over and took his bowl, stacking it with hers on the tray.

'Nice deflection, L, B,' she said, marking out the initials deliberately, almost mockingly. 'Shall I leave the bread?'

'Mmm. Please. Is it home-made?'

'Yeah. I don't like shop bread.'

While she was away fetching the next course, LB leaned back in his chair, thinking. He still couldn't piece this woman together. She was trying not to be her parents who'd surely been the epitome of flower-power, given her name and the scraps she'd revealed, yet she appeared to have an inherent aversion to a conventional way of life, so hadn't fallen too far from the tree.

Her return broke his thoughts and he shuffled slightly in his seat. She placed a dish of vegetables on the table and a plate bearing a fillet of fish in front of him.

'Can I get you another drink?' she asked, pointing to his now empty glass.

'Same again? Thanks.'

She put her plate down and disappeared with his glass, returning a moment later with it replenished and with her bottle of wine.

'Sure you don't want a glass of wine? I can always call you a cab.'

'No thank you.'

'Help yourself.'

She waved her hand over the dish of vegetables, waiting for him to finish serving himself. He offered to serve her but she shook her head firmly and took the spoon from him.

'So why you? Why, when something bad happens, does he call you?' he asked, hoping he wasn't picking too hard at what was obviously a sore wound. 'From what you've just said, I wouldn't have thought you were his first choice. No offence.'

'I don't know,' she said after a long pause. 'I really don't know. That's what doesn't add up for me.'

LB lowered his eyes. To him, there was a lot more than this that still didn't add up. He said nothing, concentrating on the meal.

'I wondered if my number was just top of the list,' she went on. 'But phones tend to store them alphabetically and if I was listed as Summer, I would be way down. A name like Adam would be at the top, right?'

'True. Perhaps you were on speed-dial?'

'Still? Maybe. It's as good a reason as any, I suppose.'

She sipped her wine, looking unconvinced.

'So, that's me and Patrick. Can we talk about you now?' she said pointedly.

'Me? What about me?'

'Why are you a cop? Following your father? Or mother?'

'No. Neither. I like to solve puzzles. I like the whys in life.'

She cocked her head, looking expectantly at him.

'Why someone has done something is far more interesting, to me at least, than the when and the how. The when and the how are usually someone else's job anyway. The why is the important thing.'

'What did your parents do?'

He smiled at her question. People's backgrounds and upbringing shaped their lives so much. Did they choose to follow them? Or rebel?

'What's so amusing?' she asked.

'Nothing. It's a very 'why' question. Why are you what you are? What has influenced you? Are my parents middle class, conservative, conventional people or are they bohemian rebels? … How do *you* relate to your parents' lives?'

'Uh-huh. I asked first.'

'Okay. My father was an architect. He's retired now.'

'And your mother?'

'Was a mother. Is a mother. I guess you don't retire from that.'

'Do they live in Edinburgh? Your accent is pure posh East Coast, if you don't mind me saying.'

He laughed.

'I don't mind you saying at all. It's what I am. No. They live in France now. My father has arthritis that doesn't appreciate Scottish dampness. My mother is French.'

'Ah. The auld alliance.'

He sighed involuntarily. He'd heard the phrase a thousand times and was bone-weary of it. She glanced away, her regret at the quip writ large and he tried to scrub the hard edges off his expression when she looked back at him.

'So. Half French. I wouldn't have got that from your accent.'

'You would if I spoke French.'

'Ah. Presumably you would sound French and not be butchering such a beautiful language?'

He shrugged modestly. It was merely a reflection of his parentage. He could butcher most other languages, sounding either Scots or French in the delivery.

'But you're not Scots,' he said, catching her eye. 'Or maybe one parent is Scottish, because you have a twinge of an accent, laced very loosely over Home Counties.'

'Neither parent is Scots. Or Home Counties. I've just lived here for a long time.'

'Where did you grow up?'

'Lincolnshire.'

'That's not a Lincolnshire accent either though, is it?'

'No.'

He found her reply very deliberate. More backlash against her upbringing?

'So why do you live in Scotland now?' he asked.

'Bugger all mountains in Lincolnshire. Too much sky. Makes for piss-awful photos.'

He laughed, a deep rumbly sound that came from the heart and wore no pretences. She smiled at it.

'So how do you relate to your parents' lives?' he asked again. 'I sense that they were less than conventional and you've tried hard not to follow them.'

'Tried. Not sure I've succeeded.'

'No, I'm not either,' he said lightly. 'Why are you rebelling?'

'Ah, the why questions again. Their being unconventional, as you put it, led to me feeling like I never fitted in when I was young. Everything about me was just too different.'

She said the last word as if it had spines cutting her tongue.

'Different name. Different clothes... Different.'

'Were you bullied?'

She lifted her chin in the merest of nods and LB tiptoed away from the topic, understanding that it wasn't something to talk about over dinner.

'So what do your parents do?' he asked, piling the last of his food on to his fork.

'Mum's an artist. Dad's a musician. And makes furniture. Which pays more than the musician side but is not how he likes to be defined.'

'Siblings?'

'None. Think they ran out of stupid names. Or I inhibited their lifestyle too much for them to contemplate another. I think I was an accident. You?'

'One brother. Frank. François, as my mother would call him.'

Summer sat back, watching him.

'I read an article about you today,' said LB suddenly, making her shuffle in her seat. 'Which talked about you having synaesthesia.'

'Oh. The interview in *The Guardian*. What about it?'

'I hadn't realised you were famous.'

'I'm not. I won some awards for my work. No one would recognise me on the street. Are you about to ask me about the synaesthesia?'

'If you don't mind.'

She shrugged.

'Everyone always asks about it once they know. I wish I'd never revealed it. Go on. What do you want to know?'

'The article said you felt emotions as colours. How does that work?' he asked, partly wishing he hadn't.

'It does what it says on the tin,' she replied. 'My days are suffused with colours that are in my head that correspond to how I feel.'

LB was struggling to understand.

'In the article you said it helped you to judge when a picture was just right,' he said. 'How? How do you know when you've really nailed a picture?'

'It's red – the feeling I have about the picture. Blood-coloured if it's perfect. I don't see the colour in my vision, but in my head. It's almost impossible to describe.'

He wished he hadn't asked. She seemed prickly talking about it and all her lightness had gone.

'I suppose you want to know what colour I'm feeling now,' she said with heavy resignation.

He shook his head.

'No. Unless you really want to tell me.'

She smiled softly.

'Shall I get dessert?' she said. 'I assumed you were a pudding man.'

'Based on what evidence?'

'Your size. I guessed it takes a fair number of calories to maintain that frame.'

As soon as she'd cleared the plates and was out of the door, LB self-consciously ran a hand over his stomach. Was he getting fat? He didn't think so. He sipped his drink feeling uncomfortable. He was out of practice talking to women socially. Perhaps he would feel more in control once they got back to discussing Patrick and his disappearance.

Was he getting fat?

Summer pushed the door open with her hip and rested the tray on the edge of the table. She put a bowl in front of LB and a jug of cream in the centre of the table. Her bowl had a smaller helping of the dessert – a dark chocolate torte – and she drizzled some cream over it once she was seated. She offered the jug to LB but he eschewed it. She twisted her mouth to one side, looking amused.

'I meant you were big-framed. You're not overweight. The torte needs cream because the chocolate is extremely bitter,' she said, matter-of-factly.

He met her eye, hesitating, and then added cream to his dish.

'Who says I'm concerned about my weight?'

'Your face did when I said you were a big man.'

They locked gazes. LB broke first.

'What are you thinking?'

She smiled, but it didn't reach her eyes.

'I'm wondering how well I'm being rated. You've asked a lot about me. I've told you a lot. I assume that you were asking because you want to evaluate how good a witness I am and where any bias will lie. I wondered how I was doing. Am I still wrong? All wrong?'

'Oh.'

He dug his spoon into the torte and watched the cream fill the space, letting her question still lie.

'Ben?' she chivvied.

He glanced up, startled by her use of the name and paused, measuring her, needing to wrest control back. He breathed deeply. Judging by how she had reacted so far, he was likely to offend her, however he phrased things.

'Okay. Please don't get upset. If I was judging you as a fresh-faced detective on their first case, I would tell you that I think your assumptions are narrow. That you don't consider widely enough. That you jump to the obvious.'

He shook his head as she blinked angrily, and carried on.

'Don't get upset! Why should you suddenly think like a detective? I don't think like a photographer.'

She looked mollified. Just.

'You assumed I was asking about you to gauge your value as a witness,' he said. 'But the wider picture would also include whether I was genuinely interested in you, whether I was being polite—'

'And which was it?'

'You also work in either/or terms,' he said, almost mowing her words down. 'Your categories don't overlap. I could have been asking for all the reasons stated. Or none.'

Summer chewed her lip, her pale eyes growing flinty.

'You are a very irritating man.'

'I irritate you,' he said, playfully. 'Does that automatically mean that I irritate everyone? Or do I irritate you because I challenge you, make you think outside the narrow confines you live in, question you and your belief system, make you look at yourself from another perspective, and you're just not used to that?'

She glared at him before gulping down a mouthful of wine, her eyes spitting venom. He waited until he thought she might have accepted his assessment of her before speaking.

'I honestly don't mean to offend you,' he said softly. 'I was merely answering your question. And trying to challenge you to widen your perspectives. You're too intelligent to think so narrowly.' He held his hands up rapidly. 'And take that as the compliment it is!'

'Have you always been like this or did it develop when you became a cop,' she said.

'Either/or question,' he countered evenly. 'Maybe I was always like this and it became accentuated by being a cop.'

'Okay! I get your point.'

She stood up abruptly and cleared the table, piling things on to the tray and then kicking the door open and leaving without looking at him.

'Go back through. It's comfier,' she called over her shoulder. 'I'll be with you in a moment.'

LB waited until he could hear the clink of crockery in the kitchen, picked up his glass and returned to the lounge. He settled himself back in the corner of the sofa and waited, wondering whether he'd pushed her too much and why he was trying to. He was either too relaxed or too on edge and he couldn't quite work out which. He laughed at himself. Maybe it was both. He stood up and started to look at the titles of the million paperbacks that filled the walls.

He was still scrutinising her books when she arrived and he turned and smiled at her.

'Eclectic taste.'

'Thanks,' she said without warmth.

She took up residence in the chair again, coiling long legs up beneath her. She settled her notes on her lap and waited for him to sit down. LB picked up his notebook.

'Shall we continue?' she asked, her voice clipped.

LB nodded.

'We'd got to you going to the MSA and talking to Ed,' he said. 'What next?'

She worked her way through the rest of that day, taking her

time and being careful to be logical and dispassionate about everything. LB made copious notes, occasionally stopping her to seek clarification. Finally, he asked to hear the recording from Patrick's answerphone. Summer handed over the small recorder and he played it, listening carefully and replaying it several times.

'The machine doesn't have a date stamp?' he asked.

'No. Just the day.'

'And Patrick often screened calls when you were together, and may well still do that, so the day needn't be this week or last?'

'Correct.'

'Caller ID log on the phone?'

'Only the last number that called. Which of course would be me. Probably something else that makes me wrong.'

He glanced up, his mouth twitching.

'Probably. So, you think that the first message and the last are from Kate Hampton?' He played them again, his eyes closed, and then frowned. 'Maybe. I wouldn't have immediately picked her out as the caller but I can't say I know her well enough to be sure one way or the other. They do sound like the same woman and I agree with you that the first male voice sounds like a loan shark or at least someone he owes money to. He's quite menacing.' He played through the tape again, stopping after the second message. 'And no idea who this is?'

Summer shook her head.

'The appointment could have been today, or last month, or maybe next month, though if it were next month it would probably have said May in there,' he thought out loud. 'How long did Patrick keep messages when you were with him? Could this go back beyond last month?'

'I doubt it. If the appointment had passed, he'd probably delete it. My guess is that it would have referred to today on that basis.'

'Okay,' he said and clicked the play button. 'This sounds like someone demanding money, so maybe a shark, maybe one of the grand schemes, maybe nothing of the sort, just someone he owes money to from the pub, but no real indication of which Monday the call was, other than it was after the last message, which didn't have a month stated. But if he hasn't just kept that message for reasons unknown, it would therefore be a Monday after the twenty-seventh of March. That gives us… potentially… the second, ninth or sixteenth. Potentially.'

LB was scribbling down possible dates for the previous message, drawing up a grid of them, cross-referencing them to the potential dates of the threatening message. He moved on to the next message and then looked up at her.

'There's absolutely nothing to say that this is Paul Hampton, Kate Hampton's husband. It fits your theory about Patrick, but that's the wrong way around. The evidence should lead to a theory. You had a theory and now you're saying the evidence supports it. This could be anyone.'

He finished the rest of the tape, scratched the back of his head with the end of his pen as he reviewed his notes and then shrugged.

'Three angry messages. Higher than your average I would say… it's two days since he called you. Time for your theories. Where do you think he is?'

Summer lifted her chin and squared her shoulders.

'I don't know. He must be mixed up in something. Money would be my first choice. Child trafficking in Malawi would be my second choice.'

LB flicked through his notes to find the relevant bits of information.

'Why that order? Is it an either/or? You think he might be blackmailing Kate Hampton, so obviously you think that's something he would do. Could he be blackmailing someone at work? Could someone in the MSA be involved with a child-trafficking ring?'

She leaned back, considering the options.

'Fair point. Patrick was a journalist at the start of his career. Fancied himself as an investigative journalist I think. Moyenda thinks Patrick has disappeared because of things he was digging up in Malawi. That seems a bit faraway though. Unless there *is* someone involved here at the MSA who knew what he was looking at.'

LB leaned over and took the sheet with the mind-map from her. She waited quietly as he scanned it, flicking between it and his notes, deep in thought. Finally, he straightened his shoulders and looked at her.

'It's two days,' he said carefully, knowing she'd catch his drift.

She nodded, biting her lips together.

'I know. Even I had considered widely enough to think he might be dead.'

She closed her eyes and screwed her mouth up.

'Hey,' he said, reaching over to take her hand. 'Hey. I didn't mean to upset you.'

She pulled away and laughed hollowly.

'If you'd asked me on Monday what I felt about Patrick, I would have said he was an untrustworthy piece of shit,' she said. 'But now? Now I feel gutted that I was the person he chose to call for help and I've not only been useless but according to you, I've possibly screwed it all up too.'

'Hey. You've not been useless and you haven't screwed it all up either.'

He hoped he was right on that last point.

'Look, I'll talk to Lothian again tomorrow,' he said. 'You never know, they may give the case to me to get on with since they're so busy. Either way, I'll push for something to start happening with this.'

'Thank you.'

She chewed the knuckle of her thumb, her index finger pressed against her nose. LB glanced at his watch and was surprised to see how late it was.

'Unless you have more you want to talk to me about, I should go.'

She shook her head.

'I've told you everything I've found out. Thank you for agreeing to help.'

He smiled, gathered his pen and notebook together and slipped them into the attaché case. In the hall, he stood waiting for her to retrieve his jacket. She helped him into it and he turned to face her.

'Thank you for a very tasty and interesting dinner. You're right, you can cook very well. I'll keep in touch.'

He moved towards the door.

'Ben?'

He turned.

'Mmm?'

'Is Ben your middle name?'

'Almost. Benedict.'

She smiled.

'Benedict suits you better than Ben.'

'Then feel free to call me Benedict.'

'What's the L?'

He locked gazes with her, his eyes soft.

'Goodnight. Thank you again for dinner.'

He pressed his palm against her cheek, kissed her other cheek and left.

FRIDAY MORNING

Moyenda opened up the office, his brain whirring over his day ahead. It was still early and the air was cool. Already one of the children in the project had come to the building and he smiled at him.

'*Mwadzuka bwanji?* How are you?' Moyenda said, ever trying to encourage the boys to speak more English.

'*Ndadzuka bwino, kaya inu?*'

'*Ndadzuka bwino, zikomo*. I am well, thank you.'

The small boy followed Moyenda as he went into the building. Moyenda unlocked the office, smiling to himself as the boy headed straight to the kitchen.

'No breakfast, Charles?'

'No breakfast, Uncle Moyenda. I gave it to Tuesday.'

His little sister, Moyenda recalled. He leaned back to watch Charles.

'Some fruit?' he called through to the kitchen.

Charles reappeared with a banana in one hand and a hunk of bread in the other, his eyebrows raised. Moyenda nodded, watching the scrap of a child as he ran back out into the grounds.

'*Zikomo!*' Charles called over his shoulder, his mouth full of bread.

'Don't be late for school,' Moyenda called back.

Moyenda sat at the desk and started up the computer. While

it warmed up, he checked the diary, looking to see who was doing outreach and what plans there were for the day. He was scheduled to go to one of the communities to help coordinate a health clinic just before lunch, and afterwards take the footballs and strips to the recreation ground for a training session. He had a little time yet.

He logged in then went to make himself some tea. By the time he returned, the computer was fully warmed up and he sat down. He had a newsletter to finish ready for sending to various fundraisers, a task which took an hour to complete and format, leaving Moyenda wishing he had left it to Joy to do. He opened the top drawer of the desk, relieved to see that Joy had produced sheets of address labels in readiness for him. He printed several copies of the newsletter, found envelopes and stamps, and put it all together ready to post.

His main chore done, he clicked on the accounts folder. He needed to check how much money there was available. Several of the boys at secondary school had gone through a growth spurt and could do with new shirts. He assumed there would be enough money to buy cloth and take it to the tailor to be made up, but he wanted to be sure. It wasn't his responsibility to maintain the accounts – that was done by Isaiah, one of the volunteers and an accountant – but if the funds were there he could order the material. He also wanted to check something Patrick had asked him to investigate almost a month ago. He opened the spreadsheet of current accounts. The amount in the daily account surprised him. He usually knew about most of the money coming in and had expected there to be about 180,000 kwacha in total – about £300. To his amazement there was far more than this and he wondered where it had come from, a feeling of unease spreading though him. He scrolled up through the figures, recognising most of them. All the donations he had expected to see were there, with a note next to each of the sums explaining its origin. There were several other deposits though, with no explanatory notes. Moyenda frowned. They weren't for small amounts, but ran to millions of kwacha in total. Who had donated almost £50,000 to Samala without him hearing about it? Without the whole team having a party to celebrate? They did occasionally get big donations for specific projects, but these were always labelled and usually kept in different accounts, with transfers to the daily operations account made when needed.

Moyenda stared at the screen. The spreadsheet was broken down into different pages – each one covering a specific project. Maybe all this money had come from Oxfam or Unicef or someone and had been added to the wrong sheet by accident. He clicked through the other sheets, mentally checking off the project grants that he knew of. They were all there, carefully labelled and broken down and it was clearly indicated when there had been a transfer to the daily account. None of the figures matched with the unlabelled ones. He returned to the daily account. There they were, seven deposits, all unlabelled and all unrelated to the big projects. He could have written off one as an anonymous deposit from a well-wisher, but not seven.

Seven.

Seven boys were missing.

Moyenda felt sick. He looked again at the dates of the deposits. Had Patrick been right after all? He had said that he thought he knew where some of the boys were and warned Moyenda to be careful and keep a close eye on the other children. That had been almost a month ago and since then, Patrick had gone missing too.

Out of curiosity, Moyenda looked at the email account for Samala. Isaiah had sent a copy of the accounts file to Patrick at the start of last week. Moyenda read the message that accompanied it. Evidently Patrick had given up waiting for him to look at the accounts and had asked Isaiah for a copy to help him with his fundraising. Isaiah had sent it through, unlabelled large deposits included. Did that mean that Isaiah knew where the money was from?

Moyenda closed the email and looked at the numbers for a final time. He scribbled down the size of each deposit and the dates when they had arrived in the daily account. He had sent his last message to the photographer lady in Scotland without full confidence that it was true, but now he was in no doubt. He just had no idea what to do about it.

***

LB awoke early and stared at the ceiling, allowing his sleep-leaden body to emerge into full wakefulness. When his limbs became light enough for him to contemplate moving, he rolled out of bed, rubbed the sleep from his eyes and hit the shower. He soaped himself before letting the water pour over his cropped hair and down over his body. Only when he'd used as much water as if he'd run a bath did he turn the flow off, scrape the water from his skin with his hands and step out, towel himself roughly and wrap his body in a robe.

His brain was still sifting through the night before. How many of Summer's suppositions and leaps of faith were true? There had been some pretty serious accusations being made.

He strolled to the kitchen to fix a pot of coffee and contemplate breakfast. On a normal work day, breakfast would comprise no more than a mug of bitter black coffee but on weekends and rare holidays he would indulge in bacon and eggs and two rounds of toast. There were the remains of an artisan loaf in the bread bin and he carved off two thick slices then raided the fridge to put two eggs and a parcel of bacon from the local butchers on the worktop.

Back in his bedroom he slid open the wardrobe doors, revealing an ordered rail of suits, shirts and trousers. He smiled. He dressed slowly, matching his tie and cufflinks carefully to his shirt, and put in his contact lenses, blinking as they settled on his corneas. In the kitchen, he set the toast going and the bacon and eggs to cook, humming lightly to himself, his day beginning to settle nicely.

It was about to be derailed.

He switched on the radio and tuned it to the local station, waiting for the news. As he buttered his toast, the seven o'clock headlines came on. His attention was only half on the news but he stopped abruptly when he heard Patrick Forrester's name, his hand poised as he reached for a jar of marmalade.

'News just in this morning. It's been revealed that Kate Hampton, the minister for health in the Scottish Parliament, was having an affair with Patrick Forrester, a journalist working for the Malawi–Scotland Alliance.'

There was no mention that he was missing. The news rattled on to the two murders which were no closer to being solved, and then to the elections, before finishing with the weather forecast. LB breathed deeply. So, the news about Patrick and Kate was out. The question was, how? Who had leaked that? Summer? Yet there was no mention that Patrick was missing, which slimmed the likelihood that it had been her. So if not her, who? And why? Did he genuinely believe it wasn't Summer who'd leaked the story, or was he just hoping?

He slid the bacon and eggs out of the pan on to his plate and carried it over to the table in the corner of the lounge along with a mug of coffee. He took the seat which allowed him to look out of the window and watched the traffic, eating slowly, his brain running over what he knew about Patrick Forrester. Once his breakfast was over, he took the plate and cutlery back to the kitchen and put them on the side, his feet on automatic. He emptied the dishwasher, drying off any excess water remaining on the crockery and tidied it all away before placing the dirty things in the machine, chunking through a well rooted regime while his brain worked on other things. Another cup of coffee poured, he settled back at the table with his notes from the night before.

On the windowsill next to the table there was a pot of pencils alongside a mechanical pencil sharpener and a sheaf of clean paper. LB put them all on the table before methodically sharpening each pencil to a perfect point, taking his time, letting his mind run back over the previous evening. When the entire pot of pencils was done, he replaced the sharpener on the windowsill and started writing on a fresh sheet of paper. He worked steadily, mulling over each piece of information that Summer had revealed. Until hearing the headlines, he'd been leaning towards Patrick going missing because he'd discovered a child-trafficking ring and had possibly been stupid enough to try and blackmail someone about it. But if Summer hadn't been the one to reveal that Kate and Patrick were having an affair, someone else had. Maybe she was right and Patrick's disappearance was linked to that.

He drew his notes to a close, gathered all the sheets together and slipped the pile into the attaché case.

Merde.

***

'Some holiday, Ben,' said Sandy over the top of his computer screen as LB sat down at his desk.

'I know.'

LB logged in, smiling wryly at his partner.

'You still hooked on the photographer's missing friend?'

'Mmm.'

Sandy tossed a selection of newspapers over the desk to him.

'Not surprised.'

LB read over the headline article in *The Scotsman*. The key facts were as Summer had surmised – Kate Hampton had been having an affair with Patrick and her husband Paul had found out, which was why he'd left. The tabloids were more salacious, embroidering the basic story with racy comment. None of the papers that LB looked through mentioned the fact that Patrick was missing. Each article showed a variation on the same paparazzi shot of Kate going into work, shielding her face with a folder. LB flicked to the editorial section. The tabloid didn't think that Kate could possibly be re-elected given the situation and was scandalised that Kate, 48, was having an affair with a man fourteen years her junior. LB shook his head. If the roles had been reversed, it would barely have raised comment. *The Scotsman* was more reserved but also wondered how Kate could come back from a scandal like this so close to polling day.

LB started searching the police database. Sandy looked at him.

'So, are you interested in this guy's disappearance because that photographer is cute, or because you think there's something in all that?' he asked, pointing to the pile of papers.

'You're as bad as her. Why is it an either/or situation?'

He smiled at his partner and printed out the results of his search. Sandy smirked.

'There's more going on than this,' said LB, tapping his finger on the papers. 'Last night she also outlined a potential child-trafficking racket out of Malawi.'

'Last night? Aye, aye?'

Sandy raised his eyebrows, still smirking.

'She cooked dinner for me if you must know, to tell me her latest theories about Forrester's disappearance.'

'Oh aye? Don't let the fact she's a fine lassie cloud your judgement.'

LB shook his head, a smile poking into the corner of his mouth. He retrieved the search results from the printer and held them up to Sandy.

'Bruce Macdonald?' Sandy said, his eyes scanning the paper. 'Jeez, he's a nasty piece of work. What's he got to do with this?'

'Maybe nothing. Maybe everything. Blood ties.'

Sandy frowned but LB didn't enlighten him. Instead, he picked up the phone.

'Good morning. Could I speak to Andy Watson please? DS Stewart, Fife constabulary. Thanks.'

He fiddled with his cufflinks while he waited on hold.

'Hello? Andy? It's LB. How are you doing?'

'Running round like a blue-arsed fly with these fucking murders! What can I do for you?'

'You're the name to contact on misper. Patrick Forrester.'

There was a pause on the other end of the line.

'Yeah. Haven't given it much thought to be honest. Called in by someone who doesn't seem to have any relationship to the guy. All sounded a bit weird and the guy's probably just gone on holiday and forgot to tell anyone. And I'm also meant to be helping out on these murders, so it hasn't exactly floated to the top of my to-do list. Why are you interested?'

'Seen the headlines today?'

'What, Kate Hampton dropping her knickers for some toy-boy? What about it? I wasn't going to vote for her anyway.'

'Look at who the toy-boy is.'

'Hang on… oh shit.'

'Yeah. You know who Bruce Macdonald is?'

'Oh fuck. You're shitting me. I don't have time for this.'

'I do. Want to second me on to the case?'

'Why the hell would you want me to do that?'

'I know the woman who called it in. She thinks that Forrester was blackmailing Kate Hampton over their affair.'

There were more expletives on the other end of the line and LB held the phone away from his ear. Sandy laughed on the other side of the desk.

'So, will you second me to the case?' LB asked. 'Because I'd like to talk to Kate and Paul Hampton but it's not in my jurisdiction.' He held the phone to the side again and waited until it went quiet. 'Fine. If you've got time to go into it, then do it. I was just offering to help out. The woman lives in my jurisdiction, the guy's missing in yours. I thought it would be a good example of those cross-boundary collaborations that the big cheese is always wanting us to get into. I'm happy to do the leg-work. I know you're busy.'

There was a long silence on the other end of the line.

'Let me run this past my boss and get back to you. He won't want you going near Kate and Paul Hampton though. Not this close to the election.'

'I understand that, but I'll be tactful and discreet.'

'If you go anywhere near them, you won't be talking to them alone, LB.'

'I understand. Run it past your boss and call me back.'

'Why the hell would you want to add to your load anyway?'

'The woman's cute,' said LB, winking at Sandy. 'And I'm on holiday and bored.'

'Right. Let me get back to you. She really worth the effort or are you finding it that difficult to get laid these days?'

LB laughed.

'Call me back.'

***

Rob smiled as he flicked his eyes over the headlines. That would teach that little bastard. And that stuck-up bitch. If it hadn't been for her, things could have been okay. He put the paper down on the counter and paid for it and his fuel, adding a chocolate bar to the bill at the last moment. The cashier smiled prettily at him as he handed over his credit card.

'Haven't seen you for a while, Robbie. How's it going? You got work here again?'

'Still the same job as before. There was a cash flow problem though so my services were on hold for a bit. I'll be here for a while though now, I reckon. Did you want to meet up for a drink sometime?'

She nodded eagerly and Rob smiled to himself. He was a good-looking man, still with the physical fitness he'd had in the army. She should be flattered to receive the attention.

'That would be great. You got my number?'

'Write it on the paper, then I'll be sure I have it.'

She scribbled her number in the top corner of the paper and handed it back. Rob thanked her, grinned and waved as he gathered his things and left. Outside, he tossed the newspaper on to the passenger seat of the van and tore the wrapper off the chocolate bar, taking a bite as he pulled away. He headed north, his mind still on the headlines.

His mobile rang and he checked the caller display before answering.

'Hello, sis, how are you doing?' he said.

'Feeling sick again, but that's as expected. Where are you?'

'Why?'

'I wondered if you'd be able to start on the painting this weekend at the Crail house? Shall I pick the paints up this afternoon?'

'Ah, I'm not going to be back in Edinburgh before next week. I can do the Crail house next weekend.'

'Sure. No worries. That was the original date they agreed to. I just wondered if we could start early.'

'Not and be done by Tuesday. Did you tell the McKays I could start on their hall then?'

'Of course. No problem. Where are you?'

'West coast. I'm catching up with a couple of old pals.'

'Whisky and solitude?' she asked.

Rob grimaced.

'Hang on, I'm driving,' he said. 'Let me pull over so I can talk.'

'So, how's the fishing going?' she asked.

Rob stared out of the window at the thin rain that had started. Trust her to read him so well.

'Crap. Given up on it. I'm going to head to Skye tonight. Archie's place. He's still overseas, but I've got the keys. I can work on it while he's away.'

Archie was in the same regiment as Rob, but had stayed in when Rob had left. Rob knew Helen wasn't sure if their continued friendship was healthy. Too many reminders of things past. It was good to be able to talk to someone who really understood though.

'Okay,' she said, breaking his train of thought. 'Are you back Sunday or Monday?'

'Monday. Look, I've got to go, I'm blocking the road a bit. Talk to you later. Hope you feel better soon.'

Rob ended the call, pulled away and headed for the islands.

***

Summer's phone buzzed in her pocket to indicate a new text. She looked at the number. Malawian. Not anyone she knew; not the same number as the last text from Malawi. She clicked to open it. The message had just one word. 'No'. She frowned. What was the last question she'd asked Moyenda? She checked her email. 'Have any of the missing boys been adopted? If so, when? And by whom?' She made a clucking sound with her tongue and sat down at the table to rummage through her notes. Seven boys were missing. One of them was Limbani and she was certain he was the boy who'd been adopted by the Saunders. The name wriggled in her brain. Where else had she seen it? She puzzled for a moment, trying to catch hold of it, finally opening Patrick's laptop and doing a search. The file of family trees came up in the results and she opened it. Limbani was one of the children whose family tree had been mapped out and his great-aunt's name was boxed in red. Summer flicked through all of the family trees, the names suddenly connecting, firing like gunshots, citrus orange and lime billowing through her as she realised what was happening. The seven missing boys were all in the files. All of them had relatives with red boxes around a name on the tree. Summer printed the whole file out, adding it to the collection of notes she already had. Then she stared at it. The great-aunt, Asala Kalanga, would be about seventy. Not unheard of in Malawi, but rare enough. She picked up her phone.

'Oh, good morning. Mrs Saunders?' she said when a woman answered. 'Hello. It's Susan Morris again. I wondered if you'd managed to have a word with your husband about the article I'm doing?'

'Er, yes. We're happy to talk about it as long as it's a positive story. We'd hate to see even more negative press about Malawi. And we would like to see a copy of it before it's published and be able to correct anything that's wrong or misleading.'

'Of course! That's no problem at all.' Summer pulled a notebook towards her and pulled the cap of a biro off with her teeth. 'It's definitely going to be a positive article. We wanted to do something about adopting Malawian children, but cover what the realities of the process were for ordinary people rather than celebrities, and, of course, how beneficial it all is for the children themselves.'

Summer paused and heard a begrudging assent on the other end of the line.

'What do you want to ask?'

'Oh, just about what processes you had to go through, that sort of thing. You know, with everyone saying that actress, Saffy Latimer, basically just bought that little girl. It's a good-news story, don't worry! It's going to be more about the new lives the kids have now; trying to put a positive side forward after everyone has been so negative about celebrity adoptions.'

'Okay,' Mrs Saunders said slowly.

'Would you mind telling me about how hard or how easy the process was, to start with?'

There was a hesitation and Summer wondered if she'd gone in too quickly.

'Well, it wasn't what Saffy Latimer went through,' the reply came at last. 'John and I, we'd been out to Malawi with the church and the little boy we have now was in an orphanage attached to the church, you know. Anyway, we both fell in love with him and wanted to help him and asked the minister at the church what we had to do; whether it was even possible really. He was very helpful actually. He really helped out at the Malawian end. We needed to get agreement from his remaining family – a great-aunt – to even start the process and then once we had that, there was an official in the government who had to sign the papers.'

'Which church was it in Malawi?'

'St Agatha's Church in Blantyre. We have long-standing links with it from our church.'

'Thank you,' Summer said, scribbling furiously. 'And who is the minister there? The one who helped you?'

Again there was a long pause.

'Er, Bradley Collinson.'

Summer caught her breath and quickly hid her reaction as a laugh.

'Gosh, that doesn't sound a very Malawian name,' she said.

'No. He's American. He's working as a missionary there.'

'Oh, right. Thank you. And which minister in the government had to sign everything?'

'Er… let me think… Moses. Moses Chizuna. Sorry, the Malawian names are a little tricky to remember sometimes.'

Again Summer swallowed, blinking hard. She had met these people.

'That's great. Thank you for all this, it's really helpful. And was it expensive? I mean, did you have to pay for the processing of the paperwork and all that?'

She could hear ice beginning to form again on the other end.

'Well, there were some fees of course. And we made donations both to the church and to the orphanage. It was very hard to leave the other children there, so we tried to help all of them at least a little. But we didn't *buy* Limbani, if that's what you're implying.'

'Not at all, not at all! I'm sorry. I really didn't mean to imply that. I was just trying to get the full picture.'

Summer back-pedalled as quickly as she could.

'And how have things turned out? Is your little boy enjoying the UK? Has he made friends here? How long has he been here now?'

'We adopted him at the end of last October. It's still hard for him, I'd say, because he doesn't speak English fluently yet, but he's certainly gained some weight and height since he arrived!'

Summer looked at the accounts file on Patrick's laptop. Large donation in late October. Unlabelled.

'And of course,' Summer said, 'Limbani will be getting a good education and the love of a family, which is what's really important. It's so good that you were able to give him all that.'

'Absolutely. That's why John and I just had to do something. These kids have nothing. I know people might not agree, but surely, it has to be better to give these children a chance in life. If Limbani had stayed in Malawi, he'd have had nothing at all.'

Did she detect a slight thawing the other end?

'Limbani…? What was his surname?'

'Nyirenda. But of course he's Limbani Saunders now.'

'Of course,' Summer said, keeping her voice easy despite her rising disquiet.

'Incidentally, how did you know that we had adopted a child from Malawi?' Mrs Saunders said suddenly, cutting across her thoughts.

Summer floundered.

'Oh, I was just given a list of people to contact from my boss. I'm not sure where he got it. Anyway, I think I have all I need. Thank you for your time and for answering all my questions. You've been really helpful.'

'Which paper did you say you were from?'

'*The Scotsman*,' she said, her gaze falling on yesterday's newspaper in front of her. After all a big lie was as bad as a small one.

'Oh. We don't get that in Kent. But you're sending us a copy before it gets published, yes?'

'Yes of course. Well, thank you very much for your time and I'm sorry for disturbing you at home.'

She rang off and breathed deeply.

'Shit, shit, shit, shit, shit.'

Perhaps Benedict… she rolled his name around in her head, trying it out… was right, and Patrick's disappearance had nothing to do with Kate Hampton and everything to do with Malawian children being adopted illegally. But maybe it wasn't illegal. Maybe the Saunders had received the blessing of the great-aunt and had followed protocol.

She texted Moyenda: 'When did Asala Kalonga die?'

She swung her feet down and slithered off the chair, needing another coffee. While she waited for the kettle to boil, she forced herself to think widely and consider other options. If all this was above board, what would Patrick have been writing about? Exactly the sort of article she'd pretended to be researching just now? The evidence that there was anything wrong was circumstantial. The timing of the money could be a coincidence. It could have been a donation from either the orphanage or the church to Samala to support the work they did with the orphans. It could be completely unrelated to Limbani's departure to the UK.

She had met both Bradley Collinson and Moses Chizuna when she was in Malawi. They'd seemed nice guys. Moses was a bit flashy and wore a lot of bling, and Bradley was very evangelical and irritating, but did any of that make them into child traffickers?

Her phone buzzed. A text from the same Malawian number as the day before. She opened it.

'2004. Leave it alone.'

If it was all above board, how could a dead woman have signed the paperwork? And why was Moyenda so scared that he was changing SIM cards almost daily to reply to her? She remembered they were really easy to get hold of – most Malawians in the city had mobiles; few had a landline – the country had largely skipped that phase of telecoms technology – but he was obviously reading texts to his old number so hadn't changed his phone.

She took her coffee back to the table in the window and started to re-draw her mind-map, trying to stick to facts and question all her assumptions. She added in all the information from Mrs Saunders, and the details of the money arriving in the account. If only she could find out where the money had originated. Maybe Benedict would be able to trace it? Would she ask him?

She drew up a list of all the large unlabelled deposits and the names of the missing children. Leafing through her photograph albums from the trip to Malawi, she found pictures of three more of the children and printed them off, stapling them to the family trees and searching through Patrick's notes to find out when they'd gone missing. Each of them had gone missing at around the same time as a large deposit had been made into the Malawian account. The payments were all the same value, give or take a few hundred kwacha. Summer chewed her lip. One identical timing could have been written off as a coincidence, but this many? She started again on Patrick's laptop, chasing up the blogs and web pages he'd bookmarked, this time looking for specific faces. The only other boy that Patrick seemed to have got very far in tracing was Mabvuto, now living in Chicago. He'd gone missing in late November and the new family in Chicago had posted pictures of their Christmas meal in the family blog. The couple were very religious and much of the blog was taken up with thanking God for bringing them a son. Evidently they'd been childless but they now had Mabvuto, although they seemed to have changed his name to Matthew. She stared at the pictures. Mabvuto had appeared in a number of her pictures and had a thin scar on his right arm and the twisted, rippled skin all down his face that resulted from falling into a fire when he was smaller. Matthew had the same scarring.

Shaking her head, she left the notes and brewed herself another coffee. How did these missing children fit in with everything else? Was there really someone at the MSA involved who hadn't taken kindly to Patrick discovering all this? Were Patrick's bruises nothing to do with a loan shark but the result of a warning about investigating this? Was Patrick actually short of money even after he'd sold so much of his stuff?

Her coffee poured, she returned to his laptop and opened up the files of accounts.

'Jesus. No wonder you were in and out of money – these are a complete mess!' she muttered, picking up a pen and starting to make notes.

There were several worksheets in the Excel workbook but she didn't understand the coding of them. Numbers had never been her strong point – she was a visual person who remembered scenes and faces brilliantly. She stared at the figures on the screen and pulled out the sheet of paper she'd retrieved from Patrick's flat. None of the numbers were the same as in the spreadsheet. She tussled with it all for a few more minutes and then gave up. Maybe Benedict could look at them. She printed out each sheet of accounts, labelled them and added them to the growing file at her side.

She wondered whether to email Moyenda again. If he was so scared, did he doubt that his email was safe? Or his phone? Could she ask him about the children without getting him into danger? He didn't have a computer at home and relied on work or internet cafes to check his emails. In the end, she asked him in a text if he could access his emails safely. He replied 'yes but only soon' almost immediately from his usual number. She quickly composed a message to him, outlining what she suspected was happening with the boys and asked him where the money had come from on the dates that coincided with the boys going missing. She also asked him if any of the people whose names were boxed in red in the family trees were still alive. She told him that Patrick was still missing, but that a good policeman was helping her to find him. She hoped that the last part was true and clicked on send.

The mind-map was to one side of her pile of notes and she glanced over it. Where the hell was Patrick? What had happened to him? Was he even still alive?

To quell the flush of green the last question had brought, she started to draw up a timeline, working backwards from Tuesday and using the information she had garnered from Ed, Grace and the dates of the files that Patrick had been working on. It took her the best part of a third cup of coffee to complete and she was pleased with it, even though many of the dates were sketchy. She wasn't sure that it helped in giving her any answers to her questions, but it did pull some things together. She printed it off and stared at it. Why had Patrick been beaten up? That seemed to be a key point, but as far as she could tell, it could relate to owing money, uncovering a child-trafficking ring, Paul Hampton finding out Patrick was screwing his wife or none of these things.

She was roused from her thoughts by a hammering on the door. She leaned forward and peered out of the window. The person was turned away from her but she was sure it was Benedict. She downed the dregs of her coffee and went to answer the door, pleased to see him. The expression on his face quashed her enthusiasm.

'Have you talked to the press?' he said curtly, looming large in front of her.

'What? No!'

'You swear?'

'I swear. What are you on about?'

He thrust the latest copy of *The Scotsman* into her hands. Summer ran her eyes over the headline article and the name Patrick Forrester leaped out at her. She looked up, eyes wide.

'Not me. I promise you. Not me.'

He nodded, his face softening.

'Get your things. We're going to Patrick's flat.'

'What?'

'I called Lothian this morning and got seconded on to the case. Get your things. I need you to talk me through anything we find at his flat.'

'Would you be asking me if you didn't need me to do that?'

'Yes.' He smiled. 'I need your keys too. Get your things.'

Summer ushered him into the hallway to wait while she grabbed her handbag and her keys to Patrick's flat. She picked up her camera bag, slung it over her shoulder and rejoined Benedict in the hallway.

'What's that?' he asked, nodding at the bag.

'Camera.'

His lips thinned but he didn't comment. Summer followed

him out to his car, threw her camera bag into the back and settled into the front passenger seat. Benedict waited while she buckled up and then pulled away briskly. Summer looked across at him, trying to read his mood. Why had he thought she would've gone to the papers? And even if she had, did he think that she wouldn't have mentioned it last night? She was disappointed he thought so little of her.

'So. There's a proper case now and you're on it?' she asked.

'Apparently. Albeit leashed.'

'Sorry?'

'Lothian, while being grateful to me for taking some of their workload, don't want me to go stamping around, sullying the reputation of the health minister,' he said, glancing at her.

'Oh. I thought she'd sullied it enough herself.'

He laughed, making the atmosphere finally lift.

'So, Lothian have let me work on the case since I know so much already, but within boundaries. One of those boundaries, naturally, is that the press don't get wind of things.'

He looked across at her meaningfully. She threw her hands up.

'Hey, I didn't tell the press about Kate Hampton and Patrick.'

'I believe you. But I don't want anything else to leak out. You're in a privileged position, Summer. Don't break my trust in you.'

'I won't.'

She fell silent, wishing that he respected her more. LB focused on the road. Her mind churned for a moment.

'If I didn't tell them and you didn't tell them, who did?' she asked.

'Good question. Don't know. *The Scotsman* wouldn't reveal their sources. Who else knew? The ned at the MSA? Who else could he have told after you saw him and he put two and two together?'

'Anyone. Everyone?'

'Hmm. Did anyone else know?'

'Well, Paul Hampton of course, but it doesn't seem likely it was him.' LB inclined his head noncommittally. Summer continued, 'Who else? I guess Patrick could have told someone.'

'Who were his confidantes? Who was he closest to?'

Summer reflected, staring out of the window.

'I don't know. He had a huge circle of friends, but none who were bosom pals, I would say. I didn't see anything that pointed to a best friend. He talked to me when we were together. My guess, uneducated and narrow as it undoubtedly is, was that he talked to the people he was seeing, when he was seeing them.'

LB glanced across, grinning.

'Don't be touchy! Siblings?'

'No. I mean yes, he has a sister, Lauren, but they're not close. She lives in London with her husband. He wouldn't talk to her. Certainly not about having an affair. I got the impression she was a very straight-laced woman from the way he spoke about her.'

'So is Kate Hampton from all accounts. Why do you think she'd get involved with Patrick?'

'He's a charmer. He knows how to flatter, how to be liked. He's very charismatic. Maybe things with Paul were difficult? Maybe she was in need of a bit of attention?'

LB shrugged.

'Okay, so, why would Patrick go for Kate Hampton?'

'Hmm. Trickier one to answer without knowing her. I wouldn't have said she was his type, but perhaps he fancied a challenge. Perhaps she's much warmer and sexier in real life than how she comes across on TV. Maybe he was feeling randy one evening, she happened to be the one he shagged and she was shit-hot in bed. Who knows?'

'Would he have targeted her deliberately in order to be able to blackmail her?' he asked carefully.

'I don't know. I don't think so. He isn't that smart at long-term planning for one thing and I honestly don't think it's in his nature to be that manipulative. It would be much more likely that something happened with her and *then* he saw the possibility of leverage.'

They fell silent again, LB staring at the road, Summer wondering whether Patrick might have confided in someone and if so, who that someone might be.

'Why are we going to the flat?' she asked.

'I just want to have a look around. See if there's anything that seems more important than it did when you went there. You're coming as a guide.'

'Why has your order of priority changed? Last night you thought it more likely to be linked to the illegal adoption of children. What's changed?'

He paused for a moment before replying.

'The fact that Patrick's name has come out into the open, but the fact he's missing hasn't. It makes me wonder if the person who leaked the story knows something about his disappearance.'

'Or maybe they don't know he's missing and it's just one of Ed the Ned's friends trying to make a bit of money.'

LB nodded, appearing unconvinced. Summer laughed suddenly, making him glance across.

'Sorry. It's just that last night you thought it was more likely to be to do with Malawi and I was going for the Hamptons and today the roles are reversed.'

'Why have you changed your mind?'

'I did a bit more digging on the kids in Malawi today and went back through some of Patrick's notes on it all. I think that the pastor at the church and one of the Malawian government ministers are selling some of the orphanage kids to Westerners and that Samala might be involved, because it seems to be on the receiving end of some donations that appear at exactly the same time as the kids go missing. I'm waiting to hear back from Moyenda.'

LB blinked as she gabbled out the information.

'If Samala *is* involved, will Moyenda tell you?' he said, frowning.

'I think so. He seems genuinely worried about the kids.'

'He could be genuinely concerned for the kids but see that a new life in the West has more advantages than disadvantages for them.'

Summer bunched her lips.

'Hmm. He's not like that. He acknowledges all the disadvantages of Malawi but would rather change the country than sell the kids.'

'Changing countries is a noble idea, but not one that'll happen in his lifetime. Maybe he's working at changing the country *and* trying to achieve a decent future for the kids. I'm not saying this is my view, but let me play devil's advocate for a moment. The kids have no family and a precarious future living in an orphanage with none of the network that I assume smoothes paths in Malawi as much as it does here? Some Westerner sees these kids, feels really sorry for them, knows they can offer them a life of plenty over here. They find out how to adopt them. Legally, this might be difficult but the pastor of the local church knows someone in the government and knows that things can be arranged and the correct paperwork obtained. The Westerners pay a fee, shall we call it, for these services, some of which lines the pocket of the pastor, some of which lines the pocket of the minister and some of which goes to Samala and the orphanage to keep them sweet and, more importantly, quiet. The kid gets a great new life in the West, some people in a very poor country make some money, the charity and the orphanage get some money which helps the kids who are left. Tell me who is losing out?'

'The kid, who loses all his roots and culture.'

LB shrugged.

'Maybe not too high a price to pay to have all the advantages he'll gain.'

Summer chewed her lip, finding it hard to argue. LB looked across.

'Well?' he demanded.

'It's just wrong. And the picture you paint is very rosy. Where's the guarantee that the kid *is* better off? He could be sold into the sex trade or abused.'

'Fair point. Maybe the pastor vets the couples?'

Summer looked out of the side window, wishing she had a stronger argument.

'Maybe. Maybe we'll never know.'

'So how does the scam work, do you know?'

Summer looked back, running her thumbnail under the other nails on the same hand. She paused before answering, trying to ensure that her evidence supported her theories and checking mentally where the weak spots were, determined that LB wouldn't pull the rug from beneath her again. How much should she tell him about what she'd done?

'This is all based on what little Patrick had put together. As far as I can tell, the pastor makes the arrangement at the orphanage and the minister signs the paperwork. Usually there would need to be permission from any remaining family to allow the child to leave the country. Patrick had got family trees drawn up of the missing kids and some of the names were outlined in red.'

She stopped. Gentle violet had leached away at these half-truths, and clashing colours were almost overwhelming her. Why was it so important to tell him everything? She didn't know. She just needed to.

'The one family I have managed to talk to said that it was this relative who agreed to the adoption,' she said, relieved that the jarring mosaic started to subside with her words. 'Except that the person died years ago. Long before the couple had even met the child, never mind started the adoption process.'

'Hang on. You said the one family you've managed to talk to. Who have you spoken to?'

Summer explained while LB's eyes popped and he shook his head.

'What else have you not told me?' he said, his hands gripping the steering wheel, his tendons tight over his knuckles.

'Nothing.'

'Seriously, Summer.'

'Seriously! I called Mrs Saunders yesterday as part of a fishing trip. Then this morning I called her again before you came over. The only other thing I've done is to look at the file of accounts on Patrick's laptop and try and draw up a timeline of his life. I've got both of them with me and you're welcome to have them! I wasn't deliberately hiding the fact I'd contacted Mrs Saunders from you, we just hadn't got round to talking about it. You've been full of questions about Kate Hampton.'

LB nodded, his jaw set. Summer stared at him for a moment.

'Why *are* you more interested in Kate Hampton today? Is it really just because the news of Patrick has broken? Ed could have broken that and still not be involved in Patrick's disappearance.'

He smiled, his eyes twinkling.

'Something I tried to teach you last night has stuck. Yeah, Ed could have said something. You're a reporter for *The Scotsman*, say, and have this big scandal about a politician you want to reveal, but you know that you have to be right because otherwise, the aforementioned minister is going to sue your arse. Would you take Ed's word?'

'No. Not without proof.'

'Bingo. What proof has been offered? And who would have it?'

'Kate. Paul. Patrick. But none of these are likely to have talked, are they? Not Kate and certainly not Patrick, and Paul would be shooting Kate in the foot.'

'Not the action of a loyal husband,' LB said drily, glancing across.

Summer caught the look on his face, making her pause for thought. LB waited, a light smile playing on his lips and reflecting in his eyes.

'He's moved out,' she said. 'Not very loyal this side of the election either. You really think Paul would do that, though?'

'I don't know. I don't know him personally. He may have done it in a fit of anger and revenge. He may have done it cold-bloodedly. He might not have anything to do with it. He might have everything to do with it and not know Patrick's missing. That's why I'm talking to him and Kate this afternoon.'

'What?'

'You heard.'

Summer opened her mouth and closed it again, her temper tickling with navy and pink.

'What else are *you* not telling me?' she asked after a while.

'Lots,' he replied, keeping his gaze on the road ahead.

'That doesn't seem very fair.'

He didn't respond. Summer waited him out.

'How do you manage to read so many books?' he said finally, glancing across at her.

She blinked at the change in topic.

'Er. Well, quite often photography involves a lot of sitting around and waiting. Waiting for the light, or for the clouds to develop or clear, or for sheep to move in or out of pictures. I read while I'm waiting.'

'But you keep all the books. So do you expect to read them again or are you just a hoarder?'

She shrugged, still piqued.

'Just a hoarder. I've always got more books that I want to read and rarely return to ones I've finished. You're right. I could clear most of the bookcases in the house and give myself another few square metres of wall space. I like to look at them, though. It reminds me of when I read them. Sometimes the edges of a book are wrinkled because I read it in the mizzle at The Old Man of Storr, waiting for the cloud base to lift. Sometimes the spines are shattered because I dropped it, or used it to wedge a leg of the tripod or something.'

'Don't the photographs themselves remind you of these times?' he said, looking puzzled.

'They do. But they're in albums that need taking off the shelves and opening. The bookcases are just there. Do you read much?'

He shook his head.

'Not as much as I'd like. Certainly not as much as you. I don't have the time. Okay, you need to start directing me. How do we get to Patrick's?'

To Summer's relief there was no sign of the nosy neighbour when they got there, though presumably LB would deal with him if he appeared. She swung the door open, distracted momentarily by the squealing hinges and then looked into the flat, eyes widening as she did so, orange fear flashing through her whole body.

'Holy shit!'

FRIDAY, MID MORNING

The air was cool and fresh inside Ryalls Hotel. Moyenda felt shabby and out of place, the dust from his trip to the community coating his shoes. He nodded to the doorman as he entered, greeting him in Chichewa. The doorman smiled and greeted him back, but without the warmth reserved for guests. Moyenda walked in and turned right, passing a wicker sofa and a brass-bound wooden trunk that served as a table. As usual, staff from the College of Medicine were here, drinking coffee and using the wi-fi – the strongest signal in the town. He continued past the small round tables, his eyes darting as he looked for the man he was meeting. The ground floor opened out to create a small dining area and beyond that was a bar with more sofas and wide, comfortable, wicker chairs. Mzondi Malilo was seated at the back wall, next to the French windows that opened into the courtyard. He had a cafetière of coffee in front of him and his eyes were on official-looking papers in his hand. Moyenda took a moment to look at him. He looked impeccable in a cream linen suit that was barely creased, his skin smooth and almost glossy and his hair cropped very short. At thirty he was still young, a junior member of the government who kept a house in his home town of Blantyre. He was also one of the board members of Samala and someone Moyenda hoped he could trust.

At that point, Mzondi glanced up and waved, beckoning Moyenda over and indicating the free chair.

'Ah, Moyenda. Good to see you. You are looking well. And how is Chifundo? When are you going to have children of your own to worry about?'

Moyenda smiled.

'We have more than enough children in Samala to worry about! How are you? How is Malita?'

Moyenda took the free seat, waiting while Mzondi told him about his wife and family. The waiter came over and Mzondi raised his eyebrows at Moyenda.

'Yes, coffee. Thank you,' Moyenda said, still feeling like a fish out of water.

Ryalls was the best hotel in Blantyre, one that most of the population of the city would never set foot in. It was where all the ex-pats met, where businessmen dined clients and customers, where foreigners with money stayed; it wasn't the place for people like Moyenda, with the dust from the streets on his shoes. The tiled floors were always spotless, there was wi-fi with a strength to satisfy the overseas guests, a swimming pool and a restaurant – '21 Grill' – which served the best food in town. The staff wore shirts the colour of egg-yolk and black trousers or skirts and sported brass name-badges on their chests. They were trained not to laugh at the guests' pronunciation of their names and to recognise who was important and who wasn't. Moyenda wasn't.

The waiter withdrew discreetly and Moyenda wondered how to start. Mzondi was looking expectantly at him, and Moyenda felt his mouth grow dry. How much should he trust this man?

'I wanted to talk to you about Samala,' he said.

'How is it going? There seem to be fewer children begging than there used to be, so the work must be going well. And I read that the children are playing football. There is a match this weekend, isn't there?'

'Yes. I'm going to the recreation ground this afternoon. The children were delighted to get footballs recently. They have made up their own rules about using them – no football unless you have been to school.'

Both men smiled and Moyenda relaxed slightly.

'So what is it about Samala that you need to speak to me about?' Mzondi said, settling back into his chair.

'Nothing significant. Nothing that warrants coming to Ryalls,' said Moyenda, glancing around, having decided upon the story he would use.

'I will pay, if that is what is troubling you. Ryalls is cool and quiet and it does excellent coffee. Malawian coffee.'

Moyenda bowed his head.

'I have to prepare the accounts for the half-year progress reports. To send to Unicef and so on.'

Mzondi nodded, smiling at the waiter as he brought another cafetière of strong coffee and a cup and saucer over. The two men waited while the crockery and drinks were placed on the table, only continuing once they were alone again.

'The accounts,' Moyenda started again. 'There are payments in them and I do not know where they have come from.'

'You run a charity which has more money than you expected and you are *worried*? Most people would take the money and stay quiet!'

Moyenda laughed thinly.

'I am just a bit concerned that it is linked to something bad. There are some children missing and…'

He tailed away. Mzondi's eyes narrowed, the muscles of his face tensing.

'The children live on the streets, Moyenda. Many of them will go missing. You know that. They think that they will have a better chance in Zomba or Lilongwe, or they go to live with their grandmother or an aunt or uncle. Why are you worried about them?'

'They normally tell me they are going.'

Mzondi nodded, sipping his coffee, his gaze resting on Moyenda.

'I know that you worry about the children and see them as your responsibility, but if the children run away or disappear it is the orphanage that has to account for them, not you or Samala.'

'Not all of the missing children were in the orphanage. Some of them were still on the streets.'

'But then they are even more likely to have decided to go to Zomba or to Lilongwe. They might not have wanted to tell you because they would know that you would try and talk them out of it.'

Moyenda nodded. He knew that was true.

'Anyway, it is the money that you need to account for in your reports, not fewer children,' Mzondi continued. 'Why do you think I can help you with that?'

'You are on the board. You oversee the accounts. I thought you would be able to tell me if the money was good or not.'

'Ah. Yes. Have you brought the accounts with you?'

Moyenda nodded, fishing in his leather satchel for his print-outs. He laid them on the table between them and pointed out the payments, indicated with a star in pencil at the side. Mzondi drew the papers towards him and Moyenda poured himself a cup from the cafetière. Suddenly, Mzondi tipped his head back, roaring with laughter.

'Oh, Moyenda! You had me so worried! These payments. They are from my department!'

Moyenda blinked.

'Did Moses not tell you? There is a big push to try and reach at least some of the millennium goals. His Excellency the President thought that our goal for literacy was one that should be attained and is putting extra money into projects supporting schools and education. Moses spoke up strongly for Samala. These payments that trouble you, they are part of this literacy project. I cannot believe that Moses did not write to you about this!'

He pushed the papers back, still chortling. Moyenda nodded, not sure whether to be reassured or frightened. He put the papers in his satchel and breathed out heavily, smiling widely.

'Oh, I am so relieved. I had been wondering and wondering what they were for. I was very worried. But if it is from yours and Moses' department, it is all fine.'

Mzondi's eyes bored into him, but Moyenda wreathed his face with smiles and laughed hard. Mzondi joined him.

'These worries almost always have a simple solution. Chifundo tells me that I worry too much. Moses should have told me!' said Moyenda.

Mzondi nodded. A shard of ice pierced Moyenda's heart as he saw the look that was too thinly veiled in the other man's eyes.

He had been wrong to trust him.

***

'Damn it. Answer the phone!'

She clicked the phone shut angrily and hurled it into her bag only to retrieve it a moment later to make another call.

'Caroline? Hi. It's Kate. Is Paul there? … In a meeting. Oh. Okay. Would you tell him to call me as soon as he can, please? Thanks.'

The phone made another violent entry into Kate Hampton's handbag. Was he really in a meeting or just refusing to take her calls? A copy of *The Scotsman* lay on her desk and she turned it over, hiding the headline. Of course he was refusing to take her calls. Why wouldn't he?

Her office was unnaturally quiet. Most of the staff who would normally be buzzing in and out were either avoiding her or had already been re-assigned to someone else. Someone who was worth their salary. Her meeting first thing with Douglas Rae had not gone as she'd hoped. He had looked like she'd walked dog-shit into his office when she saw him, resignation back in hand, and he hadn't made any pretence over his feelings. She had brought shame on herself but worse than that, she had brought shame on the party and her timing was diabolical. And she had lied to him. He'd given her the chance to come clean about what was happening and she had lied to him. There had been no kind words or recognition of her hard work, just a grim face and a curled lip. All she could do now was to make sure things were in a decent state to hand on to her successor. It was a pitiful end to what had been a promising career. She'd been dismissed to clear her desk and get the hell out of the building.

She chewed at an already raggedy thumbnail. Patrick was missing and the police wanted to talk to her about it. Why?

She wracked her brain, trying to remember precisely what message she had left on his answerphone, grimacing as she recalled it. If he was missing and they had accessed his computer… Dear God, it didn't bear thinking about. They must be needing to talk to her because of the message she'd left and the emails she'd sent, surely? Surely it wasn't to do with Bruce?

'Don't worry about Patrick, I'll sort it out. I always do.'

That was what he'd said and God, how many times had things been 'sorted out' for her in the past?

Paul leaving had been bad enough but then the children had turned on her too. Shame and embarrassment – that was what she had scattered around herself. The children would never forgive her. Bethany was having a tough time of it at her boarding school and Henry had yelled at her down the phone, telling her that she'd ruined things for him at university and he was ashamed of having her as his mother. He might as well have stabbed her in the guts and turned the knife.

Patrick telling Paul had been one thing. Patrick telling the papers was a step further than she'd ever believed him capable of. Well, he'd overplayed his hand surely. What else could he threaten her with? Oh, God forbid. Not that terrible party they'd gone to. Had Patrick been spiking her drinks there? And what the hell had she been smoking? More than a mere cigarette she was sure, but the whole night was a bit of a blur. She had said no, but Patrick told her to live a little and badgered and nagged at her until she succumbed.

She tipped the contents of a drawer into a cardboard box,

feeling stupid and used. Tears were threatening to well and she blinked hard, squared her shoulders and took a deep breath. She only had herself to blame. Patrick had seen her as nothing more than a meal ticket and she had been foolish and vain. If she'd stayed faithful to Paul, if she'd kept Patrick as nothing more than a business contact... If, if, if. However much she would like to shift all the blame on to Patrick, she couldn't. She shook her head and slammed more files into the box.

When had he gone missing? Surely not just today? People have to be missing for more than a day before the police are involved, don't they? Should she call the lawyer? She knew nothing about him going missing but what if Bruce *had* been involved? Maybe she should give Kirsty a ring. No. Kirsty always said she kept out of these things and wouldn't speak to her anyway. Blood will always be thicker than water. Was Bruce behind Patrick's disappearance? What did Paul know?

She tried to call Paul again. His mobile cut straight through to voicemail and she hung up. Sinking down into her chair, she buried her head in her hands, her hair sticking up between her fingers. Stupid, stupid, stupid woman. She deserved everything she got.

FRIDAY, LATE MORNING

LB leaned forward, glancing into the flat, and grabbed Summer by the shoulder.

'Out.'

She hesitated for a moment but he kept up the pressure on her arm until she stepped back.

'Out. Go find a coffee shop and wait for me there. I'll call you,' he said.

He pushed her away, his eyes following her until she'd left the building, his hand fishing in his pocket for his mobile. He stepped back from the door to call Lothian, his eyes scanning the surroundings. The call over, he drew a pair of surgical gloves from his pocket and pushed the door open fully, his eyes flicking over the scene before him. He walked through the flat carefully, checking for any intruders still present, picking his way through the carnage. All of the contents of the shelves and drawers had been transferred to the floor and LB had to tiptoe between it all to preserve the scene. Whoever had turned the flat over was long gone though. LB checked the back door. It was shut and locked. He turned to the front door. No signs of forced entry, but then the lock wouldn't withstand being prised open using a credit card in the jamb.

LB peeled his gloves off, stuffed them back in his pocket and prepared to wait for the team from Edinburgh.

Andy Watson arrived about twenty minutes later with a young constable and a forensics team. He shook hands with LB, a scowl on his face.

'Trouble just follows you, doesn't it, LB?' he said, by way of a greeting.

LB said nothing. The description was not earned but he wasn't about to start trading jibes.

'I'll leave you guys to it, shall I?' he said, stepping back. 'Not my jurisdiction.'

The forensics team started their work, the constable was despatched on a door-to-door and Andy Watson glowered and turned his back. LB walked out of the building and pulled his phone out, shrugging.

'Hey,' he said when Summer answered. 'You okay?'

'Yeah. What's happened?'

'Break-in by the looks of things. Could be nothing to do with the case.'

'You don't believe in coincidences any more than I do.'

'No. Where are you?'

'Not far. There's a coffee shop about three blocks away. Want me back there?'

'No. Lothian are here processing the scene. I'll call you again when they've finished.'

'Can I do anything?'

'Not right now. Enjoy your coffee.'

He ended the call and killed time sauntering around the block several times before eventually returning to the flat. He had no intention of being in the way while forensics got on with their job. Andy Watson welcomed him with as much warmth as before but deigned to share his opinions.

'No indication of force, so either someone had keys or it was a pro.'

'Or a ned with a credit card. You seen the lock?' replied LB.

Watson sniffed.

'True. I guess we won't know if anything's missing.'

LB shook his head. Not without Summer they wouldn't but he wasn't about to offer her up to Watson as a sacrifice.

'So what do you know about Patrick Forrester? Other than he's AWOL? What's that bird who called it in said?'

LB stepped aside as a photographer came to take pictures.

'Er. He's a complicated guy. He was having an affair with Kate Hampton. Allegedly. He works for the Malawi–Scotland Alliance. Is a bit of a playboy. Might have been short of money. Might be involved in child trafficking.'

Watson stared at him.

'What the fuck? Child fucking trafficking??'

'Maybe. Maybe he just uncovered it. Maybe he's involved. Not sure.'

'Jesus fucking Christ, LB. You need to start talking.'

'Can I point out that you wouldn't need me to start talking if you'd picked up the case properly and talked to *the bird*,' his lip curled as he said it, 'who called it in.'

'No, you fucking can't.' Watson's eyes bulged and he looked as if he had just eaten a lemon. LB waited. 'Was all this in that email you sent me this morning?' Watson asked.

'Yes. I see you've not read it then.'

Watson jammed his hands in his pockets and hunched his shoulders.

'I should never had said you could come on to the case,' he muttered.

'Fine. Good luck solving it then.'

LB turned as if to leave.

'Hey! No you fucking don't!'

LB looked back, his face no doubt belying his irritation with the man.

'What's in this email?'

'Full details of what Ms Morris has told me. I suggest you read over it before we talk to the Hamptons this afternoon. It looks as if forensics are almost done here. What time are the interviews this afternoon scheduled for? And are they at the station or at the Hamptons' house?'

'The station. She's at two thirty. He's at three.'

'Good. Keep them apart?'

'Don't tell me how to do my job, LB.'

'Wouldn't dream of it, Andy,' he said, full of disdain.

He stood back and waited for the forensics team to pass by. The constable reappeared and told Watson that the neighbours who were in hadn't seen or heard anything. Watson nodded and then glared at LB.

'Get to the station for two. I need you to tell me everything you know.'

'Yeah. Read the fucking email,' LB replied, his voice mocking over the expletive.

He followed them out, careful to keep the key. Watson stared at him as he pocketed it.

'The key's Ms Morris's. See you at two.'

LB walked to his car, got in and waited until the team from Lothian had left, and then pulled out his phone.

'Drink up. I need you back here,' he texted. Then he leaned back and watched the road in the direction he assumed Summer would come from.

***

LB met her outside the flat and offered to take one of her bags from her. She shook her head.

'You okay?' he asked, thinking that she looked pale.

She nodded unconvincingly. He pulled a pair of surgical gloves from an inside pocket and handed them to her.

'They might be a bit big. Forensics have dusted and taken what they want. The flat was a palimpsest of prints so I doubt we'll get anything useful and we'll need to take yours for elimination. You probably don't need to wear gloves, but I'd rather you did.'

'To cover your back, right? Because I shouldn't really be here?'

He nodded. Summer put on the proffered pair. They were indeed too big.

'You got copies of all the photos with you by any chance? The ones you took the first time you came round?' LB asked.

'Yeah. Hold this.'

The weight of her camera bag surprised him. She rummaged in the large shoulder bag, pulling out a wallet of photos then swapped him the wallet for the camera bag.

'I need your eyes,' he said. 'We're going to walk through the flat and you're going to tell me what's missing.'

He opened the door and let her walk ahead.

'Tread carefully. There are seeds or something all over the floor,' he said. 'Any idea what they are or why they would have been thrown here?'

Summer leaned over and looked at them.

'They're from the bao board.'

'The what?'

LB closed the door behind them. Summer pointed to a piece of wood on the floor. It was a long, narrow chunk of a dark reddish wood with thirty-four hollows carved in it – thirty-two small ones making up four rows of eight and two larger ones, one at each end. LB examined it.

'What is this?'

'It's a game. Unless there are any missing, there should be sixty-four seeds on the floor.'

'A game?'

'Mmm. I can teach you if you like, although I only know the basic version. The full version in Malawi is the most complicated form of the game. The version I know doesn't make use of these two holes being different.'

She pointed to two hollows towards the middle of the board which were square rather than round.

'Patrick knows that version,' she added and turned away as her voice caught.

LB reached over and rested his hand on her shoulder.

'Come on. Let's work through these photos.'

She waited for him to shuffle them into a logical sequence

and the two of them started. LB held up a photo and they both scanned the room, checking off items in the pictures against what was scattered around the room. They were on the third photo when Summer frowned.

'Where's the phone?'

'Where should it be?' asked LB, scrutinising the photo. 'Oh, here on this table.'

Summer tiptoed through the items on the floor to peer behind the table.

'It's on the floor. Here.'

She twisted round to be able to see it better.

'There are new messages,' she said, her voice excited.

LB leaned past her and retrieved the phone, muttering under his breath.

'Shouldn't forensics have noticed that?' asked Summer as he placed the phone back on the table.

'Yes.'

He was too professional to criticise them openly. Summer pulled her Dictaphone out of her bag, readying it to record the new messages. LB unconsciously copied Summer's earlier trip, pushing the play button with the end of a pencil.

'I'm not playing games, Patrick. End of the week. You don't want to let me down again. I'm not a patient man… Wednesday: 4.06 p.m.'

Summer visibly paled. The machine continued playing.

'Patrick? Are you there? I know you're probably screening, but please, pick up? Please? … Okay, well, the scan went well… I'm sorry about what I said… I'm just scared. I would have helped you, but now with a baby coming… I can't. I'm sorry. I'm sorry for what I did. Please, Patrick, call me back? We really need to talk… Thursday: 2.22 p.m.'

LB's eyebrows shot up, his gaze raking over the abortion clinic leaflets scattered on the floor.

'Who's that?' he asked. 'It's not Kate Hampton.'

Summer shrugged. The machine clicked off and she waved the Dictaphone at LB to indicate she'd recorded it all. He leaned over to the phone and found the last caller number. It was an

Edinburgh number and he wrote it down, reading it out to Summer as he did so.

'Recognise it?'

'No. I don't know. I'm not good with numbers. If I'd photographed it I would remember!'

She smiled apologetically. LB nodded and then held up the next photo in sequence. They checked off each of the items, the only thing missing being the laptop.

'That's still at my house,' said Summer.

'I'll need to get that from you,' he said, noting her disappointment.

They completed their comparisons and stood in the centre of the lounge.

'Just the laptop then?' said LB. 'Nothing else.'

Summer closed her eyes, holding her hand up. For a moment, LB wondered what she was doing before it dawned on him that she was mentally walking through the flat again, comparing the rooms with how they were during her earlier visit that week.

'No. There's a bundle of letters missing,' she said, opening her eyes again.

'Which photo?' said LB, shuffling through them.

'It's not in a photo. I didn't photo them. They were in the drawer of the desk, along with the leaflets for the clinic.'

She hunted around the flat but the bundle wasn't there.

'You're sure?'

'Mmm.'

She closed her eyes again.

'There were three letters. White envelopes. Nothing special – the sort you get everywhere. The size where an A4 sheet can be folded into thirds and just fits. Handwritten address, not typed. They were towards the front of the drawer with the leaflets underneath, so you could see what the leaflets were for without moving the envelopes. First class stamps. Edinburgh postmark.'

When she opened her eyes, LB was looking expectantly at her.

'I didn't read them,' she said, sounding offended.

'You took his laptop and read his emails!'

'Mmm. Anyway, they're not here.'

'Okay.'

LB crossed his arms and swivelled slowly.

'Does this look right to you?' he said abruptly.

Summer glanced around the room.

'It's the first break-in I've seen. I don't know.'

'Look. Just look. You look at scenes for a living.'

Her eyes wandered over everything.

'Not scenes like this! I don't know what I'm looking for,' she said, sounding uncertain.

'And I can't tell you. It's a feeling. Just look for me, will you?'

He nodded at the room. The two of them stared at it silently for a few minutes.

'It's in layers,' she said suddenly.

LB looked across to her, rubbing his chin.

'Go on.'

'There's a methodical layer and a trashing layer on top. It feels like the chaos is too chaotic. It's the wrong colour. I can't really explain.'

'Keep going.'

'It's as if the place was being made to look as if it had been burgled. That the person wanted just some specific things but to take those would be too pointed, so the place got trashed to hide that.'

LB nodded, saying, 'Except by only taking one thing, it makes it all wrong.'

'And the fact the door's not forced,' added Summer, becoming animated.

'The lock's too rubbish to need to bother. I wonder what was in those letters?'

'Confirmation of Kate and Patrick?'

'And with Patrick out of the way, it could all be deniable. Maybe. Who's the woman on the phone? And who was the impatient man?'

'Two people who don't know Patrick is missing,' said Summer, making LB turn to her approvingly.

'Very true. What time is it? Okay. I have to be at the station at two to brief a colleague on everything. Let's have an early lunch.'

'What am I doing while you go to the station?'

'Staying out of trouble? Shopping? Catching a train back? Whatever you want.'

Her face fell.

'But not coming to the station with you.'

'Trust me. You'd rather not be there. The guy who's the lead on this end will drive you bananas. You're better off being out of his way.'

'And I wasn't supposed to be here either?'

LB smiled and nodded.

'Bingo. Come on. Let's go. We've seen all we can here.'

'Let me just feed Oscar.'

'Oscar?'

'The cat. He's semi-feral. He'll be fine if I just put stuff out for him.'

LB shrugged and Summer scooted through to the kitchen, shook some food into the bowl and returned. LB shouldered her camera bag, leaving her with the lighter tote and handed her the wallet of photos.

'Know anywhere good to eat?' he asked as she stowed them.

'Nice place around the corner.'

LB nodded. Summer glanced around the room again, and her shoulders sagged and her eyes began to glaze. LB touched her arm making her jump.

'You okay?'

'Fine,' she said, raking her hand through her hair.

'Really?'

'No.'

He extended an arm out to the side and she leaned against him. He squeezed her lightly.

'You're doing all you can,' he murmured.

'And he still might be dead, right?'

'I don't know.'

He squeezed her again, and then propelled her out of the flat, his hand between her shoulder blades.

'Come on. Lunch. My shout since you cooked dinner last night.'

He shepherded her out of the building before falling into step with her again, letting her direct the way to the cafe for lunch.

There, they read the menu in silence, sitting at a wooden table decorated with plastic flowers in a plastic vase. LB periodically checked on his companion, concerned that she looked so pale. She didn't look up at him. Once their orders were in, he pulled a small notebook out of his jacket pocket, feeling awkward.

'I know you're still shaken about things but I need to ask you some questions.'

Summer met his eyes. In hers he saw that in a trice he'd gone from someone she was beginning to think of as a friend back to a copper, and he cursed himself.

'Sure. Fire away.'

Her voice was flat and thin and he blinked, trying to soothe her.

'When were you last at the flat? Before today.'

She stared at him.

'You know that. Wednesday afternoon. I promised you I wouldn't come back. Why don't you trust me?'

'I do trust you. I just have to ask these things. What time were you there?'

'Before lunch. I suppose it would have been about half eleven when I got there.'

'And when did you leave?'

'I don't know exactly. Maybe half an hour later at most.'

'And you locked the door behind you? And the back door in the kitchen was locked?'

He was dismayed to see her looking so hostile.

'Yes. I locked the back door after it had been left open. I thought it wasn't safe to leave it unlocked like that. I definitely closed the front door after me too. In fact the neighbour, Cameron, can confirm that. He stood in the hall and watched me while I did it.'

'And you're sure there was a bundle of letters in the drawer of the desk and they are now missing?'

'Yes.'

'You never mentioned the leaflets for the clinic.'

'I forgot. It wasn't a deliberate omission.'

He looked carefully at her. She seemed weary to the bone and he wished he didn't need to ask her so many questions. Better him than Watson though.

'Who do you think is pregnant?'

'The second woman on the phone. The one whose number you wrote down.'

'Not Kate Hampton?'

'Well, the woman talked about a scan. It wasn't Kate Hampton's voice.'

Summer rested her cheek on her knuckles, settling grey eyes on him.

'I'm guessing that Patrick's views on fatherhood wouldn't have been positive? Judging by the leaflets,' said LB.

'Got it in one. He's too free-spirited to have children. And still not committed enough to monogamy it would seem.'

'Rough on whoever it is who called if she *is* pregnant. Not only is Patrick not supportive, but today she finds out he's also seeing another woman. Not ideal father material.'

'No.'

'Anything else you can think of, before I meet the guy heading up the case here?'

'You mean the guy who missed the phone being on the floor? He needs all the help he can get.'

She sipped at her glass of water, blinking shiny eyes, and rested the glass against her forehead.

'Sorry. I have a storming headache,' she muttered. 'No, there's nothing else I can think of right now.'

'What are you going to do while I'm at the station?'

She looked up. Would she ever let him be a copper *and* a friend, he wondered.

'Go to a couple of camera shops, I think. Sit in Princes Street Gardens until my head clears.'

'Do you want to travel back with me?'

She nodded, saying, 'Yeah. That would be nice. Will you be able to update me on how things go with the Hamptons?'

'Maybe. I'm not making any promises though.'

Summer sighed.

'When we were driving in, I didn't think it had anything to do with them. I thought it was all to do with Patrick finding out about things in Malawi. My pecking order had been Malawi, then maybe the loan shark, then things with Kate Hampton, but now I have no idea. I don't think it can be the loan shark because of that other message, which implies he didn't know Patrick was missing, so presumably he's not behind it. But who trashed the flat? And what was in the letters? God, I wish I had read them now!'

'I would guess they were linked to the reason why Patrick's disappeared. They probably hold evidence of whatever Patrick was about to say or what he knew that made him vanish. That might be his affair with Kate, it might be Malawi. I agree that what had seemed quite plausible – that he owed a lot of money to a nasty piece of work who was reclaiming it with interest – is somewhat less plausible now that the person still seems to be asking for his money.'

There was a TV on mute in the corner, showing a twenty-four hour news channel. LB glanced up, idly reading the scrolling message along the bottom of the screen.

'Kate Hampton's resigned,' he said to Summer, nodding to the set. 'Which removes the blackmail leverage. She was never going to be able to withstand the scandal in the papers, so I guess the key question is, who told the papers?'

'Who knew? The people at that party?'

'Not reliable enough unless there was a photograph and the papers would have run that.'

'Patrick?'

'Who's missing and not voluntarily from the call he made to you.'

'Kate?'

'Who might be foolish but presumably isn't stupid.'

'Paul?' she said hesitantly.

'Hell hath no fury… okay, he's a man, not a woman scorned, but same thing. Let's say Patrick was blackmailing Kate and to stop him, she told Paul about the affair. He could play it one of two ways – support her or not. Let's work this through. Say he supports her and Kate goes back to Patrick to say she's told him. His next threat could be to tell the press. She relays this to Paul and he makes Patrick vanish. Why would he then tell the press himself? That wouldn't make sense. So, let's imagine he *wasn't* supportive. He could ruin her without needing to make Patrick disappear.' He leaned back, irritated. 'It just doesn't add up.'

'Maybe another, more reliable third party knew?' offered Summer. 'They tell Paul *and* the press and Paul does something to Patrick as revenge?'

LB's mind skidded over a name.

'That's a very serious accusation against Paul,' he said.

'It's just an option. Maybe none of this has anything to do with Kate and Paul Hampton and Patrick has been kidnapped by someone linked to the Malawian child disappearances.'

LB's eyes narrowed.

'Could the letters have come from overseas?'

Summer shook her head vehemently.

'UK stamps. First class. Edinburgh postmark. I've told you that. And posted mail takes so long to get to or from Malawi you'd email someone or text them, not write a letter. What if it's not either/or. What if it's to do with Malawi *and* the Hamptons? Maybe Patrick's disappearance is linked to the Malawian angle, but the flat was broken into by Paul or someone Paul could employ, to retrieve incriminating letters before they're made public and cause even more embarrassment?'

LB chewed the idea over.

'What are you doing tonight?' he said.

'Nothing. Why?' said Summer, surprise lighting her face.

'Let's talk about things once I've seen the Hamptons.'

'Won't your colleague here be pissed off about that?'

He shook his head.

'Not if he doesn't know. He'll be too busy trying to solve the murder cases anyway.'

He caught the flicker of anxiety in her face. It was now three days since her friend had disappeared. In all likelihood, this was a murder case too and he knew that she knew that.

'Let's talk about all this tonight,' he said. 'Cook you dinner?'

'Can you cook?' she mimicked.

He snorted.

'My mother's French. Of course I can cook!'

'Okay. Teach you bao?'

'Is it difficult?'

'Not the version I know.'

He smiled and steered the conversation on to photography, keeping it there until they cleared their plates. After they left the cafe, they stood on the pavement together, LB's bulk dwarfing her. He suddenly thought that she looked so frail she might blow away.

'I'll call you when I'm finished,' he said softly. 'How's your head?'

'Still pounding. I'll see you later. I'm going to sit in the park then wander around a couple of camera shops and try and keep my credit card in my wallet!'

'Okay.'

He blinked slowly at her, coiled an arm around her shoulders, squeezed her warmly and dropped a kiss on the top of her head. Summer sneaked her arm around his middle and squeezed him back.

'Thanks. I'll be fine. It's just... the flat,' she started.

'Shh,' he said, touching another kiss to her hair. 'No need to explain. I'll see you later.'

She slid away from him and took her camera bag back. He watched her walk towards the centre of the city until she was out of view.

Was he about to make a career-ending mistake?

FRIDAY AFTERNOON

LB let the cool water trickle over his wrists. He stared at his image in the mirror above him, calming his breathing. He knew he could be over-zealous about detail, meticulous to the point of obsessive, but recognising this as a drawback in himself and not being irritated by others who weren't equally thorough didn't automatically go together. Andy Watson was at the opposite end of the spectrum from LB – he was sloppy, lazy, promoted above his ability and irritated the hell out of him. He still hadn't read LB's email by the time he arrived. In fact, despite instructing LB to be there sharp at two, Andy rolled up nearly eight minutes late, munching on a disgusting-looking sandwich and then asked for a précis of what was in the email and information on why they were seeing the Hamptons. It took all of LB's patience to work through the detail while Watson shovelled food down his throat. At the end of the summary, Watson suggested that he should lead the questions as it was his patch, but LB didn't agree. The discussion developed into a debate over whether LB would be tactful enough to handle the questions, at which point LB almost boiled over. He caught his temper just in time, knowing that losing it would play right into Watson's hands. Instead he insisted on leading the questions since he knew more about the case. He also used his size to intimidate Watson – standing up fully and imposing into Watson's space – something he felt slightly ashamed of. Right now he was trying to reconcile that feeling by muttering something about ends justifying means.

He shook the water off his hands and dried them briskly, balling the paper towel tightly and dropping it into the bin. Most other people had left their towels unscrunched and with a sigh, LB used his foot to compact the bin and stop it from overflowing. He glanced at himself in the mirror again, checked his tie and his cuff-links and rejoined Watson in the corridor.

'How long before they're here?' he asked Watson.

'While yet.'

A young constable approached LB, flushed with excitement.

'DS Stewart? I might have found something.'

'Oh, run along, boy. The grown-ups need to talk,' said Watson.

'He was talking to me,' said LB, more curtly than he had intended. 'DC Price, isn't it? Did you get the warrant?'

Watson's eyes bulged.

'Yes, sir. Friends in the right places,' said Price shyly. 'I got access to the accounts.'

'Whose?' snapped Watson.

'The Hamptons',' said LB, his eyes on Price.

Watson opened his mouth to start tearing strips off the constable. LB held up his hand.

'All above board, right?' he asked. Price nodded quickly. 'So what have you found?'

Price brightened visibly.

'Mrs Hampton drew five thousand pounds out of her personal account on Monday lunchtime.'

LB's eyes widened and he jotted a note in his pocket book. DC Price handed him a print-out confirming the transaction. There was another sheet in his hands and LB nodded at it.

'And?' he said, brows raised.

'*Mr* Hampton also drew several thousand pounds out of *his* personal account on Monday. Both withdrawals were in cash.'

He handed LB the papers, ignoring his boss who was steadily turning purple. LB scanned the sheets.

'Good work, DC Price. Thank you. I genuinely didn't expect you to get so far today.'

'As I say, sir. Friends in the right places.'

DS Watson harrumphed, glowering at the two.

'Watch your step, son,' he snarled.

LB stared at Watson, slowly drawing his height up, and then turned back to the younger man, handing him his business card.

'You have a bright future. Feel free to call me.'

'Are you fucking poaching my staff?' bellowed Watson.

DC Price pocketed the card with a small smile and made his escape.

'No,' said LB. 'Just giving a smart constable some encouragement and some options. We need to talk about this.'

He waved the print-outs. Watson ushered them to one of the interview rooms and sat on the chair nearest the door, forcing LB to walk round him to the far side. LB said nothing, but rolled his eyes as he passed behind Watson. Once seated, he made some more notes.

'It's not looking good for them,' he muttered, reading over what he'd written.

'Don't forget who you're talking to and that it's election day next week. She might have trashed her reputation but she still has connections.'

LB raised his gaze, unsmiling.

'And don't you forget that a man has been missing for over three days and that no one, not even the Hamptons, are above the law.'

'What do you reckon the money's for?' Watson asked.

'Paying off Forrester? So that he'll keep quiet about the affair? Paying to have Forrester removed from the picture? Let's see what they say.'

DC Price tapped the door lightly and poked his head in.

'Mrs Hampton is here.'

Watson nodded.

'Put her in Interview Room Two.'

'Offer her a tea or coffee,' added LB. He wanted her relaxed.

Watson's breath snorted in his nostrils but he didn't cavil. LB continued to read through his notes, preparing his questions. Watson glared at him. Eventually, LB re-capped his pen and looked up.

'Ready?' asked Watson sarcastically.

'Of course.'

The two returned to the corridor. LB brushed past Watson and grasped the handle to the interview room, squaring his shoulders.

'Good afternoon, Mrs Hampton. Thank you for coming in.'

Mrs Hampton was thin-lipped and holding herself with a frosty self-control. LB smiled warmly and slid into the seat opposite her, Watson taking the free chair next to LB. A cup of weak tea squatted next to her folded hands. Watson introduced them before LB leaned forwards, wresting back control.

'We need to ask you a few questions about Patrick Forrester,' said LB, watching Kate's face carefully. 'Who was reported missing earlier this week.'

Kate said nothing, looking as if she was waiting for something.

'Do you know Patrick Forrester?' asked LB.

'Yes. I didn't know he was missing until you called me though.'

'What is the nature of your relationship with Mr Forrester?'

Kate's lips thinned further and she swallowed.

'As I am *sure* you are aware from the newspapers, I had an affair with him. Which is over.'

LB nodded slowly, jotting a note.

'Could you talk me through that? How did you meet? When was it over? Why is it over?'

'It's over because I came to my senses after being foolish,' she snapped, her words brittle.

LB waited, his face open. Watson had shifted uncomfortably in the seat next to him and he tried not to let that distract him. Kate stared at him for a moment before eventually continuing.

'We worked together on a project. It was about health in Malawi. He was an adviser to the committee that I was chairing.

We started out as friends, colleagues. It should never have developed into more.'

'When was this committee formed?'

'February.'

'And it developed into more than a working friendship?' LB said, trying to keep his voice warm to offset the arctic chill emanating from across the table.

'Yes. That was a mistake and I'm trying to rebuild things with my husband. This questioning isn't helpful.'

'I understand that, Mrs Hampton, but Mr Forrester is missing and we're trying to put together a picture of his life, to see if we can locate him.'

'I have nothing to do with that. I had no idea he was even missing until you called me. I don't see how raking up the past is at all helpful.'

LB ignored her outburst, keeping his voice calm and low.

'When did the relationship end?'

There was a pause.

'At the weekend. Sunday.'

'And could you tell me why?'

Kate hesitated, folding her fingers together.

'I came to my senses,' she said eventually. 'The thing had run its course. I realised that I'd been very foolish and that the relationship with my husband was more important.'

LB nodded, thinking, 'Save it for the papers,' but said nothing for a moment. Watson leaned back in his chair and scratched his neck. LB settled his breathing.

'When did you last see Patrick Forrester, Mrs Hampton?'

'When I called things off with him – Sunday.'

'And when did you last speak to him?'

'The same day.'

'When exactly?'

'Sunday evening. I called him and said I wouldn't see him any more.'

'So you met him *and* phoned him on Sunday?'

'Yes.'

Kate shifted her weight in the chair.

'Where did you meet him?'

'At his flat.'

'What time was that, please?'

'The morning. About eleven.'

LB nodded slowly, jotting notes.

'Could you tell me more about that meeting, please? What did you say? How did Mr Forrester respond?'

'I told him that things between us were over.'

'And how did he respond?'

'He was disappointed.'

LB raised his brows. Kate swallowed, her gaze flicking away.

'Yet you called him again that day. Why was that?'

She met his gaze, eyes narrowing.

'To tell him that I had told Paul about the affair.'

'Why?'

LB studied her. Kate paused before replying.

'Because Patrick had said that he would tell him. I saved him the bother.'

'Have you ever threatened Mr Forrester?' asked LB, glancing down at his notes. He looked up when his question received no reply and raised his brows.

'In a message on Forrester's phone,' he prompted, 'you called him a little shit and asked how he could have done that to you. What was "that"?'

Kate's face hardened suddenly.

'I don't recall. I was upset.'

'You went on to threaten to kill him,' said LB, his voice soft. He could almost hear Watson's attention snapping on.

'As I said, I was upset. I didn't mean anything by that. I was upset.'

'Did Patrick Forrester ever threaten to blackmail you over your affair?' LB asked.

He heard Watson cough slightly as if startled but he kept his focus on Kate. A flash of fear shot through her eyes.

'No.'

LB held her gaze until she shuffled uncomfortably in her seat and looked down at her hands.

'When did your husband find out about the affair? When you told him?'

'Yes. At the weekend. After I'd seen Patrick.'

'And how did he take the news?'

She sighed angrily.

'Where is this going? It was an imprudent message. Neither Paul nor I know anything about Patrick disappearing. I don't understand why you think we do.'

'We don't necessarily,' said LB, taking care over the last word. 'We're just trying to find out some background. How did your husband Paul take the news?'

'How do you expect? He was upset.'

'Angry?'

'Yes. With me.'

'Not angry with Mr Forrester?'

'Paul has nothing to do with Patrick going missing! Is Patrick even really missing? He's probably just gone away without telling anyone. He was like that!'

Watson flashed LB a glance.

'We know that Mr Forrester is genuinely missing and have reason to believe that violence was involved,' LB continued.

He watched as Kate blanched. The moment was fleeting before she became defensive again.

'Paul has nothing to do with any of that!'

'Does Bruce Macdonald?' asked LB quietly. 'Your husband's brother-in-law?'

Again, a look of fear shot through Kate's eyes and she hesitated before collecting herself.

'Bruce may have done some foolish things in the past but he's a reformed character now. He's left all that behind. He has nothing to do with this.'

LB pursed his lips, sure she was lying.

'Foolish?' he said, his voice crisp. 'I'm not sure that any of his victims would agree with that word. The man who lost an eye in a beating from him wouldn't think that Bruce was being foolish. Or the man with six broken ribs and a skull fracture. Or—'

Kate held her hands up before he could continue.

'I get the message. Perhaps that wasn't the best word to use but as I *said*,' she half spat the word, 'he has put all of that behind him now. And I really don't see where your line of questioning is going.'

LB leaned back and steepled his fingers.

'Patrick Forrester has gone missing, Mrs Hampton. You had an affair with him. That information is splashed all over the papers, mere days before the elections in which you were to stand, causing you to resign. You phone him and threaten to kill him. Your husband was angry about your affair. Your husband's brother-in-law is a convicted criminal who has served time for GBH, ABH, aggravated burglary... All things considered, you're not in a very comfortable position, Mrs Hampton.'

She swallowed, paling visibly, and fiddled with her wedding ring. LB stared at her and asked abruptly, 'Did you ever take drugs with Patrick Forrester?'

Watson choked.

'I am *not* going to answer that!' said Kate, eyes flashing.

'Why not? It's a straightforward question.'

'I'm sorry. I thought you had asked me in to help with finding Patrick. I don't see how your question is at *all* relevant.'

LB didn't need her to reply – he had seen the truth in her eyes. Ed had been right. He pressed again, anyway.

'Mrs Hampton. Did you ever take drugs with Patrick Forrester?'

'No. I did not.'

Kate's dander was up and LB looked deliberately at his notes. He knew she was lying.

'Did you draw money out of the bank on Monday?'

She took a sip of her tea and LB saw that her hands were shaking.

'Yes. Yes I did.'

'How much did you withdraw?'

'Five thousand pounds.'

LB watched her for a moment, letting the amount settle between them.

'That's a lot of money, Mrs Hampton. Could you tell me what you withdrew it for?'

Kate fiddled with the cup, twisting and turning it.

'I was going to give it to Patrick,' she said at last.

'Why was that? You had called things off with him only the day before.'

'I'd promised that I'd help him to pay off some debts.'

LB held her gaze until she looked away.

'What debts?'

'I don't know. I just know he was in trouble over money.'

'And you felt you still had to give it to him, even though the two of you had broken up?'

Kate bunched her lips and didn't answer.

'Does your husband know that you withdrew this money?'

Her eyes flashed.

'I withdrew it from my personal account. There is no need for Paul to know anything about it!'

'Did Patrick threaten you?'

She swallowed and picked up the half empty mug of tea, taking her time.

'Yes,' she said finally. 'He threatened to expose our affair. I said that I'd help him to clear his debts if he didn't. That was what the money was for.'

'I see. And when were you going to give this money to Patrick?'

'Tuesday afternoon. I arranged to meet him in a park near the office. I claimed I needed some air. He didn't show up.' She half laughed. 'The money's still in my bag. I haven't had time to go to the bank yet.'

LB scribbled something down, his brain racing. Did they

have enough to hold her? He didn't think so. DC Price wasn't the only one with friends in high places. The chief was an old friend of Douglas Rae's and would have her out before LB could draw breath. He glanced up.

'May I summarise?' he said, but didn't wait for a response. 'You met Patrick Forrester in February when he was an adviser to a committee on which you were chair. You became friendly and this friendship developed into an affair. The affair ran its course, you ended it with Mr Forrester at the weekend and told your husband about it. Your husband was angry and upset. You haven't seen Patrick since then although on Sunday, the day you two ended, you phoned him and left an imprudent message on his answerphone. However, you cannot now recall what he had done to upset you so much.' He glanced up with a wry smile, one brow cocked. 'Mr Forrester had threatened to expose your affair and you decided to clear his debts in exchange for his silence. You had arranged to give him five thousand pounds on Tuesday but he did not keep the appointment.'

Kate nodded, looking furious.

'Thank you, Mrs Hampton.'

'May I go now?'

'Not just yet. If you could be patient for just a little longer? One of the constables can get you another tea if you would like?' said LB, his voice like honey.

Kate nodded grimly.

'Another tea would be nice. Thank you.'

LB gathered his notes together, scraped his chair back and waited for Watson to lead the way out of the room. He shut the door behind them with a click. A constable came up and told Watson that Paul Hampton had now arrived and was waiting in Interview Room Three. Watson nodded and turned to LB.

'What do you think?' he asked him.

'I think that Mrs Hampton is being economical with the truth at times and at others, she's an outright liar,' said LB. 'Shall we see what Paul has to say for himself?'

Where Kate Hampton had been the epitome of self-control, Paul Hampton was raging. As LB sat down in the chair opposite him and started to organise his notes, Paul slammed his hands on the table.

'I'd like to know why you've asked me in for questioning.'

LB glanced at Watson. That wasn't the phrase used when they'd invited him to help them with their inquiries.

'I know nothing about Patrick Forrester going missing!' Paul added, his face pinched and his eyes stormy.

'Please relax, Mr Hampton. We'd just like you to help us with our investigation at this stage.'

Paul's eyes flashed at the end of the sentence and LB wondered if he'd pushed it too far. He sorted through his notes, listening to Paul's breathing, trying to judge when he'd calmed.

'Now, Mr Hampton, I appreciate this is a delicate matter, but we know that your wife was having an affair with Patrick Forrester. Could you tell us how and when you found out about it?'

LB had intended to start with some simple cross-referencing. He hadn't expected his opening gambit to draw any significant rewards.

'I got a letter telling me about it.'

LB made a better job of keeping his face neutral than Watson.

'A letter? Who was the letter from?' he asked.

'It was anonymous, but it was from Forrester.'

'How do you know?'

'The tone of it. The phrasing of it.'

LB nodded slowly, looking at him.

'So you know Patrick Forrester then?'

'No. What I meant was, it said "I am having an affair with your wife". That sort of phrasing.'

'I see. And do you still have the letter?'

'No. I burned it. It's not the sort of thing you keep as a memento, is it?'

His lip curled on the words. LB acknowledged the point silently.

'When did you receive this letter?'

'On Saturday.'

LB blinked once.

'In the post? Hand delivered?'

'In the post. At home.'

LB made a couple of notes then looked up.

'And then what?'

'Then? Well, then I asked Kate if it was true and she said it was. Confessed all.'

His voice caught as he spoke and LB looked steadily at him. Despite his bluster, Paul Hampton looked like a man who'd had the stuffing knocked out of him. Bad enough that your wife cheats on you, but a man so much younger and everything so public? No wonder he was so hurt and angry.

'When was that?'

'Saturday night. We had a big fight. As you might imagine.'

Paul shifted in his seat, tapping his foot and screwing up his lips, his shoulders hunched. LB smiled sympathetically, as if he understood this man's pain entirely.

'Quite. And you say you don't know Patrick Forrester. You never spoke to him?'

'No.'

The response shot back clean and true.

'Have you ever called him? Left a message?'

Paul hesitated and LB waited. When the silence became embarrassing, LB added, 'Threatened him?'

LB could feel the looks from Watson slamming into him but he kept his focus on the man opposite. Paul was still floundering.

'Mr Hampton?' LB prompted, an edge creeping into his voice.

'Er. I may have made a rash call that night. It was an empty threat. I was just upset and drunk.'

'I see. And have you ever spoken to your brother-in-law, Bruce Macdonald, about how upset you were about the affair? While drunk, upset or otherwise?'

Paul's gaze was all over LB's face and he didn't answer. LB prompted him.

'Er, no,' Paul stammered out eventually.

'Mr Hampton, we're only talking about the last six days. Why so unsure?'

'I haven't talked to Bruce but I might have talked to Kirsty about it all. My sister.'

'Might? Did you or didn't you?'

'Yes. Yes I did.'

'And what was your emotional state when you spoke to her? Angry? Upset?'

'Er, both. With Kate. Angry and upset with Kate.'

He was on the back foot and LB kept pressing forwards.

'And how did Kirsty react?'

'Um. Well,' he said, shooting his gaze up to the left before meeting LB's eye again. 'She was upset for me. Naturally.'

'When did you call her?'

'Sunday.'

LB looked across at Watson.

'Perhaps you could get someone to call Mrs Macdonald to check that?'

Watson looked surprised but nodded. LB watched as Paul rubbed his fingertips together and shifted in his chair.

'Do you think your sister would have talked to her husband?' LB asked.

'I can't answer for what my sister may or may not do,' said Paul, relaxing. 'But I see what you're driving at. Bruce is no thug these days. He's a reformed character. I'd like to think that he might be upset on my behalf to hear about my wife's infidelity but I doubt very much that he would do any more than shout about it.'

LB stared at him until he was almost squirming.

'Was Patrick Forrester blackmailing your wife over their affair?'

'Not that I know,' Paul said quickly, the colour leaching from his cheeks. 'Why? Was he?'

LB didn't answer. He glanced down at his notes, letting the question hang.

'So, on Saturday you received a letter which you believe to have been from Patrick Forrester, although it wasn't signed, outlining the fact he was having an affair with your wife. You confront your wife about this, you argue, you are both upset and you are angry. You also have a few drinks. Whilst angry, upset and drunk, you make a rash phone call to Patrick Forrester, threatening him? Am I right so far?'

Paul's jaw had tightened and he nodded, thin-lipped.

'You then made a call to your sister the following night, to tell her what had happened?'

Again, a faint nod.

'But you didn't speak to your brother-in-law either then or at any other time, about Mr Forrester? And you have no knowledge of where Mr Forrester is now?'

'None whatsoever. May I go now? I've told you all I know.'

'Did you draw money out of the bank on Monday?'

Paul's jaw snapped shut. LB waited but Paul remained tight-lipped.

'It's only Friday, Mr Hampton. Did you draw several thousand pounds out of your account on Monday? Surely you can remember whether you did such a thing?'

'Yes.'

'Yes you can remember, or yes you did withdraw a large sum of money?'

'Yes, I did take some money out.'

'For what purpose?'

'Something private.'

'You need to elaborate, Mr Hampton.'

'It's a private matter. I don't care to divulge the details.'

'Mr Hampton, forgive me for being blunt. Your wife was having an affair. You found out about it and argued with her. You threatened the man in question. You drew a lot of money out of the bank on Monday and now the man is missing. You don't have the luxury of not caring to divulge what the money was for.'

'It's for my sister,' said Paul suddenly. 'She needed the money. For a very personal health reason. I won't say any more.'

LB stared at him. That would take days to check out, time they didn't have.

'What's the money for, Mr Hampton?'

'It's for my sister and a *very* personal matter. It has nothing to do with Patrick Forrester.'

'I think you'd be better telling us. At the moment it looks like the money is to make Patrick Forrester disappear.'

'Well it's *not*. It's not for me to tell you. Ask Kirsty. Though she'll tell you it's none of your damn business!'

LB flexed his knuckles, making them crack. He could ask a thousand times and Paul would say the same thing. Or lawyer-up.

'May I go now?' asked Paul, his anger beginning to return.

'We'll just check that call to Mrs Macdonald. If you could be patient with us for just a little longer?'

LB gathered his notes abruptly, signalling to Watson to get up. Watson scrambled to his feet and accompanied LB out of the room.

'Get Kirsty Macdonald's number,' said LB. 'I don't believe he's telling us everything.'

LB waited while Andy Watson got the number. Watson made the call, putting it on speaker.

'Mrs Macdonald? DI Andy Watson from Lothian police here. Could I speak to you for a moment?'

'Bruce has gone straight.'

'It's not about your husband. Could you confirm whether your brother called you in the last week?'

'Paul? Yes. On Sunday. He wanted to speak to...'

She broke off. LB heard a faint beep on the other end of the line and cursed himself. Paul was surely texting her.

'Er...' she hesitated. 'He wanted to speak to me about Kate.'

'And how was he?'

'Well, upset and angry. As you might imagine.'

'And did he speak to your husband?'

'No,' she said abruptly.

'And did Paul give you money this week?'

Pause.

'What if he did? What business is that of yours? It was for something very private.'

LB swiped his finger across his neck, looking at Watson and shaking his head.

'Well, thank you for your time, Mrs Macdonald.'

Watson ended the call and looked at LB.

'He fucking texted her, didn't he?'

LB nodded, his jaw clenching.

'Did your desk sergeant not get the contents of his pockets?'

'He was only in for questioning,' retorted Watson. 'Not under arrest. Jesus. We have fuck all on either of them. It stinks, but we have fuck all.'

'For form's sake, shall we ask them where they were between ten and twelve on Tuesday?' said LB, wearily. 'Though I doubt that if they are behind it they were the ones getting their hands dirty.'

They returned to Interview Room Three. Paul was leaning back, smug and at ease. He smiled brightly when the two detectives arrived.

'So? Did Kirsty confirm things?' he said.

LB smiled brightly back.

'Yes she did, Mr Hampton. Yes she did.'

He was tempted to ask for Paul's phone but knew the text would have been wiped the moment it was sent.

'Could you just tell us where you were each day this week, please?'

Paul visibly relaxed.

'Certainly. On Monday I was running a training course with some of our junior staff that took all day. I popped to the bank in a break. On Tuesday I was in a meeting with at least six other people in the morning and in my office all afternoon. On Wednesday I was meeting with clients all day. On Thursday I was in my office all day, as I was this morning, apart from between eleven and two when I was meeting a client and having lunch with them. I came here straight afterwards. You can check all of this with my secretary, if you want? She'll be able to give you all the contact details.'

'Thank you.'

Paul slid a business card out of his wallet and handed it over.

'That number will get straight through to her. Do you want me to wait here until you've contacted her?'

Both LB and Watson knew that his alibi was tight but Watson decided to go through the motions anyway. Once the confirmations came back, the two left Paul in the interview room and returned to see his wife.

'So sorry to be keeping you so long, Mrs Hampton,' said LB as he sat down. 'Just one last thing. Can you tell me where you were each day this week, please?'

Kate Hampton's list was as depressingly watertight as her husband's – at least half of it had been broadcast on the local news each night as part of the election coverage. LB smiled and folded his notes together. He and Watson returned to Watson's office.

'Have we got enough to hold them on?' LB asked.

Before Watson could answer, his phone rang. He answered it, his eyes narrowing before he hung up.

'Their lawyer's here,' he said.

LB clicked his tongue. Watson's phone rang again. LB watched as he took the call.

'Yes, sir… I'm not sure, sir… yes, sir.'

The call ended, Watson's shoulders slumped as he replaced the receiver in its cradle.

'Let them go?' said LB, brows raised.

Watson nodded grumpily.

'Yep. Not enough to hold them on. Alibis are watertight; sister will say anything Paul fucking wants her to. She's married to Bruce fucking Macdonald – she's had plenty of training in that department!'

'Then let them go and let's try and break the corroboration?'

'Kirsty won't serve him up in a month of Sundays.'

LB shook his head, suddenly exhausted.

'Any chance of surveillance?'

'Fuck off.'

LB shrugged. They stood in the hall together and watched Paul leave, moments after Kate had exited. Andy Watson folded his arms, also staring after Paul.

'There's something not right there. Not right at all. But we have nothing. I don't imagine there'll be anything back from the flat. Your bird has fucked up any chance of finding anything.'

'My bird?' said LB, swinging round to face him. 'Do you by chance mean Ms Morris?'

Watson didn't respond, just narrowed his eyes and jutted his chin out.

'I agree she might not have done you any favours on the flat but maybe you should have investigated it when it was called in,' said LB.

'Fuck off. We have two fucking murders to solve that aren't getting any fresher. And those two stink like week-old fish but we're no fucking closer to knowing where Forrester is.'

'No,' said LB, breathing out heavily. 'Dead in some wasteland somewhere, ready for someone's dog to discover probably.'

'There'd be no chance of a conviction after *Ms Morris*,' Watson mocked her name, pinching his top lip up as he spoke, 'has stomped all over the fucking crime scene.'

'How many messages were there on the answerphone today?' asked LB, his patience finally snapping.

'What? What answerphone?'

'Exactly. The one that had been knocked down the back of the table. The one you and your team missed. Ms Morris isn't the only one who's affected this case.'

He walked off, leaving Watson staring after him. He'd really had enough of Watson, his language, his sloppiness, his keenness to pass the blame on. The Hamptons had been the best lead and it had got them nowhere.

Outside, LB found a quiet bench, retrieved the number from the answerphone out of his pocket and dialled it.

'Good afternoon. Wright Interiors.'

'Oh, hello. Who am I speaking to please?'

'Helen Wright. Who's calling?'

'This is DS Stewart of Fife Police, ma'am. Do you know a Patrick Forrester?'

He heard a slight gasp on the other end.

'Yes. Yes I do. Why?'

'I'm sorry to tell you that Mr Forrester has gone missing. Can I ask how you know him?'

'I was his girlfriend. Until a few weeks ago. Oh God, I didn't know he was missing. When? What's happened to him?'

She sounded genuinely distressed and LB tried to soothe her.

'We don't know, ma'am. We think he went missing earlier this week. We saw that you left a message for him yesterday and wondered if we'd be able to talk to you? See if you could help in any way?'

'Oh. Er, of course. When?'

'Well, as soon as possible really.'

'Oh. Well, I've an appointment with someone in a few minutes and then having dinner with some other clients. Is first thing tomorrow okay?'

'First thing tomorrow would be fine. Where can I find you?'

She gave him details of how to get to her shop, still sounding upset. LB knew there was nothing he could say to calm her and arranged to see her at nine the next day. He rang off and leaned back heavily. Was Helen Wright another woman in Patrick's life who he'd treated like shit? The man seemed like scum. Exhausted, he called Summer.

'Anything left in the shops?' he said when she answered.

'Plenty. How are you?'

'Tired and needing to leave. Where shall I pick you up and do you still want to have dinner?'

'I'm in Princes Street Gardens and yes please to dinner. Where's the easiest place for you to stop?'

They sorted out a location and hung up. LB stretched his back and debated whether to pop his head back into Watson's office. In the end he couldn't bear to. Anyway, Watson knew everything that LB did, if he could be bothered to read his emails. LB shrugged and made his way back to the car.

FRIDAY, EARLY EVENING

Helen Wright stopped hunting around the flat and sighed, sinking down on to the bed and clutching her head in her hands. She would lose her marbles soon. Must be the hormones. She was normally so careful about things, but then, ha, wasn't that an ironic thing to say. Where the hell were those letters and that photo? She couldn't have lost them. She mustn't have.

How had she ended up in this state? However she looked at it, she couldn't see how she could run the business with a baby. She scraped her hair back and tried to call her brother again, but just as it had all the previous times, it cut straight to voicemail. He must be out of range. Network coverage on the west coast could be shocking.

She tossed her phone on the bed beside her and tried to focus on the evening ahead. Should she wear magic knickers to hide the bump when she went out? It would make the choice of clothes easier but was it okay for the baby to be all scrunched up like that? They were very important clients. She couldn't mess up. She did a quick search on the internet, finding out that Mrs Adamson was on the church council and judging by the "likes" on her Facebook page, was a strong believer in marriage. Unless she could produce a wedding ring pronto she would go for the magic knickers, she decided.

When had Patrick gone missing? Before or after Rob got into such a rage about it all?

She shook herself, appalled to think she could be so disloyal to her brother. He might not be the same man who had left for Iraq, and he might have a temper in him that put the devil to shame, but no, surely not. Maybe once, when he first returned and would throw himself to the ground at the sound of a car backfiring, white and shaking, his head full of flashbacks of fallen comrades and roadside bombs and when he wasn't right in his thinking, but not now.

So what had happened, then? Where was Patrick? Had his fears come true and the man he owed money to claimed the debt in flesh?

She blinked away the thoughts, dragging her mind back to the dinner ahead and hunted in the drawer for a pair of magic knickers, hoping she wouldn't still be showing once she was in them. She really couldn't afford to get it wrong with the Adamsons.

But however hard she tried to lock her brain on to business, it was determined to stray. How could she *possibly* cope with the business and a baby? She could hardly rely on Rob, either as a business partner or to look after the kid. She could pursue Patrick for child support but he never had any money and besides, who would look after the baby while she worked? And anyway, now he was missing. Had he done a runner from her? Had something horrible happened? It was a policeman who'd called her. Did they call if someone did a runner?

She stared around at her beautiful home and wondered how impressive it would be with toys all over the place and a smell of baby sick and nappies. It didn't bear thinking about.

Why had she not been more careful?

***

Kate clapped her hand over her mouth as Bruce Macdonald marched into the lounge and her eyes flew to Paul.

'I thought we were having an evening to talk? What's Bruce doing here?'

Bruce threw a bundle on to the table, glaring contemptuously at her. She still couldn't look at him.

'What have you done, Paul?' she whispered.

Bruce rolled his sleeves up, his tattooed arms the greenish hue of old bruises, and dropped on to the sofa next to her. She recoiled, cramming herself into the corner.

'What has *he* done? Fucking slut.'

Kate's eyes shot to the table, resting on the bundle Bruce had tossed there. She gasped as she recognised the letters she'd written to Patrick.

'What? How?' she said, feeling her eyes begin to boggle. She fought hard to lock her mask of professionalism back in place, breathing steadily.

Paul started counting notes out, his gaze fixed on the letters.

'Where's the computer?' he said levelly.

'No computer. Weren't one.'

'Shit. Where the…?'

'Not in the flat, I can tell you.'

Kate watched Bruce as he leaned back, eyeing the money as it was counted. Paul looked as if he was hesitating over putting some of it back in his wallet.

'No tape up? The place wasn't cordoned off?' he asked.

Bruce shook his head.

'And you were careful? And it looks normal?'

'It looks as normal as any fucking break-in. And no, there weren't no tape or nothin'. Place was deserted. Piece o' piss.'

'But no computer?' said Paul, his brow furrowed.

'No.' Bruce stared at Kate. 'But there were a load o' leaflets 'bout an abortion clinic. You been a bit careless?'

Shock flashed across Paul's face at this revelation. Bruce stared at Kate but she was too practised a politician to let any reaction into her face a second time.

'Not me,' she said tartly, wondering who they *were* for.

Paul handed Bruce a wad of money. Bruce counted it slowly.

'Where's the rest?' he said, glowering.

'Where's the computer? The job's half done,' replied Paul coolly.

Bruce's gaze flicked from Paul to Kate.

'I took copies of them letters,' he said. 'You really wouldn't want me to lose them now, would you?'

'I don't have any further to fall,' said Kate, her voice steady. 'So they're no use to you. If you've nothing else to deliver, perhaps you could leave me and my husband to talk?'

Bruce levered himself up. Paul ushered him back towards the kitchen and Kate could hear raised voices. Arguing over the money no doubt. Exhausted to the core, she closed her eyes, half hoping she would never open them again. The voices became heated then quiet and the back door banged sharply. When she peeled her eyelids open, Paul was standing in front of her.

'What the hell have you done, Paul? The police asked me if Bruce was involved and I told them he wasn't. We are *surrounded* by paparazzi and you have *him* come here? What were you *thinking* of?'

'Sorting out some of your mess,' he muttered through clenched teeth.

'To what end?' she asked wearily. 'The only thing to salvage is me and you, and those,' she flicked the envelopes with her foot, 'won't achieve that.'

Paul sank down in a chair, his eyes burning.

'I've had more than enough humiliation from you without them getting published as well. And judging from the emails from you to him that I read on your machine, cleaning his computer would have been a good idea.'

Kate trembled over her next question.

'Did you ask Bruce to make Patrick disappear?'

He stared at her, leaning on his knees.

'Is that what you think?'

She didn't answer. His face darkened as her silence deepened and he stood abruptly.

'I can't stay. We have nothing to talk about,' he spat and snatched up his jacket.

Kate tried to remonstrate, but he was gone, slamming the door behind him as he dashed through the paparazzi camped at the front. She stared after him, stunned. Had he really got Bruce to make Patrick disappear?

She had lost her job, her career and her husband, and the man she had thrown it all away for was possibly dead because of her. No, she really didn't have any further to fall.

She stood up, put the bundle of letters in the fire grate and held a match to them, watching as the flames licked through her words.

***

Moyenda took a final look around the building before locking up for the night. The Samala office was in an area on the outskirts of Blantyre where many of the children in the project came from. It was in a small building, set towards the back of about an acre of land – a gift from a charity. Some of the land had been cultivated into small gardens for the children to learn how to grow vegetables. These were mostly eaten by the children but any surplus was sold at market and the monies ploughed back into Samala. Two boys in their late teens were kicking a football around in the other part of the land which was roughly grassed and used as a playground. Moyenda waved to them. The two had been with Samala for almost a decade. They had achieved good grades at school and they now helped out with the younger children in their spare time. One of them, Michael, was studying to be a doctor at the College of Medicine in Blantyre, something that would not have been possible without Samala supporting his education. The other, Precious, was training to be a carpenter.

'*Tionana!*' Moyenda called across. 'See you later!'

Big grins came back along with waves, and their attention returned to their game. Moyenda smiled and put the key to the office in his pocket. He wished he could use one of the two bicycles that Samala owned but he had told Joy to use one to save her a long walk home and the other was with Manale, who had gone to one of the outlying villages to talk about Samala to the chief and see some of the children. He wouldn't be back until much later. Maybe if one of the applications for funds was successful they would be able to buy another bicycle for the volunteers to use. He waved again to Michael and Precious and turned to walk back to his house. If he was lucky, he would make it back before the light failed. He considered taking one of the many dilapidated, white mini-buses, to cut out the long walk back to the centre of Blantyre. He needed to think though, and the walk would do him good.

His mind was full as he walked. On top of constant thoughts about fundraising and worries about the welfare of the children, Moyenda was weighed down by other matters. The seven missing boys were one of them. He couldn't help but wonder where in the world they were and whether they were happy there. None of them spoke much English, having been out of school at key times, and he was afraid that they would be lonely in their new lives, unable to communicate their needs and wishes. He hoped they were somewhere safe and that they hadn't been sold into the sex trade or child slavery. It didn't bear thinking about.

He turned on to the main road and joined the throngs of people on the roadside. Sometimes Moyenda thought that Malawi resembled an ant colony – everyone always moving, walking in long lines. Walking to fetch things, walking to bring things back, walking to work, walking home. A bicycle swerved around him and he ducked to avoid the long poles the rider carried on his shoulder. The man's wife, sitting on the parcel rack on the back called out, 'Zikomo! Thank you!' as they shot past, a baby attached to her back with bright cloth, and a bucket of water balanced on her head. Moyenda smiled, recalling a memory of Patrick and Summer when the two of them had visited Zomba with him. They had been walking back to the hotel on the mountain plateau when a man on a bike had scooted past them, so heavily laden he was barely visible. Summer had whipped out her camera, shooting picture after picture, laughing at the sight.

Where was Patrick? Moyenda had told him not to investigate the boys' disappearance but Patrick had not listened and now he had vanished too. Moyenda glanced over his shoulder, nervous even thinking about this. Was he being followed? He thought he was. He had thought so for days now, even before he had met Mzondi. The look in Mzondi's eyes at the end of their meeting had scared him, shaken him to his core. Mzondi, his friend, had lied to him. Moyenda had trusted him enough to share his worries, only to realise too late that Mzondi knew all along. How high did this go? Obviously as high as Moses. Higher?

He felt sick to his stomach. Moses had been so helpful. He had cleared the paperwork through the government and made sure that Samala had been granted its community-based organisation status without hiccup. He had praised Samala for the work it did, lauded Moyenda for his dedication. He had always been a great friend to Samala. Had he been planning it all along? Had he helped to set Samala up so that he could benefit from selling some of the homeless orphans? Moyenda swallowed down bile. Since he didn't know how high this corruption went, how on earth could he stop it? There was no guarantee that ministers above Moses weren't involved. He couldn't go public, even if he had enough proof, because Samala would be the victim, not the ministers. They were untouchable. No. Samala would bear the brunt of the public's fury, losing funding and respect faster than the wind. It had taken him years to build up Samala to where it was now, and every step of the journey had been difficult, every victory hard fought and hard won. He could not bring it all down, but he despised himself for that decision.

He glanced over his shoulder again. The light was failing fast and he still had a long way to go. Many of the faces behind him were the same as the last time he had looked. He hurried on, reaching the outskirts of Blantyre, glad to finally reach somewhere with street lights, and turned down the road that led to the old part of Blantyre, with its faded grandeur and British-built houses. Many of the colonial buildings had been demolished in the sixties and seventies, an act now largely regretted, especially since tourism was booming, but some remained, an odd blend of grace and authority. The people thinned, but two faces behind him stayed constant. He hurried on, trying to convince himself they were simply going the same way as him and their presence was nothing sinister.

He turned off, on to an unlit road. There was no alternative. Only some of the roads were lit in the city and the remainder of his route home was largely going to be dark. Dusk was thickening and he quickened his pace. The two men behind him quickened their pace to match. As soon as they were out of sight of the main street, Moyenda broke into a trot and then a run. Behind him, pounding footsteps matched his racing heart rate and fear flooded his veins. Who were they? What would they do to him?

He skittered round a corner but they were almost on him. As he stole a glance behind him, the first punch landed, catching him in the shoulder and sending him staggering. Moyenda brought his arms up to shield his face. The second blow hammered into his stomach. He doubled up, nausea washing through him just as a savage kick to his knee brought him to the ground. He screamed out in pain. Would anyone help him? Even as he prayed for respite, he was conscious of the grit of the road gouging his face and then his body spasmed as a boot landed with a hideous thud in his back.

Oh, God, he was going to die. They were going to kill him. Chifundo…

He rolled, avoiding a kick to the head.

I must get up. I can't let them kill me…

Moyenda tried to push himself up on to his knees, still shielding his head with one arm. For the first time, he caught a glimpse of his assailants even as one sent him sprawling into the dirt with a kick to the ribs. Smart clothes. Shiny, new shoes. These men did not need to mug him for his money; they were richer than he by a large margin.

'Get his cell,' snapped one of them. 'And get his wallet. Make it look right.'

More kicks and blows landed and the men shoved rough hands into Moyenda's pockets, seeking out his mobile and his money. Someone had seen what was happening from the street and shouts were ringing out. One of the muggers bent down, grabbed Moyenda by his shirt and hauled him up to hiss in his ear.

'Take that as a warning. Stop meddling in things that don't concern you.'

He let go of Moyenda's shirt and Moyenda slumped back, bleeding and stunned. Some people were running down the path towards them and, dazed and scared, he feared they were coming to join in. But the two muggers had taken flight and one of the newcomers started to run after them while the others clustered around Moyenda.

'It's Moyenda Mkumba!' cried one of them, crouching down to minister to him. 'What happened?'

'I was mugged. They took my cell and my wallet,' said Moyenda.

The man who had given chase returned.

'They were too far ahead,' he gasped, breathlessly. 'Moyenda?'

Moyenda smiled through his bruises, glad to be so well known and loved. He knew many of these people by sight, even if he didn't know their names. His vision started clotting.

'I think I need to go to hospital,' he said, touching his head gingerly, feeling sick, before slowly collapsing into the dust.

FRIDAY EVENING

LB was nervous. The whole of the journey back from Edinburgh he had been debating whether it was foolish to invite Summer for dinner. If she was involved with Forrester's disappearance in any way, how would it look for them to have had dinner together, not just once but twice? Thankfully she hadn't wanted to talk in the car as her head was still pounding, leaving him space to go over everything. He was sure she wasn't involved but if a body was found, would she be able to provide any valid evidence given her visits to the flat? Would any of his work stand given that it wasn't his case, wasn't his jurisdiction and he'd invited her back to his place for dinner?

He parked in front of her flat, grim-faced.

'Are you regretting asking me?' said Summer, startling him out of his thoughts.

He looked across and realised she must have been watching him steadily for some time.

'Possibly. I don't want to jeopardise any potential prosecutions.'

'Of me?' she said, her voice brittle.

He smiled to reassure her, shaking his head.

'I wasn't thinking that you'd be prosecuted, no. I would like any evidence you might potentially give to be able to stand up to cross-examination by a bastard of a lawyer, that's all.'

She held his gaze for a moment, weighing his words.

'Don't cook for me if you'd rather not.'

He hesitated.

'Actually, I'd like to cook for you.'

He tilted his head, his eyes soft, relieved to see her relax.

'Won't that damage the case?' she asked. He shrugged.

'I'm hoping not. I'm hoping I can pass it all to Watson. And you certainly wouldn't ever have dinner with him, trust me!'

'Sure?' she asked, her eyes turned towards her flat.

'No. But I need company and you look like you could benefit from some too. Give me an hour?'

She nodded.

An hour later, she was standing in the hall, gazing open-mouthed at the abstract in the hall while he took her jacket.

'He's a *fantastic* painter. I love his work,' she said. 'Expensive taste though.' She arched a brow.

'Not when I bought it,' said LB, turning to look at the picture. 'Caught him on the rise.'

'Nice skill to have. Wish I did.'

'Ah. So do I.'

She caught his eye.

'So not you, but…?'

'An ex.'

He didn't elaborate and she didn't ask.

He hung her jacket on one of the hooks and ushered her through the door on the right of the hall that led to the lounge-kitchen-diner, waving for her to sit down.

'Bloody hell,' she muttered, glancing around.

'What?' he said, casting round him to see what had provoked her response.

'If you have a cleaning lady, can I get her details?'

He blushed and she smiled.

'Er, no. No cleaning lady. Just me.'

'I'm scared to sit down in case I crease the cushions.'

She thrust a bottle of wine into his hands and put a delicate wooden box on the small table between the sofa and the beaten leather chair.

'Bao. You wanted me to teach you?' she said.

'Is that the same thing as Patrick's?' he asked, his brow puckered. 'Or does the basic version come with a different board?'

She smiled.

'No, the board's the same. It's just that mine's the travel version and Patrick's was a posh, ornate board. The game's the same.'

LB left her standing looking at his books while he fetched her a glass of wine. She thanked him as he handed it to her.

'What can I cook you?' he said.

'Anything as long as it doesn't take too long. I get crabby when my glucose levels are low. Cheers.'

She touched her glass to his and sipped the cool white wine.

'Santé,' he responded. '*Blanc de poulet avec des abricots, des pignons et des herbes fraîches?*'

She laughed.

'Sounds marvellous even if I haven't a scoobies what it is.'

'It's very tasty and won't take long.'

'Here, I'll help,' she offered, moving towards the kitchen with him.

'No!' he said before finding some composure. 'No. No one else comes into my kitchen. You can sit there and talk to me while I cook though.'

He indicated a bar stool next to the breakfast bar on the lounge side of the divide and she slid on to it, placing her glass on the worktop before her. LB caught her smiling into her glass as he put on a large, navy blue, canvas apron.

'I'm a messy cook,' he said, embarrassed.

'I don't believe that for a moment. I do believe your shirt cost more than I sometimes earn in a week though.'

He acknowledged the point with a shrug and started to rummage through the pull-out larder at the side of the cooker.

He cooked the way his mother did – nothing was weighed; the main unit of measurement was the handful. Into a food processor he put a peeled onion, half a handful of pine nuts, two handfuls of dried apricots and two handfuls of herbs from pots on the windowsill. As the blades turned, a heady aroma of oregano and sage filled the room. The stuffing made, LB slit open two chicken breasts, pushed the mixture in and wrapped them in thin slices of pancetta before laying them in a dish.

'Do you always have food like that in?' she asked, watching as he drizzled a little oil over them and shoved the dish in the oven. He turned.

'Yes. I really hate bad cooking. I would rather go hungry than eat something out of a packet.'

He scrubbed a dozen new potatoes, dropped them in a pan and added cold water and then peeled and sliced a couple of carrots which he tossed into a bamboo steamer.

'Okay. Done for the moment.'

He walked round the breakfast bar and perched on a stool by her side.

'How's your head?' he asked.

'Clearing. Can we talk about today before dinner and then just relax? Or is there too much to talk about?'

'We can try,' he said, and smiled and sipped his wine. 'The interviews with Kate and Paul Hampton weren't very enlightening. Both of them were evasive and difficult but that alone doesn't make them guilty… You know I can't tell you any details, don't you?'

'Yeah. I know. Did you call the number of the woman who left the last message?'

'Yes,' he said, screwing his face up as he recalled her name. 'Helen Wright.'

'Helen Wright…' Summer said slowly. 'Helen Wright…'

Her brow crinkled as she ran her tongue over the name.

'Wright Interiors?' he added.

'Oh my God. You're kidding me?'

'Why? Who is she?'

'She's an extremely fine interior designer. She and I shared a feature in the Sunday papers last year – Scottish artists to watch out for or something like that.'

'Well, she said that she'd been Patrick's girlfriend until a few weeks ago. She didn't know he was missing. What's she like?'

'I've never met her. We were just in the same article. Different interviews.'

LB nodded.

'Well, I'm meeting her tomorrow morning. See what she says. She might know more about the loans for a start.'

'What was the message again?'

Summer slithered off her stool to retrieve her Dictaphone while LB put the potatoes on to boil. He turned as she played the two messages again. Summer leaned back against the breakfast bar as the machine clicked off.

'She would have helped him and she's sorry for what she did… helped him financially?' she said, looking up at LB.

'Maybe. I wonder what she did?'

'Told the press?' hazarded Summer. 'About him and Kate?'

'Maybe. It's not worth guessing tonight. We can just ask her tomorrow.'

'We? Am I joining you?'

'She's an interior designer. I can't help it if you happen to be in there choosing cushions or something when I drop round to see her.'

He took a long drink from his wine, his eyes catching hers over the rim of the glass. She grinned. He waved at the sofa.

'We might as well sit down. Other than checking the vegetables there really isn't anything for me to do in the kitchen. If you can forgive me getting up now and again?'

'I can forgive you almost anything if what's cooking tastes even half as good as it smells!'

He smiled appreciatively as he tugged the apron off. She followed him to the sofa and sat down. LB moved the side table, placing it carefully in front of them and then retrieved his pot of pencils from the windowsill and his attaché case from the hall. Summer sat quietly while he shuffled through his notes and scratched the back of his head with a pencil, composing his thoughts.

'You were telling me about the adoptions of Malawian children in the car – go through it again?' he said, raising his eyebrows, the pencil now poised.

Why did she suddenly look so wary?

Summer wriggled back into the corner of the sofa and leafed through her own file of notes. LB jotted while she spoke, glancing curiously at the papers she'd put on the sofa next to her – a scribbled set of numbers and a timeline. He nodded through the update, recalling what she'd said in the car. When she finished he leaned back, rubbing his eyes.

'How can this be linked to the break-in?' he said. 'The only things missing are the letters. Could they be to do with this?'

Summer stared into her glass, swirling her wine.

'I doubt it. What do you reckon?'

'Mmm. I doubt it too. Hang on. Excuse me? I just need to check dinner.'

'Who's Bruce Macdonald?' she asked as he reached the kitchen.

LB grimaced but didn't answer and returned quickly to scoop his notes up and away from her sight. She repeated her question. He turned to her, tired.

'No one you need to know about.'

'But he's linked to the Hamptons?'

LB rested his chin in his hand, leaning on his knees.

'What are these numbers?' he asked, nodding at the sheets lying on the sofa between them.

She stared at him. His patience hardened into determination. She pulled the sheet of figures towards her.

'I've no idea,' she said, looking over them. 'They're a print-out of Patrick's financial spreadsheets but they don't seem to add up. The other numbers were on a piece of paper by the phone.'

LB leaned back and flicked his fingers to take the papers from her. He picked up his wine and read over the numbers, glancing from sheet to sheet.

'Maths not one of your strong points?' he said, meeting her eyes with a humorous smirk. Summer still looked sullen.

'No. I'm absolutely shit at numbers. Ask my accountant. Why? What have you spotted?'

He held the two pieces of paper up.

'These,' he said, indicating the scribbles from the side of the phone, 'are what make these,' he shook the other sheets, 'add up. It's the money needed to make the other figures balance.'

He handed her the papers, pointing to where the figures fitted in and then laughed at the expression on her face as she scowled at them. If he was right, the figures on the scrap of paper she'd found indicated that Patrick was currently several thousand pounds short. LB eyed her carefully.

'Did Patrick ever tell you why he stole from you?'

Summer shook her head.

'He never admitted that he did, which is why the case against him was dropped. His word against mine.'

'Was he involved with a loan shark then?'

She shrugged.

'If he was, he never said.'

Her gaze dropped to her glass then she turned away.

'Jesus, if he's missing because of money, I could have helped him…' she said, her voice cracking.

LB leaned over and placed his hand over hers, half expecting her to pull away. She stared at his hand and then up into his face, but didn't move.

'But he hasn't gone missing because of money – whoever he owes money to didn't know he was missing or they wouldn't have called again.'

He coiled his fingers closer around hers, squeezing gently until she smiled weakly.

'Answer me honestly,' said LB softly. 'Have you had anything to do with Patrick's disappearance?'

'No!' she cried. 'Jesus, Ben!'

She tried to snatch her hand away, but he kept hold of it, gripping it firmly.

'Then you are not to blame,' he said, his voice soothing. 'Whatever is behind him disappearing, it's not your fault. If it's because he was blackmailing someone to get him out of this financial mess, you are not responsible for either the mess or his choices. If it's because he's discovered a child-trafficking ring, you did not lead him to discover it, nor are you one of the people behind it. He asked you for help and you are doing everything in your power to find him.'

'And he might still be dead in a ditch,' she said, turning away.

LB watched tears glisten her cheeks and drew her hands towards him to try and comfort her but she stood abruptly.

'Could I use your bathroom, please?' she said, keeping her face averted.

'Of course. Door at the end of the hallway.'

She scurried out, leaving LB watching her. Shaking his head he picked up her notes, leafing through them. He pulled out the timeline she'd been working on that morning, scanning over it, half his attention on Summer. Was she okay? She seemed like she was only just holding it together this evening. Had the break-in really shaken her? He thought he could hear water running in the bathroom. Was she crying? He picked up a pencil, adding in a few notes to the timeline about Helen Wright. He'd just finished them when Summer returned, her eyes slightly red and the edges of her hair wet. LB guessed she'd been splashing cold water on her face.

'You okay?' he asked.

She nodded briskly and returned to the corner of the sofa.

'What have you added?' she asked, pointing to the sheet in his hand.

'Just a note about Helen Wright. This is good work. You could make a cop yet.'

She grimaced.

'God. I'd rather be hanged, drawn and quartered first!'

Her ferocity surprised him and he gazed at her.

'Are we that bad?' he asked.

She ran her thumbnail under the nails of her other fingers as she looked at him. He wondered how well she would cushion whatever was coming.

'You are either sitting in an office, or dealing with bad people, or sitting in an office *and* dealing with bad people. I think I'm better off with the clouds and the hills for company.'

'That really all?'

Her lips made a hard straight line.

'Let's just say I wouldn't choose a cop as a friend.'

'Including me?' he said, dismayed.

She looked away, biting her lower lip but didn't answer. He shrugged, pulling a fresh sheet of paper towards him and wondering what she was railing against. Time to change the subject.

'What should I ask Ms Wright tomorrow? What do you know about her?'

'Nothing, really. I don't know how she knows Patrick. Obviously she fell for his charm and presumably the baby's his, but since she said they weren't together, I'm guessing they either broke up before she found out she was pregnant which to my mind isn't very likely, or he knows she's pregnant and isn't supportive.'

He rubbed his chin, looking at her.

'Why don't you think they broke up before?'

'Well, the first scan would be at twelve weeks and from the messages she left for Patrick, that was yesterday. She described her and Patrick as breaking up a few weeks ago, not a few months ago so I think she told him when she found out she was pregnant, and then they broke up. But I suppose you could ask her about that. Also, as Patrick had a load of abortion clinic leaflets, my guess is that he was trying to persuade her into having a termination. He's not ready for fatherhood!'

'Nor monogamy as Helen and Kate would have overlapped significantly,' said LB, tapping the end of the pencil against the sheaf of papers in his hands, examining the timeline.

'Maybe another reason why they broke up.'

'The more I hear about this man, the less surprised I am that he's disappeared. The man's a bastard,' muttered LB.

'He's just different to you,' said Summer, her words crisp. 'He doesn't fit your narrow image of decency. And while I agree that his love life is less than conventional and that he's possibly treated Helen very badly if he tried to talk her out of keeping her baby, he certainly never pretended to me that he was ever in it for the long haul and I doubt he did with Kate or Helen either. I imagine their expectations of him were similar to yours, but he isn't like that. That doesn't make him a bastard. It just makes him different.'

LB flinched at her outburst, eyes wide.

'He's a thief.'

'He was possibly desperate,' she countered.

'And a liar and a cheat,' LB added.

'There's more to him than his sex life,' snapped Summer. 'If you knew how hard he works for Samala and how deeply affected he is by the plight of the kids... He might not be a saint, but he sure as hell isn't the devil either.'

She stared at him, breathing hard. LB waited to be sure that she'd finished and then nodded.

'I'm sorry,' he said. 'I keep forgetting he's your friend. He wouldn't be someone I would warm to from what I've heard about him, but you're right, that doesn't make him a bastard. I'm sorry.'

The fire in her eyes died slowly.

'Actually, I'm trying to convince myself almost as much as I am you. His views on monogamy never bothered me, but the stealing did and if he was trying to talk Helen into an abortion he would be a bit of a bastard in my eyes too,' she said. 'Although if he's as hard up as we think, he wouldn't be able to support her anyway until he'd cleared his debts.'

LB's gaze dropped back to the timeline.

'That fits,' he murmured. 'He speculates about some new project, maybe in late February or early March—'

'No. Earlier than that. He stole from me in late January,' cut in Summer.

LB looked again at the timeline, his eyes narrowing as he marshalled his thoughts.

'Okay,' he started again. 'Patrick speculates about some new project in January, stealing from you to finance it. It's not enough, leaving him with a cash flow problem.' He tapped his finger on the spreadsheets. 'Which he funds with a loan from someone less than reputable, let's say. He's been seeing Helen. Maybe he asks to borrow from her – she said she would have helped him but she couldn't with the baby coming. Possibly that help was financial, although admittedly there's no evidence to support that theory yet.'

Summer stared at the paper, counting slowly on her fingers. LB raised his brows.

'Twelve weeks ago takes us to the weekend I was at the bothy,' said Summer. 'Or the weekend after.'

He swallowed. However much she might claim she knew Patrick wasn't big on monogamy, that had got to hurt. Stole from her *and* screwed someone else in the same weekend? Some relationship.

'Did you know?' he asked, quietly.

She shook her head, bunching her bottom lip.

He handed her the sheet of paper he was holding, wanting to distract her.

'Here,' he said. 'Write down, "ask what the help was". So, perhaps he falls behind on payments and gets a beating, though again, there's no concrete link between the two. At about the same time as Helen Wright is discovering she's pregnant, Patrick is sleeping with Kate Hampton too, so the beating could be over the money, the affair or potentially over the pregnancy. Does Helen have an over-protective brother or anything? Okay, write down, "when did she tell Patrick about the baby" and "what was his reaction".'

'I can tell you what his reaction would have been,' said Summer, looking up. 'He'd run screaming to the hills! Without any financial issues!'

LB laughed.

'Write down, "when did Helen find out about Kate".' he said. 'And "what was it that she did?" I feel that they're linked.'

'That would be one hell of a triple whammy,' said Summer slowly. 'Finding out you're pregnant, then learning that not only is the father not overjoyed about the prospect but that he's shagging someone else as well!'

'And that he's skint.'

She acknowledged the point, chewing her lip.

'Do you think he *was* blackmailing Kate Hampton?'

'No evidence to say so and both of the Hamptons denied it,' said LB frankly. 'But I see where you're coming from.'

'What's your feeling about it?'

He grinned at her.

'My feeling is that there's no evidence to say he was. But that Kate was lying and Paul knew all about it.'

'Who do you think beat him up?'

'Too many options to speculate.'

He put the papers down and stretched his back, suddenly exhausted. Summer slipped her shoes off and tucked her feet up. The two sat in companionable silence for a moment, but gradually, Summer's face fell.

'Do you think we'll ever find him? Alive?' she asked, her voice fragile.

He looked across, composing his words carefully.

'I don't know. Until we find a body, there's always hope.'

She swallowed.

'And statistically?' she said.

LB didn't answer.

'We haven't found a body,' he said softly, squeezing her hand to try and comfort her. 'Come on. Talk to me while I make the sauce for dinner. It won't take long.'

He kept hold of her hand, leading her back to the bar stool. He put the apron on again and set about finely chopping an onion. He tossed it into hot butter, stirring it with one hand while he leaned back to retrieve the bottle of wine next to her with the other. He smiled as he caught her eye.

'You look ridiculous in that pinny,' she said with forced brightness.

He laughed, letting it rumble in his chest. He held her gaze for a moment before turning back to the cooking. The wine hissed as it hit the hot pan, filling the air with the aroma of warming alcohol. He chopped herbs and added them to the pan, flicking them around quickly with a spatula.

'What just went in? I didn't recognise the smell,' she asked.

'Tarragon. French tarragon,' he said with a twinkle, turning to her.

'Surely it should be half-French tarragon,' she quipped back.

He laughed again.

'No. I learned all my cooking from my mother. And how to eat it all from my father.'

'It all smells delicious. I'm starving!'

'Five minutes,' he promised, turning the heat up under the pan.

He rummaged in a drawer and put knives, forks and napkins in front of her.

'Set the table? And draw the curtains?'

He tipped up his chin to indicate the table in the window. Summer grabbed the cutlery, slithering off the bar stool with alacrity. The room filled with the scent of herbs and meat. By the time she returned to the boundary of his domain, LB had served the chicken breasts and was adding cream to the saucepan, a look of deep concentration on his face as he stirred the sauce.

'You really do love cooking, don't you?' she said softly.

He looked up, surprised.

'Actually, I really love eating good food. The one has to precede the other.'

He smiled at her and turned back to the meal, pouring the sauce over the chicken and adding a small sprig of tarragon to garnish. He drained the potatoes and slid them on to the plates, added the carrots, and turned round and waved her over to the table.

'Grab the bottle?' He nodded at it.

She took the wine over to the table and he followed her with the plates.

'Sorry,' he said, frowning as he put them down. 'I should have put the vegetables in a dish. But be flattered. I'm normally only this informal with family.'

She laughed, shaking her head at him.

'Thank you. This looks delicious,' she said as he sat down.

He shrugged modestly and flicked his napkin across his lap. Before he could pick up his knife and fork, Summer leaned across and unthreaded his tie. He waited, watching her with raised brows as she pulled it through his collar, rolled it up and put it on the far side of the table.

'There,' she said. 'Now you look a bit more like Benedict and less like a cop.'

He held her gaze for a moment.

'But I'm still a cop. Just a cop without a tie on. Why does my job bother you so much? What's lurking in your background that makes you rail against it so much?'

'I don't know,' she said, leaning back and stretching the distance between them. 'My dad hates cops. Consequence of being busted for drugs so many times, I think. Maybe it's rubbed off on me.'

Her voice was light but its flippancy didn't convince him. He gazed at her, trying to imagine being brought up in a household where the police were distrusted so much. Coppers in the late twentieth century hadn't always been known for their liberal views and he could believe that her parents' alternative lifestyle hadn't gone down well.

'Did they ever bust the house?' he asked.

Summer toyed with her food, unable to look at him.

'Mmm. Several times. All batons blazing. Thing is, Dad never dealt. He and Mum might have consumed, quite copiously at times, but they never dealt. Possession is nine tenths of the law though, right?'

The bitterness rang through her words.

'Was he convicted? Of dealing?'

'No. Both he and Mum were fined for possession once. After that they just got smarter about hiding it. They never dealt though. Not that that stopped the cops trying to prove they did.'

LB watched her push her food around. The wounds must be over twenty years old and yet they were still raw.

'I'm sorry,' he said quietly.

'What? That my parents were hippies?' she flashed back. 'Or that the police tried to plant evidence on them? I'm sure if you'd been a copper then, you'd have done exactly the same.'

'Possibly. But I wasn't. And I didn't.' He held her gaze firmly, biting his lips together. 'Don't tar me with that brush,' he said softly, once the anger in her eyes had died. 'I'm really not that kind of copper.'

'I know. I'm sorry… I'm not really angry with you. Maybe you're just an easy target.'

'Easy? I'm six foot three. You can't bloody miss me,' he said lightly and she laughed.

He stroked the back of her hand, making her look down.

'I'm really not that kind of copper,' he murmured.

She leaned forward, still staring at his hands.

'Sorry,' she whispered, lifting her knife.

He shrugged, dismissing her outburst as lightly as he could. She cut a slice from the edge of her chicken and popped it in her mouth. Then she looked up, eyes wide.

'Wow,' she said, her mouth still full. 'This is amazing!'

He smiled modestly, thanking her.

'Your mother's recipe or one of yours?'

'One of my mother's.'

'Well, you can tell her that it's excellent.'

She took a long drink from her wine, studying him.

'Why no wife?' she asked.

He blinked at her, surprised.

'Er… not all that compatible with the job, I suppose.'

'Never come close?'

'Once,' he acknowledged. 'But it never quite happened.'

'What, did she crease the cushions too much?' mocked Summer.

He smiled.

'No. She just got tired of coming second.'

'You don't seem that sad.'

He leaned back, sighing.

'Regret is a pointless feeling. However much I regret it, however much I might wish things had been different, what changes? Nothing.'

'That's quite defeatist,' she said, frowning.

'No. That's quite realistic,' he said. 'And anyway, she would have creased the cushions too much.'

He lifted his glass, his eyes holding hers over the rim, a smile poking into his cheek.

'Well, she missed out on some great cooking, that's all I can say,' said Summer, spearing another piece of chicken. LB shrugged diffidently.

'Girlfriend?' she added. He shook his head.

'Don't have time.'

Summer smiled. They ate in silence for a few minutes, allowing him to consider how truthful his last answer was.

'Benedict?'

Startled, his head snapped up, making her smile at his reaction.

'Sorry,' he said. 'No one calls me that. I'm usually LB at work, or Ben. What did you want to ask?'

The smile on her face melted away.

'Answer me honestly. Do you think Patrick's dead?'

'Until we find a body, we hope he's alive.'

'Don't give me that! That's not what I asked,' she snapped.

He paused, and then picked up her hand, rubbing his thumb across her knuckles.

'At risk of riling you, you have to think he's alive unless we find a body. If he's out there, we'll find him.'

'But you think he's dead?'

He breathed deeply.

'I think the more days that pass without finding him, the slimmer the chance of finding him alive, yes. But I have to think he's alive until we find a body.'

He squeezed her fingers, peering into her face. She squeezed back and then withdrew her hand.

'As soon as you assume he's dead, you'll lose the urgency to find him,' he said, his voice soft, the backs of his knuckles stroking her hand.

He kept rubbing her skin until she looked up, and then slipped her fingers into his again. She nodded hesitantly.

'You have beautiful hands by the way,' she said, making him laugh with surprise.

'Thank you. What made you say that?'

She shook her head, looking away.

'They're just beautiful hands.'

They finished the meal in silence, LB fretting about her. Once the plates were empty, LB cleared the table, taking everything over to the kitchen and loading the dishwasher. He handed Summer a second bottle of wine and a corkscrew.

'I think we both need it,' he said when she raised her eyebrows at him.

More wine poured, they sat down on the sofa again, Summer still withdrawn. LB pushed the bao board towards her, hoping to distract her.

'You were going to teach me?' he said, catching her eye.

'Sure. I'll let you set it up. You need two seeds in each of the smaller holes.'

She sat back, watching him while he flicked the catches to open the board out. Whereas the outside of the box had deeply carved images of lions and giraffes covering the surface, inside were thirty-four smooth hollows arranged in four rows of eight plus another, larger hole at each end. Two of the smaller holes were square; the others were rounded. There was a muddle of black and white seeds inside, all about the size of black-eyed beans, and he started to sort them, putting white ones in the holes facing her and black towards him.

'It doesn't matter what colour you start with,' she said, sitting forward to help him. 'They'll all be jumbled up before long.'

The board set, she explained the basic rules, smiling as he looked perplexed.

'The easiest way to learn is to play,' she said. 'If you go wrong or make a mistake I'll explain. Let me start. The two rows closest to you are yours; the other two are mine. The game finishes either when your front row is empty, or mine is, or if either of us end up with only single seeds in the holes. Okay. I'll begin here.' She pointed to the third hollow in from the right hand side of the outer of the two rows that were hers. 'So, I pick up the two seeds and drop them into the next two holes, like so.'

She let the seeds fall into the next two holes, moving anticlockwise around her rows, then scooped up the two seeds in the hollow in LB's front row, opposite the point where her last seed had dropped. LB glanced up.

'I've captured these two seeds of yours and I sow them from the start of the front row, going in the same direction as I was before.'

LB watched carefully. Summer put one seed in the far right-hand hole and one in the next. Again, she then captured LB's two seeds that were opposite.

'Still with me? I now do the same with *these* two seeds as I just did.'

LB watched as she did, expecting her turn to then finish as there were no seeds in the space opposite for her to capture. To his surprise, she scraped out all of the seeds from the hole she had ended at and carried on, putting a seed in each space. Again, her final seed ended opposite an empty space on LB's side and again, she picked out all of the seeds and kept sowing.

'My go ends when my last seed ends up in an empty hole,' she explained. 'Like this.'

He nodded, staring at the board.

'Help me out? Where's good to start?'

She smiled.

'Sure. You can only capture my seeds if the last seed you sow lands in a hole that's already got a seed in it. Look at the front row of my side. I've got four seeds here and here.' She pointed to the board. 'I'd start here if I were you and work clockwise.'

'Oh, it doesn't have to be always anticlockwise?' he said, surprised.

She shook her head. LB picked up the two seeds she indicated and, checking he was correct, dropped them one by one into the next two spaces.

'Good. Now capture my seeds, and start sowing them from the beginning of the row. There.' She pointed again. 'Now, you can't capture anything, but you can scoop all of them up and keep going.'

She helped him, explaining why the direction of play suddenly had to change and when he had to count and when he could capture. The seeds clicked, crossing and recrossing the board with each capture. Every now and then, Summer would suggest a better move or point out some strategy to LB or tell him another minor rule as the situation arose. They played three games, Summer winning the first two and LB the last.

'It just needs to be twenty degrees warmer and smell of charcoal and mangoes in here and we could be in Malawi,' she joked as he emptied the last seeds from her front row of the board to win.

She closed the board up, her fingers slipping over the catches. LB touched her hand softly.

'Are you okay?'

She stared at him, swallowing hard.

'What would you do if I said no?' she said, her grey eyes blinking away a blur of tears.

'What would you let me do?' he asked gently.

'Hold me.'

He blinked slowly and offered an open arm to her. She scooted down the sofa to lean against him and he tucked both arms around her, resting his cheek against her head.

'Can you stop being DS Stewart for the rest of the evening and just be Benedict?' she mumbled from the crisp cotton of his shirt.

'I would be delighted to,' he said. 'Since I'm supposed to be on holiday.'

He shifted his position to lean into the corner of the sofa more, taking her with him.

'Still comfy?' he asked.

'No.'

He laughed, letting her wriggle and rearrange herself against him, and then settled his arms around her again. She wormed her fingers between the buttons of his shirt, stroking the hairs on his chest. Tears crept out, soaking into LB's shirt, and he smoothed her hair down with his palm. His hands carded her hair and he pressed a kiss to her forehead.

'There's nothing I can say to make you feel better, is there?' he said, his voice low.

'No,' she said, shaking her head against him. 'He's either dead or lost. And I know things between us weren't close, but he was part of my life for a while and he asked for my help. And I have spectacularly failed him.'

Her voice wobbled. LB struggled for words. None of the facts they'd uncovered about Patrick was leading them to where he was and he knew platitudes would merely irk her, so he let her cuddle against him, his hands rubbing soothingly over her skin.

'If it's linked to the child trafficking, am I safe?' she mumbled finally, her voice still shaky.

'Why wouldn't you be?' he said, surprised.

'Because I've done as much digging as Patrick.'

He breathed deeply.

'I don't think it's linked to Malawi.'

'What's your current working hypothesis?' she said, snuggling closer to him.

He rested his cheek against the top of her head.

'Gut feeling is the Hamptons. Absolutely no evidence though.'

'Hmm. Who's Bruce Macdonald?'

She tipped her head back to look at him. He held her gaze for a moment.

'I thought you wanted me to be Benedict, not DS Stewart?'

'Yeah. DS Stewart wouldn't tell me. I was hoping Benedict would.'

He shook his head, smiling, and she nodded and looked away.

'Can I stay here tonight?' she said a few moments later, her fingers still stroking his chest.

He blinked rapidly and laughed. It was a while since someone had asked him that.

'Not while I'm on the case, no. I don't get to stop being DS Stewart that much!'

Summer bunched her lips.

'You wouldn't have a case if it wasn't for me.'

'I know,' he said.

'Don't you have a spare room?'

He groaned, shaking his head.

'Yes. But you still can't stay. Why don't you want to go home?'

She burrowed against him again.

'I don't really want to be alone with my thoughts.'

He stroked her neck and she moved to look at him.

'I can understand that,' he said.

He rubbed his thumb over her cheek, gazing at the flecks of ice-blue in her grey eyes. His heart surprised him by starting to pound. Summer's eyes held his for two breaths before she reached up and kissed him, her lips soft against his. His breath caught in his chest. Her lips were still on his and belatedly he returned the kisses, letting his fingers tangle in her hair. Eventually she drew back, inky black pupils crowding out her irises.

'And I *really* can't stay?' she said.

He didn't reply, his mind still turbulent. She brushed the ball of her thumb across his mouth and he pulled her back to him, his lips seeking hers again. Her breath was warm against his cheek. Somewhere, deep inside his brain, he could hear a small voice protest. He ignored it, moving his hand down to the small of Summer's back and drawing her closer.

Many moments later, she eased back slowly, smiling.

'You kiss me like that, but I can't stay?' she murmured.

'No, you really can't,' he sighed. 'However much I might want you to.'

'And do you? Want me to?'

'Mmm.' He kissed her again briefly. 'But not while I'm on the case.'

She sat back, pulling away from him and looking down at her lap.

'You have no firm leads as to where the hell he is. What if we don't find him for months?'

He brushed her hair back from her forehead, doubting that her frustration was over his lack of availability.

'We will. And anyway, I'm handing it all over to the guy in Lothian on Monday. I'm only seconded while I'm on holiday.'

She nodded, studying her knees.

'What does the L stand for?' she asked, her gaze sweeping up to his eyes. 'In LB?'

Surprise flashed through his face and he paused.

'Promise you won't tell?' he said lightly.

'I promise. I don't promise not to laugh if it's really awful.'

He chuckled and tipped her towards him comfortably, settling his arms around her waist.

'Lucien,' he said, his brow puckering.

'Lucien?'

She stared at him, trying the name out again almost silently.

'It's actually quite a beautiful name,' she said.

He snorted.

'It isn't when it gets shortened to Lucy, in the playground.'

A long, unfettered peal of laughter burst from her.

'No. I guess not,' she said when she could finally speak. 'When did that stop?'

'When I got big enough to make it a foolhardy act,' he said drily. 'I'd adopted Ben a long time before that, but you know what kids are like.'

'You're talking to someone called Summer who has no useful middle name,' she retorted. 'Of course I bloody know.'

He smiled, shifting her in his arms. She leaned away, breaking the embrace, picked up her glass and drained it.

'I guess you should call me a cab since neither of us is fit to drive and you're determined that I can't stay,' she said, twirling the empty glass by its stem and looking at him, mischievously. 'Lucy.'

He held her gaze feeling a smile prickle his mouth and trying to maintain a more serious expression.

'I guess I should. Pick you up at half seven tomorrow?'

She frowned.

'We're meeting Helen Wright,' he prompted. Obviously it wasn't only his brain that had turned to jam in the last few minutes.

Her face cleared.

'Sure.'

She wriggled away from him and put her glass on the table as he called her a cab.

'Ten minutes,' he said as he closed his phone.

The silence while they waited felt awkward. If he wasn't on the case would he have let her stay? Would she want to? Maybe they'd both find out on Monday.

He looked up at the sound of a horn pipping outside. In the hallway he helped her into her coat then pulled her into a close embrace.

'Try and sleep. I'll see you in the morning,' he said, squeezing her.

She looked up and he dipped his head to kiss her, breathing in her scent, tasting the tang of apricots and herbs on her tongue. She stroked his cheek, his stubble rasping against her skin and he caught a groan in his throat before it could escape. Her teeth grazed his lips, making his heart race. The kernel of him determined not to let her stay, for the sake of the case, began to dwindle.

The taxi pipped again and they parted, grinning at each other. Summer grabbed her bag and scurried out to the waiting cab, waving once she was inside.

LB leaned against the doorframe until long after she was out of sight. He sighed, blinking slowly and ducked back inside.

Two seconds later and he would have seen Summer's taxi heading back towards him at speed.

FRIDAY NIGHT

Kate's hand missed as she went to pick up the glass, flumping on to the table instead. She peered at the glass, confused, and wished it would stop moving around and going so blurry, and closed her eyes. They flashed open again immediately in a vain attempt to stop the world twirling. After a bit of experimentation she found that lying on the sofa with one foot on the floor and her arm on the table made the room move at a speed akin to the London Eye which was manageable. She wanted to cry but all of her tears had been exhausted hours ago.

She had been clinging to her marriage, adrift and in turmoil. Her career was in tatters, her children wouldn't speak to her… all she'd had left was Paul and now she realised she'd married a monster. What else was there?

She made a determined effort to sit up and focus on the strip of pills on the table, pushing them through the foil and piling them into a heap. One by one she popped them in her mouth and sipped at the wine until both the pile of pills and the glass of wine were gone.

She wished he was here. She wanted him to see what he had driven her to. Wanted to tell him one last time that she loved him. She sloshed more wine into her glass and stared at her mobile, willing it to dial by itself. Eventually, she leaned over and grabbed it clumsily, punching at the keys once it was in her hand, blinking hard to see them. It took her four attempts to get them right but finally it was ringing.

'Yes?'

He sounded cross and she sighed down a gulp of air.

'Paul? Please come. I've done something really very foolish.'

The phone fell from her grip and she closed her eyes. She could hear faint voices tinkling in the background. One of them sounded so like her husband. Oh, she wished he was here. Then he could see what he had done.

***

The floor was cold under him, adding to the chills that shook his body. Despite this, sweat poured off him and he ached to his core. He curled tighter into a foetal position, unable to get warm and only marginally more comfortable on the floor than in the chair. His bound wrists pressed against his chest, his ankles screamed with pain. The basement was pitch black, a thick darkness that smothered everything. Try as he might, Patrick couldn't even see the floor beneath his face.

He rolled over, trying to stop shivering. Then he heard the bolts being drawn back on the door above him. He squinted as blinding light flooded the room, managing to discern a figure sway in the doorway before descending the stairs towards him. Patrick peered at him. The man was covered in soil, the sharp tang of it smelling better than Patrick did.

'I've just been digging your grave,' said the man, pulling up the chair and sitting down on it. A beer bottle hung loosely in his grasp. The man was very drunk. The fact terrified Patrick.

'No one will find it,' the man went on lightly. 'It's a great place for that. There could be thousands of bodies out here. No one would know.'

Patrick's body was wracked with shivers and he looked up at his tormenter, panicked. Was this it? Were his final minutes going to be spent on the floor of a basement, covered in his own blood and filth? Not the heroic ending he might have hoped for once.

'Are you going to kill me?' Patrick whispered, hoping he could keep control of his bladder and guts.

'Nothing would please me more, you little shit, but I'm still hoping to persuade you to do the right thing.'

'The right thing?'

The man didn't answer, but stared at Patrick, taking a long swig from the bottle in his hand.

'You stink of rotting flesh,' he said.

'I think it's my ankles,' said Patrick.

The man leaned over and yanked up the cuffs of Patrick's jeans to reveal blood-soaked socks and swollen, suppurating wounds. Pus oozed out around the black plastic, leaving a yellowish crust where it had dried. The man sat back.

'You're right. They don't look good. Septicaemia I'd say. Lost some good comrades to that out in Iraq. Better men than you,' he spat. 'Men who knew what their duty was and did it, regardless.'

He stood, grabbed Patrick by his collar, hauled him to his feet and threw him into the chair. The effort made him sway again. Patrick could smell the alcohol billowing off him.

His captor fixed him with a blearing eye, then he turned on his heel and left. Patrick breathed hard, trying to settle his heart rate. The lights to the basement were still on and he stared around, desperate to see a way out. The door was wide open at the top of the stairs but just as Patrick was summoning the energy to try and make a break for it, bound though he was, the man returned, his bulky outline filling the doorway. Patrick stared dully at him, and felt his guts recoil as he saw the man had a Stanley knife in his hand, the blade glinting dully. The man held it in front of Patrick for a moment, before letting it trail slowly over his throat, making Patrick tremble involuntarily. The man laughed.

'Not tonight. I'm too pissed to dispose of the mess. With any luck you'll have died of blood poisoning by tomorrow and save me the effort.'

He crouched down in front of Patrick and sawed through the cable tie around his ankles. Then he straightened up and cuffed him across the face. Patrick blinked, and watched as the lights faded from the edges again and the blackness returned.

***

Summer paid the taxi driver, scrambled out of the car and ran to LB's flat. She hammered on the door, leaning on the frame. LB swung the door open and stared at her. She pushed past him into the hall, the bright tangerine of fear filling her head.

'Summer? What the hell are you doing back here?'

She didn't answer. She wished he sounded kinder. Softer. She was into the lounge as he was closing the front door and she screwed herself into the corner of the sofa, chewing her thumbnail. Within seconds, LB was in the room.

'Summer? What's wrong? What's happened?'

She tried to control her breathing, her shoulders lurching as she drew air in. LB walked around to face her, his face full of concern.

'Summer? What's happened?' he said, crouching down in front of her so that she was looking at him. 'Summer?'

'It's Moyenda,' she said, thrusting her phone at him and then coiling her arms tight against her body again.

LB read over the message.

'Dear Summer. I hope you are well and that you remember me. I know you are in much contact with Moyenda and so I have to tell you he is in hospital. He was beaten up today evening. Police here are investigating. I will text again when news. Wilson.'

'Who's Wilson?' LB asked softly, moving to sit next to Summer.

'He helps out with the kids. Plays football with them.'

'How violent is Blantyre? Could this be a coincidence?'

'No. I mean, you shouldn't go out when it's dark because it is rough, but Moyenda is too well known and liked. No one would attack him.'

She looked at him over her knuckles, still trembling, her eyes wide.

'They've taken Patrick, they've hurt Moyenda...' she said. 'What will they do to me?'

'Nothing. Nothing.'

He drew her towards him, sliding his arm around her shoulder and cradling her against him. She resisted at first and then relaxed, resting her forehead on his neck. He stroked her neck, his touch gentle. Orange began to mutate into purple and green.

'How would they know where you live?' he said, sounding infuriatingly practical.

'How did they know where Patrick lived? In fact, there's more ways of finding me, because I run my business from home!'

She pulled away roughly, dragging her hands through her hair. Then she leaned on her knees, staring blindly at the carpet.

'Did you want me to come back with you? Check it's safe?'

Her face contorted in a scowl and she didn't reply. LB sighed.

'Summer, I know you're scared, but you can't stay here. I won't compromise the case any further.'

Summer ground the heel of her hand into her cheekbone.

'You have a spare room don't you?'

Her words rat-tatted out and LB closed his eyes.

'I can ring round hotels if you want?' he said.

Summer turned her head away, muttering about bloody rules and conventions.

'Stop being a hippy liberal,' he said. 'And let me come back with you and check your place is safe. If you stay here, even in the spare, there would be too many reasons to throw away all the research you've done and all my police work and I won't let that happen.'

Cop first. Friend last. She'd been stupid to ever believe he could be different.

'Summer, I will not risk compromising Patrick's safety by torpedoing the investigation. You can get in a taxi and go to a hotel or you can get in a taxi with me and I'll check out your place. The one option that is not on the table is you staying here.'

His voice was calm and reasoned but his position was as malleable as granite. Summer tried to out-stare him for several minutes before giving up without grace. She snatched her bag up.

'Okay. Don't you ever call me a hippy again.'

LB caught her gently by the wrists, his face soft.

'I would love for you to stay. But not as much as I would love to be able to put away whoever has attacked your friend. Please understand that.'

She jutted her chin up briefly, but suddenly all the fire died in her and she nodded. LB drew her into his arms.

'We'll check out your place and if you're still not sure, we'll find you a hotel, but honestly, I think you're safe. I wouldn't even suggest going to your house if I didn't think that.'

He kissed her temple and rubbed her back, his hands comforting against her. She sucked in a long, shaky breath before stepping back.

'You'd better call a cab,' she said, her head cast down.

She perched on the edge of the sofa while he called, reading over the text from Wilson again. She hoped Moyenda was okay. Had she brought this on him with her meddling and questioning? It didn't bear thinking about. With a start, she realised that LB was watching her.

'Don't blame yourself,' he said quietly, sitting next to her.

'Are you a mind reader?'

He shrugged.

'I read people for a job. And anyway, it would be a natural thing for you to do. But it's not your fault.'

'Easy for you to say.'

'People have free will. They chose to do this; you didn't make them.' He nudged her gently. 'Come on. Taxi will be here. I think it's the same guy!'

It was the same guy, who looked as if he half expected them

to go round in another circle. At Summer's, LB asked him to wait and then took Summer's keys from her. Summer waited as instructed – in sight of the taxi, on the threshold of the house – while he checked through the rooms.

'It's fine,' he said, when he rejoined her. 'It's fine. Put me on speed-dial though and call me if anything happens.'

'Patrick probably called me on speed-dial.'

He pulled her into his arms. Her head nuzzled into his shoulder and she bit her lips together trying not to shake.

'Mmm. But with all due respect, one, I know where you are; two, I'm a lot closer; and three, I'm built like a bear.'

She smiled and acquiesced. He kissed her tenderly.

'I'll come and pick you up at seven thirty,' he said and kissed her again. 'Sleep well.'

She watched him leave, her hand trembling on the doorframe. Please God, let him be right.

SATURDAY, EARLY MORNING

Moyenda cracked open his eyes, blinking at the light that was streaming into the hospital ward. He was lucky. He had a bed. There were several people on rags on the floor in the spaces between the beds. The Queen Elizabeth hospital was always full to overflowing. Between the ravages of HIV, TB and malaria, there were always too many patients.

Outside he could hear the early morning stirrings of the guardians – the relatives or friends of the patients who would bring food to them and who would wash and care for them. He wondered if Chifundo would come for him. Did she even know he was here? His mind flicked to the children. Who would do outreach today? Who was scheduled to man the office? His head hurt with the effort of thinking so he stopped and stared at the ceiling and listened to the flies instead, feeling the fresh air blow over him from the open windows.

The ward round had just started. A gaggle of students from the College of Medicine surrounded a tall, white doctor – one of the many who came to do VSO and then stayed. There was a small, slightly bent Malawian with the throng, acting as both interpreter and clinical officer. Moyenda knew both the British doctor, Dr Charlie Brackman, and the clinical officer, George. The unfortunate confusion between L and R in Malawian speech regrettably rendered the doctor Dr Blackman, which had

233

always made both him and Moyenda smile and had entertained the children enormously as the man was white-blond, blue-eyed and Scandinavian pale in his skin, even in the Malawian sun. He ran a monthly clinic out at the children's centre and his brow was furrowed as he approached Moyenda's bed.

'Moyenda! Is that you under all that bruising? What's happened to you?'

'I do not know,' said Moyenda, only half truthfully. 'I was walking back from the centre last night and I was attacked. Someone brought me here but I do not remember who. I need to go. I need to make sure that the children are okay.'

Dr Brackman rested his hand on Moyenda lightly, stopping him from rising.

'Right now, you need me to check you over. The children will be fine.'

Moyenda sank back and allowed himself to be examined, listening to the medical jargon and explanations for the students. Once the examination was concluded, Dr Brackman stood at his friend's side.

'And you've no idea who did this?' he asked.

Moyenda shook his head.

'You can't drive for a few days, but then, you don't have a car do you?'

'No, Charlie. I am not a rich doctor with a BMW!'

'You can go, but mostly because we need the bed. Is there someone you can call to come and collect you? I assume Chifundo knows you're here?'

'I do not know. Wilson has a car. He could collect me.'

'Do you still have your phone?'

Moyenda shook his head. Dr Brackman handed him his.

'Here. Call Chifundo and Wilson. I'll get it back when I've finished this bay.'

Moyenda thanked him. Dr Brackman moved on to the next patient. Two short calls later and Moyenda was ready to leave. He thanked Charlie and returned his phone to him as he passed.

'Is Wilson coming to get you?' Charlie asked.

'Yes.'

'Okay. Take care. I'll stop by your house when I've finished work.'

He shook hands with Moyenda and moved on to the next bay, the stream of students trailing after him. Moyenda gathered his things and went outside to wait for Wilson.

The air was fresh on his face. In late April the rains had ceased but the temperature was still holding up before the cool months of June and July. The scorching heat of October seemed far away. The hospital had small gardens surrounding the building and the vegetation was lush with many plants covered with flowers. Moyenda waited under what was called a flamboyant tree, looking up into its branches. It wouldn't be long before it would be covered in orange-scarlet flowers, looking from a distance as if it had burst into flames. With a pang he remembered the time when Patrick had asked him what kind of trees they were and he had told him, only for Patrick to laugh and say how apt the name was. Moyenda blinked painfully and looked down, wondering if he would ever see his friend again.

He was roused from his thoughts by Wilson's arrival. Wilson greeted him like a brother and ushered him towards a beaten-up, dusty, white Toyota pick-up truck. Moyenda climbed in the front seat, weary to his core and desperate to go home to his wife.

'I called Chifundo last night and told her you were here,' said Wilson, climbing into the driver's seat. 'Samson called me. One of the people who brought you in is his brother.'

'I know. Thank you for calling her. I managed to speak to her this morning. Charlie lent me his cell.'

'Charlie Blackman?'

Wilson looked over, his eyebrows raised. Moyenda smiled.

'Yes. He was on duty at Queen Elizabeth's. That's how I called you too. Do you know if anyone is doing outreach today? And who is in the office?'

'Moyenda, Moyenda. It is fine. I called Manale and Joy and

they are making sure someone will do outreach. Joy is in the office. I will take the children for football this afternoon. You must concentrate on yourself today!'

'Thank you. I think you worry about Samala as much as I do.'

Wilson smiled, driving carefully. As ever, the road was lined with people going about their day; pushing or riding bicycles laden with people and goods, children running in and out of the road, dodging the ruts and the ditches in their paths.

'I also texted your friend Summer and told her,' Wilson said, negotiating some young boys who were kicking an improvised football around.

'Summer? Oh. Thank you. She will be worried.'

They drove in silence until they were on the outskirts of Blantyre. Wilson looked across at his passenger.

'What happened?'

'Some young men attacked me for my wallet and cell phone,' said Moyenda.

Wilson scrutinised him, his eyes narrowing.

'What aren't you telling me?' he asked.

Moyenda looked across, took a breath and shook his head.

'Let me get home and see my wife.'

Chifundo fussed and clucked when they arrived, appalled at the sight of her husband. Moyenda went to bathe, inviting Wilson to stay. As he smoothed the clean water over his wounds, he thought hard about what to say to Wilson. He owned a haulage business and had negotiated large donations to Samala from the Blantyre Rotary Club of which he was a member. He played football with the children every Saturday and gave his time and money to the project as freely as he could. The children adored him. Moyenda had a sneaking suspicion that Wilson was gay but it was not a topic that would ever easily be discussed and, as far as Moyenda was concerned, it had no bearing on Wilson's involvement with Samala. Moyenda trusted him as a friend; could he tell him what was going on?

He dried himself carefully and rejoined Chifundo and

Wilson who were drinking tea together. They both looked up, falling silent, and Moyenda wondered what they had been talking about. It wasn't long before he found out.

'Chifundo has been telling me of your worries,' said Wilson.

Moyenda shot a look at Chifundo, eyes wide, but he was too tired to keep fighting on his own.

'I do not want you to get hurt too,' he said cautiously, pouring himself a cup of tea and sinking down into a chair.

'I'm old enough to make that choice for myself,' said Wilson. 'Perhaps you can fill me in on the details. Chifundo has not said much but now we know you were not hit for your cell and your wallet.'

'Maybe for my cell,' said Moyenda. 'But I have been changing SIM cards so they won't find anything.'

'Start at the start. What is happening with the missing children?'

Moyenda closed his eyes, leaning back in the chair. It would be such a relief to share this burden. He started slowly, trying to be logical, even though his head was pounding and all he really wanted to do was to sleep. Gradually the story unfolded – the missing children, the link with pastor Bradley Collinson, Mzondi Malilo.

'Mzondi is involved?' interrupted Wilson. 'I went to school with him!'

'He is involved,' said Moyenda harshly. 'And he knows what I found out, so I imagine Moses knows too. Moses Chizuna,' he added for clarification. 'Mzondi is the middle-man. Collinson finds the families, selects the child and tells Mzondi. Mzondi gets Moses to sign the papers. Bribes all round and a consolation donation to Samala to make it all right.'

'How many children?' asked Wilson.

'I think seven. I think that Patrick Forrester had found out about two of them – Limbani and Mabvuto – but there are five others missing too. And now something has happened to Patrick.'

'And to you,' said Chifundo, folding her arms across her ample bosom.

Moyenda bowed his head, defeated.

'What can I do? I can't bear it but if I expose what's happening, it could endanger Samala.'

'We would lose all the funding,' said Wilson. 'All the big donors would pull out immediately if there were suspicions of trafficking.'

He sat back, his shoulders slumped but his eyes darting back and forth.

'Joseph will help,' he said suddenly, straightening up.

'Joseph?'

'My cousin Dalita's fiancé. They got engaged in March. He is in the government. He is a special adviser and has the respect of a great many people who would not want to see this happening in Malawi. If he knew, he would help, there is no doubt. He would be able to stop it without Samala being affected I am sure.' Suddenly, Wilson's face was full of enthusiasm. 'Let me call my cousin,' he said, jumping up.

Moyenda was horrified.

'Is your cell safe?'

Wilson shrugged.

'I am only going to invite her and her fiancé for lunch. When they come, we can tell Joseph everything. No one else will know.'

He called his cousin quickly. Moyenda listened with Chifundo, barely able to breathe. After the introductory pleasantries and exchange of family updates, it was agreed that Dalita and Joseph would come down from Lilongwe the following weekend to have lunch with Wilson. Wilson ended the call, a triumphant look on his face.

'He will stop it. I know he will.'

SATURDAY MORNING

'*Merde alors!*'

LB threw the covers back and scrambled out of bed, still cursing as he hit the shower. In two minutes he was washed and standing in the middle of the room, towelling himself roughly. He put his glasses on, dressed rapidly and ran downstairs. He flicked the radio on and poured himself a glass of orange juice. He'd just taken a first gulp when he nearly choked, spitting the juice into the sink.

'*Returning to our main headline this morning, Kate Hampton, who resigned as minister for health in the Scottish parliament yesterday, was rushed to hospital last night after a suspected overdose. Her condition is said to be serious but stable. Her husband is by her side.*'

His mobile started ringing and he snatched it up.

'You heard the fucking news?' demanded Andy Watson on the other end of the line.

'Yes. Just now on the radio. What's happened?'

'Hoped you might tell me. Far as I know she tried to top herself last night then called the hubby who took her to hospital. I don't imagine anyone will be allowed near her today and certainly not you or me. This is a fucking disaster! I can see the fucking headlines now. Health minister tries to top herself after being questioned by the police!'

LB stared at the clock. There was nothing he could do about

Kate Hampton and if he was going to collect Summer and make it to his appointment with Helen Wright on time he needed to leave now.

'Your call,' he said. 'What do you want to do?'

'I want you off this fucking case. If it comes out that you questioned her about taking fucking drugs...'

'Fine. Take me off. Officially.'

'What do you mean, officially? What are you playing at?'

'Nothing,' lied LB. 'Take me off the case if it'll make you happier. I'm supposed to be on holiday.'

'It won't just make me happier, it'll make the boss a lot happier too.'

'Okay. Fine,' said LB, pulling on a jacket and juggling his phone. 'Whatever you want. If I find anything out, unofficially, I'll let you know.'

'What are you up to?'

'I have to go. I'll call you later.'

LB ended the call abruptly, and dialled Summer.

'Hey, Summer,' he said, breathless. 'Any chance you can make me some toast?'

'Sure. What's up? Why do you sound so stressed?'

'Turn the radio on. See you in five.'

He snapped his phone shut, slammed the door behind him, and jogged to his car.

Summer was waiting on the doorstep for him when he pulled up at the kerb, clutching her bag and a cup of coffee. She climbed in and handed him two slices of toast, blinking as she looked at him.

'Glasses?'

'Up late. I normally wear contacts. Thanks for the toast.'

'You always this grumpy in a morning?'

'I'm always this grumpy when I'm late,' he replied, waiting for her to buckle up.

She laughed. He put the two slices of toast buttered side together, jammed them in his mouth and drove off, driving one-handed until the toast was gone.

'Thanks. Nice bread.' Then he looked properly at her. 'You okay? You look tired.'

'Didn't sleep much.'

He reached over and squeezed her hand.

'I'm sorry I couldn't let you stay,' he said.

'It's okay. I understand. I shouldn't have put you in that position,' she said, sliding her hand away from his. 'What the hell's happening with Kate Hampton?'

He glanced across.

'I don't know any more than you. And I'm now off the case.'

'Why?'

She turned, surprise filling her face.

'Because it's easier for Lothian? Yesterday afternoon I questioned Kate Hampton and yesterday evening she took an overdose.'

'Are the two connected?' said Summer, humour ringing through her words.

'Andy Watson thinks so. He rang me just before I rang you. Personally, I wonder whether her actions paint her as guilty as sin. And unofficially, I'm still helping. Hence us still going to see Helen Wright.'

He concentrated on the road for a few minutes, giving Summer a chance to drink her coffee. She sipped carefully, staring out of the window.

'Why do you think Kate Hampton's done that? Really?'

LB glanced across.

'People take overdoses because it's a cry for help or because they really want to end it all. Since she called Paul, it was either a cry for help or she had second thoughts. My instinct is that it was the former. She's lost a lot – career, status, respect, husband, lover – and perhaps she thought that making the grand gesture was the right thing to do.'

'Risky. The news said she was serious but stable.'

'They always say that. Any of that coffee left?'

She passed him the cup and he took a deep drink from it before handing it back.

'You make good coffee as well as good bread,' he said.

'Yeah. I know.'

He smiled.

'Okay, let's go through the questions we talked about last night. What might Helen be able to tell me? Patrick's financial situation; whether the beating was linked to him owing money… what else?'

He glanced across. Summer's mouth was hard.

'You? Not us?' she said. 'I thought I was being allowed in with you when you went to see Helen?'

'Allowed in. Not allowed to question.'

'Oh.'

LB looked across. Her lips made a tight circle.

'I thought you'd rather be dead than a copper so why so pissed off?'

'I thought I was trusted enough to help. I was obviously mistaken.'

LB sighed.

'At risk of repeating myself,' he started, but Summer cut in, her voice still splintered.

'I know, I know. Evidence standing up in court and all that. But at risk of repeating *myself*, there wouldn't be much evidence if it wasn't for me.'

'I'm not having this fight with you again,' said LB. 'You might not have any rules governing your life and work, but I do.'

'What's that supposed to mean?'

'It's not *supposed* to mean anything. It *means* I have to work within boundaries. You're a freelance photographer with your own business – you don't have a boss breathing down your neck or threatening to haul you over the coals for not following procedure. I do. Please? It doesn't mean I don't *want* you there. Or that I don't respect you.'

She scowled but he knew he'd won the argument.

'Money, beating… pregnancy… what else?' he asked, his voice soft. 'Did she know about Kate Hampton? Before the papers broke the news.'

'Indeed. I can't think of anything else.'

He might have won the argument but he hadn't won her over. Summer turned to stare out of the window. The two lapsed into silence. After a few minutes, LB cleared his throat.

'What's wrong?' he said.

'Sorry?'

Summer snapped out of her reverie and stared at him.

'Last night… we seemed like we were… close. But today you're back to being prickly and edgy around me. What have I done?'

'Nothing. I just like you better when you're not a cop.'

'Oh.'

'Oh?' she mocked.

'Just oh… I am a cop.'

'I know. I wish you weren't.'

He looked at the road, letting out a deep breath.

'I mean, I'm glad you're helping. I just don't have a great rapport with cops. And I know I'm being unfair. I'm just being honest.'

He bit his lips, his eyes narrowing. She was as prickly as a porcupine and infuriating with it, but despite all that, he found he wanted something more than mere acquaintance with her. Maybe a lot more.

'Tell me what happened? When you were young?'

She stared out of the windscreen at the raindrops that were starting to muster against the glass. LB waited, wondering what could have shaped her prejudices so irrevocably.

'My parents were distinctive. Are distinctive. Although less so now I guess. Anyway, they stood out. Didn't conform. Not enough rules and certainly too few observations of convention.' Her mouth twisted then she swallowed. 'They were an easy target. My childhood memories are peppered with policemen bursting into the house, tearing it up, smashing things, spoiling everything. As soon as we straightened the place out they would be back to tear it apart again. There was no point trying to have nice things because they'd just be damaged. The first time they came, they found a tobacco tin with probably less than half an ounce of dope in it and charged my parents for possession. They were determined Dad was a dealer though. They searched, time after time, and when that didn't uncover anything, they threatened us. And when that didn't work, they planted evidence.'

She still didn't look at him.

'What did they plant?' he asked softly.

'A shoebox with bags in it and a list of alleged customers. The case fell apart when no one on the list could be called for questioning. All the names were made up. But Mum and Dad were labelled for life. They were shunned in the street, my mother was called names, people refused to serve her in shops… we ended up moving. Fresh start where we had no history dragging us down. So I guess they won in the end.'

LB swallowed, and flicked the indicator on making her finally look across at him. He parked and held her hands, his eyes searching hers.

'Summer, trust me. I hate that kind of policeman as much as you do. What they did to you and your family is unforgivable and I understand why you're so angry. But it wasn't me. I would *never* do that. And if I ever came across a copper who did, I'd blow the whistle on them, get them removed from the force. Please believe me?'

He reached across and pressed his palm against her cheek. She smiled faintly and he leaned in to kiss her tenderly. She hesitated before kissing him back.

'I know,' she said as she pulled away, stroking his jaw. 'But you have a hell of a lot of bad memories to overcome.'

'I get that.'

He kissed her again and then moved back, squeezing her hands.

'Let me try?' he asked, his dark eyes locked on hers.

She stared for a moment, silent. Then she nodded. He smiled. 'Thank you.'

He drew her towards him again, his mouth brushing hers.

She smiled as he eased back, letting him believe that she might eventually see him as more than just a cop.

He pulled back on to the road and they drove in silence until they were in Edinburgh, all conversation seeming trite.

Eventually, Wright Interiors loomed into view. The roads around were choc-a-bloc with cars, forcing LB to park several streets away. LB grabbed his briefcase, checking the notes from the previous night were easy to access.

'So what's the plan?' asked Summer.

'Helen has never seen you? In person?'

'No.'

'Okay. Since I'm not officially helping with the case any more and you shouldn't really be there either, you'll have to look like a customer but only if you're sure she won't recognise you. Not from an advert or that article or anything?'

Summer hesitated.

'Possible. Though in the photo of me in the article I'm wearing a hat.'

LB sucked his teeth and screwed one side of his mouth up. A hat was no disguise for those eyes.

'If there's ever an issue, we wouldn't be able to write it off as coincidence since I drove you here.'

'Well, I need to look for wallpaper anyway,' said Summer walking on. 'It's not my fault that you want to talk to the woman selling it.'

LB smiled ruefully, shook his head and hurried after her. Summer pointed out the shop and strode off purposefully. LB watched as she ducked into the shop. Would she be recognised?

He waited a few moments before following her. A bell jangled above his head and a slim, smiling woman approached him. He scanned the room rapidly, matching her smile. Summer was tucked in a corner, sitting on a chaise longue, leafing through books. She flashed him an okay sign from behind Helen's back.

'Ms Wright? Hello. I'm DS Stewart. We spoke on the phone yesterday.'

'Oh yes of course. Come in. Um… I have a customer who's looking at samples at the moment. Perhaps we could talk in the back?'

LB dropped into step behind Helen, thinking quickly. He glanced at Summer and flashed his phone at her. Hopefully she would realise he was calling her and would keep quiet but follow the conversation with Helen.

Helen led LB through to a tiny office off the main part of the shop and waved her hand at a chair. Next to the chair was an antique desk with a computer and some neat paperwork on it and a shelf of folders above the desk. A modern filing cabinet sat next to the desk. LB sat, placing his phone face down on the desk to hide the fact it was active and looked up at Helen, waiting for her to sit on the other chair.

'Thank you for agreeing to meet me this morning and I'm sorry it's under such difficult circumstances,' he said, keeping eye contact. She glanced away.

'Oh. Yes. Er, coffee?'

'No, thank you. I need to ask you some questions about Patrick Forrester. To get some background information and so on.'

Helen nodded, looking miserable. LB found his notes and uncapped a pen.

'Could I ask you how long you've known Patrick Forrester?'

'I met him at a New Year's party, but we only started seeing each other a couple of weeks later.'

LB jotted a note, wondering how Summer would take the confirmation of her suspicion that she and Helen had overlapped in Patrick's bed.

'You said yesterday that you and he broke up a few weeks ago. Could you tell me when you last saw him?'

'Hang on.'

She pulled a leather organiser towards her and unsnapped the fastener. She leafed through the pages rapidly and then looked up.

'We broke up on March thirty-first but I did see him again, on April the sixth.'

She looked up, and LB saw that her eyes had lost their earlier sparkle and were flinty.

'Ms Wright. I realise this is a difficult and private thing to talk about but we're investigating Mr Forrester's disappearance. Could you tell me why you broke up and what happened at your subsequent meeting please?'

Helen breathed in sharply, turning her head away.

'I haven't spoken to Patrick since that day. I had no idea he was missing until you told me.'

'I understand that and I really am sorry to be asking these questions. I need to get as much background information as possible from those who know him.'

He stared at her, waiting. She fiddled with the catch of her organiser and then nodded.

'Er. Well. We broke up for a number of reasons really. The main one is that I'm pregnant and Patrick was not supportive. He would have preferred me to get rid of the baby.'

She paused again, her focus on the desk, her lips thin.

'And the other reasons?' prompted LB after a few minutes.

'He owed me money. He'd borrowed from me and couldn't pay me back. And I realised he was also involved with someone else. But you'll have seen all that in the papers.'

She jutted her chin at a copy of *The Scotsman* on her desk.

'Could I ask how you found out that Patrick was involved with Kate Hampton?'

She paused, running her fingertip over the corner of her organiser.

'I saw them together. Coming out of a hotel.'

She ground to a halt.

'They could have been attending a meeting,' suggested LB. 'What made you believe there was anything going on?'

'I read his emails. And her emails to him.'

'Was it you who told the papers about Mr Forrester and Mrs Hampton?' asked LB, watching her carefully.

Helen shifted in her seat.

'No.'

She snatched her gaze down to the surface of her desk. LB waited. She looked back up after a few moments.

'No. Not the papers. But I did tell Kate Hampton's husband,' she said quietly, looking up at LB's questioning gaze. 'I thought that she – Mrs Hampton – was why Patrick was reluctant to support me over the baby. I guess I was wrong about that.'

Her bitterness reverberated around the room.

'Why do you say that?'

'Because he still didn't come back,' said Helen. 'I'm still pregnant, out of pocket and single. He hasn't returned my calls since we met up again.'

'And what happened at that meeting?'

'I told him that I knew about him and Kate Hampton and asked him if she was the reason he didn't want the baby. He said he didn't want the baby because he couldn't afford one and that it had never been his plan to become a father. He said that if I'd got myself pregnant, then it was my problem.'

'That's not a very nice response.'

'No.'

Her expression was hard. LB glanced down at his notes.

'You've said that Mr Forrester owed you money and that he said he couldn't afford a child. Do you know if he'd borrowed money from anyone else?'

'Yes. Not sure of his name. Ken? Kevin? Something like that.'

'Keir Bevan?' hazarded LB, thinking that if Patrick had crossed Bevan, he should start trawling the Forth now.

'Mmm. That's the name. I think.'

LB worked hard at keeping his face neutral.

'We know that Mr Forrester arrived at work about a month ago looking like he'd been beaten up. Do you know anything about what happened?'

'That was his first warning, as they called it. It was to do with the loan repayments and the fact that Patrick was behind with the money. It's why I said it didn't matter about the money he owed me.'

She stared at LB for a moment.

'Is that why he's gone missing?' she asked. 'Because he owes this guy money?'

LB shrugged.

'We don't know. That's why we're making these inquiries. On the message you left on his phone, you said you were sorry for what you had done and that you would have helped him, but with the baby coming, you couldn't.'

She nodded cautiously.

'Could you explain what you did and what the help was?'

She sucked in a deep breath, tipping her head back briefly.

'What I did was to tell Paul Hampton about his wife and Patrick,' she said. 'And I would have tried to help with the loan repayments except I can't afford to with a baby on its way.'

'Do you know if there's anyone else who might have had a grudge against Mr Forrester?'

Helen laughed lightly and said, 'I expect there's quite a queue! I can't imagine Mr Hampton was all that happy but I don't know him personally. I doubt Kate Hampton will want to be a bosom pal any more.' She tailed away, obviously thinking of something else, and smiled. 'I guess lots of other people like him.'

'Why do people like him so much? He seems to have treated you quite badly, if you don't mind me saying.'

Helen's lips thinned.

'Well. I suppose so. But he was a lot of fun to be around. Until I told him about the baby he was very loving and generous. He made people feel welcome and at ease. I think the timing with the baby wasn't great for him. He said he felt backed into a corner and that he was struggling with everything when I last saw him.'

Her hand flew to her mouth.

'Oh God. You don't think he's done something stupid do you?'

'There's absolutely no evidence to suggest that,' said LB soothingly.

Helen nodded, her fingers twisting together. LB glanced over his notes.

'Is there anyone else who might have a grudge against Patrick? Other than the Hamptons?'

He watched her carefully. She fidgeted for a moment.

'I guess my brother was quite angry,' she finally ventured. 'When I told him about the baby and Patrick's reaction.'

LB nodded encouragingly.

'But I can't imagine he would do anything,' she said hurriedly.

'Where is your brother at the moment?'

'Er. Skye. He's doing up a house for a friend.'

'Do you know where he was in the week?'

She paled.

'Rob wouldn't…'

LB waited.

'Er. On Monday he was decorating a bathroom in Livingstone – he works for me sometimes. On Tuesday, he went to do a job in Edinburgh, but they hadn't cleared the space so he left. He said he'd gone over to the west to go fishing with a friend when I spoke to him on Tuesday night, but then he said he'd given up on that and was off to do up Archie's place in Skye.'

'When did you last see your brother?'

'Tuesday at breakfast. He's been staying with me. He's been over in the west since then.'

'With Archie?'

'No. He said Archie was away. He could be staying at Archie's but he could also still be staying with whoever he went fishing with.'

'Do you know that friend's name?'

She shook her head.

'Sorry. He didn't say. I'm sure he's got nothing to do with this though.'

'We just want to be able to eliminate him from our enquiries.'

She nodded.

'Yes of course. Did you want me to ring him now?'

AMANDA FLEET

She didn't wait for an answer but pulled out her phone. Her face fell a moment later.

'Oh. It's gone straight to messages… Hi Rob. Can you call me back when you get this? It's Helen.'

She rang off and looked at LB.

'Do you know the address in Skye? Or Archie's surname?' he asked.

She shook her head.

'I have them at home somewhere. I can check at lunch.'

LB delved in his wallet for a card and wrote his mobile number on the back.

'Well, thank you for your time, Ms Wright. If you think of anything else that might be helpful, please give me a call? And could you ask your brother to get in touch?'

He handed her the card and stood, smiling at her. She ushered him back through to the shop. LB surreptitiously clicked end call on his phone, thanked Helen again, and while her back was turned flashed his hands at Summer to indicate ten minutes. He hoped she would understand and play along.

The bell jangled above his head again. As soon as he was out of sight he texted Summer to again ask her to stay and tell her that he'd be at the coffee shop across the road.

He chose a table by the window and kept his eye on Wright Interiors while he ordered a black coffee.

Summer stuck to the plan, joining him almost a quarter of an hour later.

'I think I've just agreed to redecorate my dining room,' she said, looking flustered.

He smiled.

'You know it would have looked weird for you to have left straight after me! How much did you manage to catch?'

'All of it I think. What now?'

'Now? Breakfast.'

He pushed a menu over to her and Summer laughed. They were the only customers in the place. LB put their orders in,

251

pulled out the sheaf of notes he had accrued over the past few days and shuffled through them until he found the timeline.

'I need to call Andy Watson,' he said apologetically, glancing at Summer.

She shrugged, dropping sugar cubes into her coffee, watching him while he dialled.

'Andy? It's LB. I talked to Forrester's ex-girlfriend this morning. Apparently he'd borrowed money from Keir Bevan... I know... and he was behind on the payments. He'd been given one of Bevan's warnings...'

LB held the phone away from his ear, waiting for the torrent of expletives to cease.

'Just thought you should check it out. My gut instinct is that it's not him, because there was another call about the money, after Forrester went missing... I know it's your case... handle it however you like... oh, and it was the ex-girlfriend who told Paul Hampton about Kate... a letter... yes, I guess it is the same one... no, nothing else.'

Summer mouthed, 'She's pregnant,' across the table at him.

'Oh, no, hang on, she's pregnant... no he wasn't happy... Helen Wright.'

He passed on her contact details and hung up.

'The poor woman is probably going to get a visit from Watson,' he said, picking his coffee up.

'You don't seem to like him.'

'No. He gives policing a bad name. He's exactly like the image of coppers you have.'

He watched the shutters come down between them and took a bite out of his croissant. Chewing, he pushed the timeline between them. Before he could speak, Summer asked, 'Who's Keir Bevan?'

'He's a nasty piece of work. Loan shark. If he hadn't called again after Patrick went missing, I'd be suggesting we get a team of divers searching the Forth,' LB said bluntly.

Summer swallowed and LB realised too late that he should have cushioned the blow. He slid his hand over hers.

'But he called after Patrick disappeared, so I don't think he can be involved,' he said.

'Who do you think is?'

'Well, Helen has every reason to hate him, but I don't think it's her. She does have a brother with no alibi though, who is conveniently unreachable out in the west somewhere. My gut feeling is the Hamptons though. I think Helen sent the letter to Paul, Paul confronted Kate about it, Kate called things off with Patrick and then Patrick threatened to blackmail her over the affair in order to pay off the loan shark. Although much of that is supposition.'

'So where is he?'

'I don't know.'

'And possibly won't ever? The Hamptons are too savvy to say anything.'

He bunched his lips in acknowledgement. Summer leaned her head forwards, rubbing the skin above her eyebrow.

'Why do you think Kate tried to kill herself?' she asked, her eyes meeting his.

'I don't know. Maybe she felt she'd lost everything that meant anything to her – husband, career, respect? Maybe she realised her husband was behind Patrick's disappearance and couldn't bear it.'

'He's not just missing though, is he? He's dead. You don't take someone out of the picture for this long and then be able to just put them back. Patrick would report them; it would come out. No, if Paul Hampton has made Patrick disappear, it's permanent,' said Summer, her voice quavering.

LB picked her hand up and pressed her fingers against his lips. There was nothing he could say that would help. Yes, the party line was always that you didn't give up hope until you found a body, but she was right. Whoever was behind Patrick's disappearance wouldn't keep him hidden somewhere indefinitely. He was more than likely already dead. The only real hope was that he might have been left for dead somewhere and be found in time, but the more days that passed, the less likely that was.

'Who's Bruce Macdonald?'

LB snatched his gaze back to her and hesitated.

'Paul Hampton's brother-in-law,' he said at last.

'And?'

'And he has a violent past.'

Summer stared at him.

'Why aren't you searching his property? It won't be Paul who's taken Patrick, it will be him! Why aren't there search teams going through his shed, his house, his…'

She tailed off, tears choking her throat.

'Because we don't have enough evidence for a search warrant,' he said softly.

'That doesn't normally stop you!' she snapped. 'Why don't you just make something up?!'

LB's patience had reached its end.

'I know that's your experience. I know the police treated you and your family badly when you were young, but it's not like that now. What you're wanting me to do is to become the very thing you despise! The very thing *I* despise.'

She tried to pull her hand away but he kept hold of it.

'Look, once we finish here, I'll go to the station and see if I can persuade the team there to go and check; I'll comb through everything again and see if there's enough evidence to search his properties, but I can't promise anything.'

He released her hand and she snatched it down to her lap. LB rubbed his jaw.

'I'll get someone to check out Helen Wright's brother too. I don't have a sister, but I can imagine if I did, I'd be less than happy if she got treated the way Patrick treated Helen.'

Summer nodded.

'I'll get these,' she said, flicking her head towards the waitress.

LB shrugged. Summer plonked her bag on her lap and started half emptying it to find her purse. One of the first things out of the bag was a pair of thin rubber gloves. LB picked them up and stared at her, his face hard.

'Care to explain?' he said.

Summer met his eyes levelly.

'I always carry a pair with me. Years ago I helped out at an accident – a cyclist was knocked off his bike and I worried because of all the blood. I've carried a pair since then.'

He nodded, relaxing. Summer continued to pile object after object on to the table, making LB laugh, first at the quantity of stuff she had and then at the size of the bunch of keys she deposited on top of the files.

'You look like a jailer,' he said, hoping to lighten things.

'Yeah, I know. House, car, my parent's house… I have to keep them all together or I'd lose them. You've seen my place!'

She paid for the breakfasts and repacked her bag, still stony-faced.

'How long will you be at the station?' she asked.

'Don't know. Why?'

'I have some business I could do in Edinburgh if you'll be an hour or more.'

'Then do your business. Call me when you're done?'

She nodded.

At the doorway, LB caught her hands and pulled her towards him.

'I will do my absolute most to get someone looking at Bruce Macdonald's properties. I promise.'

He pressed his lips to her forehead. She smiled weakly and drew back.

'I'll call you when I've finished,' she said, starting to head towards the Royal Mile.

He watched her walk away, feeling sick at the thought that Patrick could still be alive in one of Macdonald's properties. Dear God let them be able to get a warrant.

SATURDAY, LUNCHTIME

Helen Wright's brain clicked over things. Where were those print-outs of the emails and photos? They weren't at home – she'd searched the place when she'd got back from meeting the Adamsons – and they weren't here in the office either. She could have sworn that she'd left them at home on the coffee table. Maybe Rob had moved them.

Click, click, click.

His anger had been directed equally towards Kate Hampton and Patrick. Had he given those emails and photos to the press? She had used them to confront Patrick; she hadn't intended for them to be made public.

Click, click, click.

She dialled his mobile.

'Hi sis!'

'Hi Robbie. How are you? Why didn't you call me back?'

'Huh?'

'I left a message.'

'Oh. Haven't checked them. What's up?'

'Er. There was a folder on the coffee table. Did you pick it up?'

'Folder? What was in it?'

'Some pictures and some emails.'

'Oh. Of the slut and the bastard? Yeah. I got rid of them.'

'Why?'

'I thought they were too upsetting for you.'

'Did you give them to the press?'

'What? Fuck, the reception's bad again. What?'

She didn't get to answer as he rang off, leaving her in no doubt. He'd never been able to lie to her, even as a little kid. She chewed her nail. Then she looked out the business card the tall policeman had given her.

***

LB had called Summer twice and twice it had rung though to voicemail. He was sitting in his car, going through his notes, wondering if he should call again, when his mobile rang.

'Hey,' she said as he answered. 'I'm done. What were you calling me about?'

'Tell you when I see you. Where shall I pick you up?'

They arranged a meeting place where LB could park. When he arrived, he leaned across to open her door and kissed her cheek as she got into the car.

'Good news,' he said before she could speak. 'Someone said they saw a man matching Macdonald's description leaving Patrick's flat on Thursday.'

'Is that enough to get a warrant?'

'Yes. There's a team organised to search all of Macdonald's places.'

'All?'

'He's got a number of places linked to him over the city. Two warehouses, a lock-up, plus of course his home. Watson says he'll keep me posted.'

Summer's face was wreathed with smiles.

'Thank you,' she said.

LB shrugged.

'And, Helen called me. She thinks her brother, Rob, told the press about Patrick and Kate Hampton.'

'Why?'

'You remember she said she'd seen Patrick leaving a hotel with Kate Hampton? And read his emails? Well, she'd taken pictures of Patrick and Kate entering and leaving the hotel. And after reading his emails, she forwarded them to herself and then printed them off. She says she used all of this to confront Patrick the day they broke up, but that they're now missing and her brother said that he got rid of them. She's sure he gave them to the press.'

'And how does this help to find Patrick?' said Summer, her brow wrinkling.

LB checked himself.

'Well, it doesn't. But it does solve something that had been bugging me.'

Summer grinned.

'And did anyone find out anything about Rob?'

'Not much so far. Ex-army. Address currently the same as Helen's. Sandy's doing some more digging for me.'

'Right. So what's the plan now?'

'Go back to Fife. Have a late lunch. Wait to see what turns up in the searches?'

She seemed crestfallen.

'What if they find him?'

'Even if they do, you won't get to see him today. He'll either be in good enough shape for Lothian to question him, or he'll be getting checked over by doctors. We might as well head back. Your turn to cook I believe.'

'Fine.'

He drove them back to her house and helped Summer to make sandwiches. The atmosphere around them fizzed with excitement and expectation although they talked about anything and everything except Patrick. Just as LB was swallowing his last mouthful of lunch, his phone rang.

'DS Stewart ... what? ... You're kidding me? ... *nothing*? Nothing at *any* of them? Shit ... when? ... Okay, thanks for letting me know.'

He hung up and looked across at Summer, his eyes dark.

'They've finished searching the Macdonald properties,' he said. 'No sign of anything. They're questioning Macdonald at the moment though.'

He watched as Summer crumpled visibly, standing quickly to catch her. He lowered her to the chair and held her as tears rolled down her cheek.

'Where is he?' she sniffed, clinging to him.

'I don't know. I don't know,' he whispered, feeling wretched. He'd been as certain as she was that they'd find something at one of the places.

He pressed light kisses to her head, cradling her against his chest. She wormed her arms around him, cuddling in close.

'What now?' she asked, her voice still thick with tears.

'Let's see what he says.'

They didn't have long to wait. Watson called again a few minutes later. LB relayed the crux of the conversation to Summer.

'He's confessed to breaking and entering in order to steal letters back from Kate to Patrick, but swears blind he knows nothing about Patrick going missing,' he said. 'And he has a watertight alibi for Tuesday.'

Summer nodded.

'Okay. Say he's telling the truth. Who else could it be? Someone at the MSA? Maybe the child-trafficking thing involved someone there?'

LB shook his head.

'Possible, but we've nothing to go on. There's been no indication from Moyenda or anyone else that there was a Scottish angle to it all. None of the adopted kids came to Scotland did they?'

Summer shook her head.

'And it isn't Keir Bevan because he called after Patrick went missing, so who is it? Helen? Helen's angry brother?'

'Going to the press only punished Kate,' said LB slowly, sounding his thoughts out.

He pulled his mobile out again and called his partner.

'Hi Sandy. Any update yet on Rob Wright? Yes, I'll hold.'

He waited, his mind running over all the options. It seemed to take an age before Sandy came back on the line. LB's expression hardened and his eyes widened. He flicked his fingers at Summer, demanding a pen and paper from her, and scribbled furiously. The call went on for several minutes. Finally, LB rang off and looked at Summer.

'Ex-military, as we knew. Left the army under a bit of a cloud after an incident in Iraq. Hasn't held down a job since but seems to be working for his sister at the moment and living at her house. Known to have a temper. Been involved in some brawls after hours outside pubs and warned by the police several times, though no charges against him.'

Before Summer could respond, LB was back on the phone.

'Ms Wright? DS Stewart again. I wonder if you could tell me the address in Skye, where your brother is? … Could you look please? Thank you.' He jotted down the address when it came. 'And you said the owner of the house was called Archie. Do you have the surname? … Finlay. Thank you … No, nothing serious. We just wanted to see if he really had given the press those things. Thank you very much.'

He looked at Summer as he dialled again.

'Sandy? I know! I'm on holiday … what's the number for the police in Skye? Can you look it up for me? Thanks.'

He noted it down, rang off and dialled the new number.

'Hello? This is DS Stewart of Fife constabulary. We're looking into the disappearance of an Edinburgh man called Patrick Forrester and we have some evidence that points to him being on a property on Skye. Would it be possible for an officer to go out to the place and check for me, please?'

LB relayed the address, adding more details about the case and giving his number. The call finished, he looked at Summer who was piling things into her bag.

'Come on,' she chivvied. 'Let's go.'

'Where?'

'Skye of course!'

'Whoa! Let's see what they say before we go charging off there!'

Summer faced him squarely.

'It's four days since I got that call from him. Everything at this end is going nowhere. It might take them hours to go out to the place; hours he might not have.'

'It'll take us longer to get there!'

Summer stared at him and then closed her eyes.

'I can't do nothing!' she cried.

He caught her hands.

'Sit down. It's pointless going haring off. Let's see what they say.'

His voice was low and soothing. Summer sank down into a seat, head bowed, rocking herself slowly.

'Oh God. Please let them find him,' she whispered. 'Please let him be alive.'

***

The thin light barely lit the room, never mind warmed it. Patrick's body was convulsed with shudders. The relief he had felt the night before at having his ankles freed had been short-lived as the pain and infection from the wounds seemed to be spreading. If he didn't end up with his throat slit by his enemy, he would probably die from his injuries, he thought.

He'd spent the day in fear of hearing the bolts being drawn back and his captor reappearing. Woozy as his head was, Patrick could clearly remember the man saying he had dug his grave. Would anyone find him before the man killed him and buried him? Was anyone even looking for him? Probably not. Work thought he was on holiday and neither Kate nor Helen were very likely to be seeking him out. What about Summer? Would she have done anything? Or was he going to die in this shithole?

He wasn't sure if he was hallucinating, but he thought he could smell paint. Was the man redecorating the place? Why? To get rid of forensics? But he hadn't got rid of Patrick yet. It didn't make sense.

Patrick rubbed his face gingerly with his wrists, trying to remember all the things the man had said, seeing if he could work out why he was here. Money? Maybe. But why hold him for so long? Surely the idea would be to scare him into paying what he owed and then release him. Or just kill him immediately. Kate? Paul? He shook his head. He didn't imagine Paul had the muscle for this, however mad he'd been and however many threats he'd made.

His stomach knotted at the sound of the bolts being drawn back. He shrank back into the chair as far as he could. The man stepped lightly down the stairs.

'You're a lucky lad,' he said cheerily, standing before Patrick.

Patrick gazed greedily up into the room beyond the top of the stairs, seeing kitchen cabinets and bright light. He looked back at his captor, trying to see if he had a knife or a weapon on him.

'Have you come to kill me?' he asked, fighting hard to keep the terror out of his voice.

'Not yet. My boss says hang on. Change of plan. Again. What a fucking carry-on.'

Patrick stared at him. The man's pupils looked unusually dilated. Had he been taking drugs?

'It's not really *my* boss pulling the strings,' the man went on. 'You've been shagging the wrong woman, from what I hear. If it was my woman, *I'd* fucking kill you.'

Patrick blinked.

'Who's your boss?'

The man laughed.

'No one you know. I've told him you're sick and he doesn't care. Thinks the Big Man's wrong not to have had you offed already.'

'The big man?'

'Just big with money. Got no balls or you'd be six feet under in the woods. Keeps havering over what to do. Twat.'

The man crouched down to look at Patrick's ankles, and then up at Patrick's face.

'I'd better find something for these, in case he finally settles on wanting you alive. Don't go anywhere.'

He laughed sarcastically. Patrick watched him leave, his vision receding from the edges, returning him to a blackness he was beginning to find reassuring.

***

Helen locked the door to her flat, her mobile clamped to her ear by her shoulder. Still no reply from Rob. Could he really have done something to Patrick? Surely not. *Surely?*

She still hadn't got an answer by the time she reached the shop and she sank down in a chair, her head clasped in her hands. Rob had been so mad! Not just about Patrick cheating on her, but over his suggesting she get an abortion. He couldn't bear the thought. After losing his own child like that – aborted by his first real love while he was fighting in Iraq. Put in a clinical waste bag like it was just a lump of meat, with Rob only finding out after the event. Mind you, Robbie would have stood by the mother, poor as he'd been at the time, but she'd said she was better off without both of them. He hadn't seen it the same way.

Was he really at Archie's place? Had he taken the keys with him when he went off fishing? Why? He didn't normally plan so far ahead. She didn't even have a number for Archie – just his name and the address in Skye on a scrap of paper that Rob had stuck to the fridge.

'Oh Jesus, Rob,' she muttered. 'What have you done?'

***

The two policemen picked their way up the rough drive to the house, inching the car around potholes.

'This it?' asked the driver. His colleague nodded grimly.

They parked next to a white van and rapped on the front door of the house. There was a long delay before there was any response and the two men were about to start walking around the outside, checking windows.

'Hello?'

A man with short-cropped blond hair answered the door, wearing overalls that were shrugged off his torso with the arms knotted around his waist. Under them he wore a paint-splodged khaki T-shirt. The two policemen flashed badges at him.

'Oh hello, sir. We're looking for either Archie Finlay or Rob Wright.'

The man's brow furrowed.

'I'm Rob Wright. This is Archie Finlay's house. I'm doing it up for him as a holiday home.'

'Could we come in and have a look around?'

'Why?'

'Just a routine enquiry, sir.'

He paused, and then indicated for them to come in.

'Sorry about the mess,' he said, waving his hand at the dust sheets and brushes in the hallway.

'Do you have any ID?' asked one of the policemen.

'Oh. Yes. Of course. Hang on.'

The man left them in the hall, returning a moment later with a wallet. He took out the driver's license and handed it over.

'Had my hair cut since then!' he laughed as the men looked at it.

'Can you confirm your date of birth?'

'Sure.'

He trotted out the date, the words coming easily.

'Is there a problem?' Mr Wright asked.

'Could we have a look around the place?'

'Of course. Help yourself. Just mind the mess.'

Again he waved his arms at the empty house. The policemen nodded and picked their way through the building before returning to the hallway.

'Sorry to have troubled you, sir. We were asked to check it out. As we said, just a routine enquiry. I'm sure it's just crossed wires somewhere. Thank you.'

Mr Wright showed them out, smiling broadly.

'I bet it's that nosey neighbour up the lane. She does love to know everything! Did she think I was a burglar?'

The policemen laughed.

'Thank you again, sir. Nice set of tattoos! Army?'

'Black Watch,' said Mr Wright, his eyes lighting up.

The policeman nodded, smiling.

'Well, sorry to have disturbed you.'

The police car bounced its way back up the lane, the driver watching the receding figure in his rear-view mirror. The man gave a wave, but stayed in the doorway.

'He strike you as okay?' he asked his colleague.

'He struck me as washed-up ex-army. Just like my mate's brother.'

'Hmm. Maybe. Call it in.'

SATURDAY AFTERNOON

Summer was screwed into the corner of the sofa but only two minutes earlier she had been pacing the room, working hard on not crying. The tears were mustering. LB sat next to her and coiled his arm around her, his brain full of platitudes he knew she'd hurl back at him if he voiced them. She lifted pale eyes in a wan face, meeting his gaze and leaning against him, before resting her forehead on his neck.

'I can't bear waiting like this,' she said.

'Do you want me to hold you?'

They sat in silence for a moment before Summer jumped up and started walking round the lounge again.

'We should have gone to Skye!' she said.

'There would be no point,' he said, keeping his voice soft and soothing. 'We could never have got there before the police.'

'Do you want a coffee?' she said abruptly.

He smiled, recognising her need to be doing something. He was awash with coffee.

'Yes please. That would be great.'

Summer nodded briskly and left him to his thoughts. LB leaned forwards, grasping his hands together, his elbows resting on his knees.

'If he's not in Skye, where is he?' he murmured, turning things over in his head. His phone rang, causing Summer to shoot back into the room, eyes agog.

'DS Stewart. Oh, hi … okay … okay … Well, thanks for letting me know. And I meant it when I gave you my card earlier. You're an intelligent cop. I would gladly have you on my team.'

He rang off and looked up at Summer.

'Young constable from Lothian, chasing up Keir Bevan. Bevan said he was owed a lot of money by Patrick – thousands – but that he had no idea he was missing. Which would fit with him calling Patrick after he vanished. DC Price seemed sure he was, well, let's not go so far as calling him innocent, but not involved with the disappearance.'

Summer nodded and turned silently back to the kitchen. LB knew how she must feel. All alleyways seemed to be turning into cul-de-sacs before their eyes.

As Summer returned with a mug of coffee, LB's phone rang again, startling Summer and making her spill the drinks. LB juggled his phone and fished a pristine white handkerchief out of his pocket which he threw to her to mop up with while he answered the call.

'DS Stewart … Oh hello. Hang on a moment?'

He switched his phone on to speaker and put it on the table.

'Okay. You're on speaker phone,' he said, motioning Summer to sit down. 'Also listening is the woman who reported Mr Forrester missing, Ms Morris. What can you tell us?'

'We checked the house for you. A Mr Rob Wright was there, decorating it for a friend, Archie Finlay, who's turning it into a holiday home.'

Summer's lips trembled.

'We went into the house and looked around. There was no one except Mr Wright there. We checked his ID and he is who he says he is. Sorry not to have more news for you, but your missing person isn't here.'

'Basement? Outhouses?'

'No. Neither. We had a good look around. No one other than Mr Wright there.'

'Okay. Thanks very much for checking that out for us.'

The call ended and LB switched his phone off, his eyes meeting Summer's.

'I'm sorry,' he said. 'It had seemed like a decent possibility.'

Summer's tears spilled as she blinked, and she turned away.

'I'm here if you want me,' said LB quietly.

She shook her head. LB watched her, torn between wanting to comfort her and wanting to be on his own to be able to think. Summer looked up with red-rimmed eyes, scrubbing her face with the heel of her hand.

'If he's not on Skye, and he's not in one of Bruce Macdonald's lock-ups and the loan shark hasn't done anything, where the *fuck* is he?'

LB bit back the truth. They were hunting for a corpse who would probably only turn up when a dog-walker called it in.

'I don't know,' he said softly.

'Is it linked to Malawi?' she asked, with more hope than certainty lacing her voice.

LB sighed. They had no leads at all in that direction.

'I don't know,' he repeated.

Summer nodded, her lips bitten together.

'Excuse me,' she said, picking up her coffee and leaving.

LB watched her back disappear and heard her feet on the stairs, wondering what she would manage to bury herself in to get through this. It could be days or weeks before Patrick's body was found. Maybe even years. The chance that he was alive four days after going missing was slim; the fact they had no leads at all for finding him was just nailing the coffin lid down.

He picked his phone up and called Sandy.

'Hi. You busy? I mean, I know you're always busy, but…' he said when his partner answered.

'Jeez, you sound rough. What's up?'

'We just ran out of leads on the Forrester case. I have no idea who has made him vanish or where the man can be. Our best leads were that he'd been taken to Skye or that Bruce Macdonald had him but both of those have just fizzled out.'

'Shit. I would have put money on Macdonald having had him. You checked all the properties?'

'As far as I know. Several lock-ups and garages in Edinburgh.'

'What about the one under his other name?'

'What?' asked LB, sitting up straight.

'Er, oh hell, the one where he stashed all that knock-off stuff. Shit, it was years ago. Don't think you worked the case. God, what was the name? Something like Frankie…'

'Frankie?'

'Hang on. Shush. Frankie, Frankie, Frankie… Frankie Belmont! You checked that name?'

'No. Thank you, Sandy. You're a star!'

He hung up promptly and called Watson.

'Check out properties owned by Frankie Belmont,' he said.

'Hello to you too. Who?'

'Frankie Belmont. It's a name Macdonald used several years ago – he had a property registered under that name where he used to store stolen goods. Just check it, will you!'

There was a long pause on the other end of the line and LB could hear the clicking of computer keys.

'Fucking hell,' muttered Watson down the line. 'You're fucking right. It's a place out by Kinross.'

He relayed the address and LB tried to place it, thinking the name sounded unfamiliar.

'Can you get someone out there?' he asked, his brow still wrinkled.

Watson sucked his breath in noisily.

'Not my jurisdiction. Ask Fife!'

LB tipped his head back, biting down his annoyance.

'Okay. Thanks for your help,' he said, barely bothering to hide the traces of sarcasm in his voice.

He hung up before Watson could respond and dialled Sandy again. A few minutes later he'd organised a backup team to be sent out there, although he thought that because the case was Lothian's it probably wouldn't be the A-team getting called out. LB closed his phone, strode out to the hallway and bellowed up the stairs.

'Summer! Get your coat!'

Summer popped her head out of her study door and peered over the banisters.

'I've pulled?' she joked.

'New lead. I would tell you to stay here but you'll only do yourself a mischief pacing about and climbing the walls. Come on.'

Summer pounded down the stairs, her face suddenly wreathed with light. LB hoped it wasn't another false dawn.

'What? Where?' she demanded.

'Another property owned by Macdonald. Out by Kinross.'

'Where?'

He showed her the address, shaking his head.

'Not entirely sure. Have you got a map?'

Summer pushed past him to the lounge, grabbed a map from one of the shelves and opened it out. After a moment scouring the sheet, she jabbed her finger on a tiny black square, up a track, well off the beaten track.

'There,' she said triumphantly.

LB took the map and ran his eyes over it, working out the best route to follow and looked up at Summer.

'Don't get your hopes up. I don't know he's there. It's a pretty slim possibility.'

'I'll get my keys.'

'*Your* keys? Mine's out the front. And, forgive me, it's going to get us there faster than your tin can on wheels.'

Summer laughed.

'On these roads? Your shiny beast will get stuck in the mud. My tin can on wheels has four-wheel drive.'

She turned sharply and headed into the hallway, grabbing her keys and her bag.

'You can navigate,' she said, nodding briskly at the map in his hands.

'Summer,' he started, but she was already out of the door.

***

Patrick's eyes opened enough to allow him to see a sliver of his surroundings. His head was humming like a Tibetan singing bowl. He raised his cuffed hands to his ears and felt dried blood on his fingertips. He wanted to sit up but couldn't move, so lay sweating and shivering on the cold concrete. He could hear noises above him but it sounded as if he was listening from the bottom of the ocean. He closed his eyes again. Perhaps he could go back to sleep? Perhaps he could just drift away?

The blackness stripped slowly back to grey when he opened his eyes. He stared dully at the steps about four feet from his nose, letting his eyes follow them upwards until his gaze rested on the doorway. Was the door open? Just a crack? He still couldn't move. Everything was such an effort.

He had to escape. He didn't want to die here. If the door was open a crack, he could get out.

And then what? From the lack of traffic sounds, the house was far from any road and he had no idea where he was.

Defeat washed through him.

'Your choice is to die here on the concrete or die in the fresh air,' he said to himself, screwing his eyes shut again.

He summoned all his strength and forced himself to sit up. Instantly, dizziness swirled and his vision turned to fireworks but he stayed upright. It took another ten minutes before he could drive himself up on to his feet, steadying himself on the chair. His mouth filled with thick saliva as nausea welled but he swallowed it down and breathed deeply until it passed. The steps were five paces away. He looked down at his arms. The skin on the underside of his forearm had tiny dots speckling it, scarlet against a greying background. He looked away, turning his focus to the steps. His eyes were too swollen to open properly. He wondered what he would do if he made it to the top of the steps and the door was still locked, and forced himself not to think about that.

He grasped the rail on the wall with his hands and climbed the first stair, gripping tightly as the world tilted and swayed.

One step. Nine more to go. The climb took him twenty minutes. Finally, he stood on the top step. He leaned his head towards the door, trying to listen but the ringing in his ears made it impossible. Trembling, he took hold of the door handle. He turned it slowly until it reached its limit and pulled it.

It didn't move.

He tried again to no avail, before collapsing on to the top step, sinking his head into his arms and sobbing, his salt tears stinging. He sat there, his last hope dashed and his resources drained, not having the strength of body or mind to return to the concrete floor and wooden chair below. Utterly defeated, he leaned his head back against the door. Through his tinnitus he suddenly heard a voice. A female voice.

'Help,' he said. His voice was inaudible. He swallowed, licked his cracked lips and tried again.

'Help.'

This time someone in the same room could have heard him but certainly not whoever was in the kitchen above. More tears rolled down his cheeks and his head lolled to one side. He sobbed and took a deep a breath, trying to summon every atom of remaining strength and focus it into one last attempt.

'Help!'

The effort emptied him and his head collapsed back on to his knees, the edges of his vision starting to disappear. He heard footsteps, a man's voice snarling, and then the bolts being drawn back.

'Help,' he whispered again.

The door opened inwards, smacking hard against Patrick and pitching him back down the stairs to his prison. With his hands still bound he could do nothing to break his fall, even if he'd had the strength. His head ricocheted off the steps and he tumbled, legs flailing, before landing on the concrete with a thud. He opened his eyes and had the sensation of being above himself and looking down quite dispassionately. His captor had run down the stairs and rolled him over. The woman's voice came more clearly from the doorway and with a sinking heart, Patrick realised it was coming from a radio. The ringing in his head got louder and yet the sounds became muffled.

'Help me?' he breathed, fighting to keep the blackness at the edges.

'Jesus,' muttered the man, staring down at Patrick's body.

***

'If we'd come in my car we'd have had a blue flashing light to put on the roof,' said LB, irritated.

'If we'd come in your car, we'd be tip-toeing around these holes at two miles an hour and the blue flashing light would mean fuck all!'

The Land Rover lurched, bouncing through potholes as it raced down the narrow roads, making LB grip the strap above the window fiercely. Grimly, he acknowledged the point of bringing Summer's car. He wished it was Sandy at his side. Sandy might not be as burly as he was, but he was big enough and knew how to handle himself. He could also talk to Sandy about what might be up ahead. He wasn't so sure he could do that with Summer. He stared at the road.

'Do you think he's dead?' Summer asked, negotiating a deeper hole with skill.

'Until we find a body, we have to assume he's alive,' said LB, though as he said it, he realised there was no conviction in his words.

Summer reached across and hit LB, though the angle she was at and the need to keep her eyes on the road made it pathetically weak.

'Don't fob me off with that! I am not a child!'

'Okay, yes!' snapped LB. 'You want me to stop feeding you the party line? Yes. I think he's dead and probably disposed of. I think when we get there, things will be damned difficult because so far, I see no sign of any blue flashing lights coming to assist us. I think that Macdonald or more likely one of his henchmen has killed Patrick and that he will not be an easy man to deal with. And if you step out of this fucking Land Rover when we get there I will knock you to the ground myself. Are we clear on this?'

He never swore normally. He thought it weak and pointless. But his stress had boiled over and now it had dissipated. He looked across and tried to touch her arm to apologise but she snatched it away as if he'd branded her. Her face was tear-stained and blotched and she wouldn't look at him. He tried to remember that this was her ex-lover he'd just described. He felt a complete shit.

'I'm sorry,' he said, his voice low.

'No need to apologise. I kept pushing. Did I hurt?'

He laughed and shook his head.

'Not really. Not as much as my words. Turn right here.'

She turned her head away, slowing the car and nosing it into a side track.

'How far from here?' she asked.

'A mile. A difficult mile.'

The Land Rover jolted its way over the rough track, slowing as it ploughed through the rutted and broken surface. Finally they approached the house.

'That's it,' said Summer, slowing down. 'And there's a van.'

As they inched forwards, LB raised his hand slowly.

'Pull in here, out of sight.'

She edged the Land Rover into a small clearing just off the track.

'Stay here,' said LB.

He popped his seatbelt and leaned over to curl his hand round the back of her head and kiss her quickly.

'Stay here,' he repeated.

'Or you'll knock me to the ground yourself?' she said, lips thin.

'No.' He smiled, abashed. 'That's really not my style.'

He kissed her again and slid out of the car.

As he approached the house, he looked over at the van, but there was nothing to distinguish it from any of the million white vans on the roads. He walked up to the front door, all senses alert. He could hear voices inside. He cocked his head, listening, finally convincing himself that what he could hear was a radio. He tried the front door but it was locked. He turned to check the rest of the house and almost walked into Summer.

'I told you to stay in the car,' he hissed through clenched teeth.

'What if you need help?' she said.

LB shook his head, planted his palms on her shoulders and propelled her backwards.

'Go back. Now.'

Her eyes were wide as she looked at the house, the tinny sound of the radio filtering out. She held her ground. LB took her face in both his hands.

'Summer. Please. Go back to the car, lock the doors and wait until I fetch you. This is dangerous and likely to be very unpleasant.'

She stared at him. He stared back. He would carry her back if he had to. It wasn't necessary. She nodded meekly. He watched her go back to her vehicle and then crept round to the back of the house. The door to the kitchen turned in his hand and he leaned gently on the door to open it. There was no one in the kitchen and he lifted the snib to stop it locking behind him. Stacked against one wall were crates of counterfeit whisky, the branding freshly painted on the sides, the tang of the paint prickling his nose.

His feet treading softly, he walked through to the hallway, glancing into empty rooms on either side. He swallowed. Could he wait for backup? He made his way back to the kitchen, hugging the wall, careful to avoid the wet paint on the crates. There, he saw another door that he'd originally assumed led to a pantry. He opened it silently to check and found himself peering into the gloom of a basement. At the bottom of the stairs, he saw the inert form of a man, sprawled on the floor.

LB's pulse quickened. He stepped back silently into the kitchen and pulled out his mobile, clicking his tongue as he saw there was no signal. His eyes darted around, searching for a weapon, finding nothing. He tip-toed back to the doorway, ears pricked for sounds. All senses pinging, he jogged down the steps to the body, glad that Summer couldn't see it. The room stank – a pungent mix of excrement, blood, infection and fear. LB bent over the man, his fingers seeking the groove next to the Adam's apple. He dug his fingers in, his eyes on the doorway above him. If anyone came back, he was trapped.

He could feel a weak pulse. He pulled his phone out again but still had no signal. He was about to return to the main house when he heard the sound of footsteps in the hallway. He half hoped it was Summer disobeying his instructions but the weight of the footsteps as they approached the kitchen told him it wasn't. He stood quickly and ducked under the steps. A thickset man jogged down the stairs towards Patrick. LB recognised him as Gavin Tolland, a no-nonsense thug who'd worked for Macdonald in the past. Before Tolland could do anything, LB stepped forward.

'Police,' he said, holding up his warrant card. And as he did so, he saw the Stanley knife in Tolland's hand.

'Gavin Tolland, I am arresting you for the kidnap and unlawful imprisonment of Patrick Forrester. You are not obliged to say—'

He didn't get any further. Tolland sprinted up the stairs with LB close behind him. At the top, Tolland turned and lunged at LB. The pain took a moment to register. LB looked down to see the Stanley knife embedded in his shoulder. One centimetre deeper and the blade would have pierced his lung. LB grabbed Tolland, his hold slipping. He was aware of a warm feeling spreading out across the left side of his chest and knew he wouldn't be able to fight for long. He tried to wrench Tolland's arm behind his back but the ferocity of Tolland's resistance threw him backwards. He twisted, desperately maintaining his grip on Tolland and the two tussled at the top of the stairs. A solid forearm connected with LB's jaw, throwing his head back, and he felt his balance begin to go. He tightened his grip on the thug's arm, dodging blows.

'Just come quietly!' he said. 'There's no way out of this.'

Tolland punched again, knocking LB to one side. LB lost his footing and lurched diagonally, seeing the steps veering inevitably upwards to meet him. He locked his grip on Tolland's arm and the two fell heavily down the steps, landing only inches from Patrick. The fall twisted the Stanley knife out of LB's shoulder and he yelled, releasing his hold on Tolland who scampered up the steps. It felt like half his shoulder had been ripped out along with the blade. LB struggled to his feet and staggered up the stairs after Tolland. As he lurched through the doorway into the kitchen, he saw Tolland disappear into the hallway and out towards the front door.

'Oh God. Summer,' he said.

As Tolland hared for freedom, someone stepped out behind him and swung something at his head. Tolland slumped to the ground, poleaxed. Summer stood beside Tolland, a car jack hanging limply in her hand, staring at him as if she couldn't believe what she'd just done. Tolland started to get up.

'Summer! Get out of there!' yelled LB, willing her to move, but she stayed rooted to the spot.

Tolland was on his feet and making a grab for her. His fingers were millimetres from her arms when LB rugby-tackled him back to the ground and pinned him down with his weight. He wrenched Tolland's arms behind his back, blood streaming from the wound in his shoulder.

'Gavin Tolland,' he gasped. 'I am arresting you for the kidnap and unlawful imprisonment of Patrick Forrester.'

He moved to hold Tolland's legs still with his knees, his head hanging.

'You are under caution. You are not obliged to say anything,'

LB continued, closing his eyes. 'But anything you do say will be written down and used in evidence.'

He breathed heavily, pausing before being able to complete the caution.

'Do you understand the caution?'

Silence.

'Do you understand the caution?'

Silence.

LB wrenched Tolland's arms back viciously, making him howl.

'Do. You. Understand!'

Tolland grunted a yes.

'Do you have anything to say?' said LB, screwing his face up.

Tolland shook his head. LB watched as Summer pressed buttons on her phone. He shifted his weight so he could inspect his wound, his vision swimming.

Merde alors!

'Police and ambulance.'

LB locked eyes with her, relief flooding through him as she made the call.

'You didn't arrest him for murder,' she said once help had been summoned.

'Patrick's not dead. Summer, do you think you could come and apply pressure to this,' he nodded at his shoulder, 'before I bleed to death?'

Summer glanced round the muddy ground. Seeing nothing useful, she took her coat off, peeled off her blouse and put her coat back on. Balling the shirt, she kneeled next to LB and jammed the wad into LB's wound. He hissed and screwed up his face but didn't shift his hold on his captive. Summer wriggled to support him, letting his head rest against her neck.

'What happened?' she asked. 'How's Patrick?'

'Alive, but he's not in good shape. I'm sorry... Press harder.'

'What happened to you?'

'Collided with a knife. I told you to stay in the car.'

'Good job I don't listen to you.'

'Mmm. For once…' He screwed up his face with the effort of breathing. 'It's welcome.'

The discordant noise of sirens billowed loudly across the countryside and LB turned to look. Against the dark green of the hillside, he counted three vehicles – an ambulance and further back, two police cars.

'Not long now,' Summer murmured to him, kissing his brow.

He nodded. Her white shirt had turned crimson and he knew that if Tolland tried to make a run for it, he wouldn't be able to stop him. He was pinning him down by sheer mass at the moment. She pushed her hand harder against his shoulder and he winced.

'Sorry,' she whispered.

The ambulance arrived a few minutes later. Paramedics rushed over to LB.

'Basement,' he said, inclining his head to the house. 'Worse than me.'

One of the paramedics headed over while the other tried to treat LB.

'I can't move. I'm holding this man under arrest. Go and treat the man in the basement until the police arrive,' he wheezed.

Summer glanced up as the police car rattled its way down the track.

'They're here,' she said.

***

A few minutes later, Tolland was cuffed and in the back of the police car and LB was lying on his back with a drip in the back of his hand, his wound dressed and bandaged. Patrick had been stretchered out to the ambulance. Summer had gasped when she'd seen him and run to his side. The kaleidoscope of colours almost overwhelmed her – horror, shock, fear, relief. She felt battered by them.

'Patrick?'

His eyes opened a crack and he stared dully at her.

'Summer? Huh? You found me.'

'Oh Jesus, what happened to you?'

She didn't get an answer. The paramedics elbowed her politely out of the way and carried Patrick to the ambulance. LB joined him a few moments later, leaving Summer staring into the vehicle, still rocked by intense colours.

'I'll follow,' she said as the paramedics closed the doors. Her eyes were on the receding image of the ambulance as the policeman nodded.

'Are you okay to drive?' he said, scrutinising her.

'What? Oh. Yes. Thanks. Yes, I'm fine.'

She looked down at herself, her hands still bloodied, her trousers covered in mud, and smiled. Yes. She was fine.

SATURDAY EVENING

'Well. Aren't you a sight for sore eyes, wrapped up so sexily in that.'

LB's eyes fluttered open and he took a moment to register where he was. As his eyes met Summer's she nodded at his hospital gown, tucked a sweet wrapper into her paperback to mark her page and laid the book on his bed. His eyes rested muzzily on her.

'Hey,' he said. 'I do my best.'

He struggled painfully to sit up, still groggy from the anaesthetic.

'Where the hell did you get that?' he asked, indicating her book. 'Do you just sprout them?'

She laughed.

'It was in the waiting room.'

Her brow furrowed and she flicked to the inside cover.

'"Placed here by the Rotary Club of The Howe of Fife",' she read. 'Well, presumably not *here*, but somewhere nearer *there*… "To promote literacy in the community. Please take this book and when you have finished reading it, leave it in a public place such as a bus station or waiting room, so that someone else may enjoy it."'

She closed the cover and arched her brows at LB over the top of the book.

'It's travelled a bit then,' he said, his fingers picking at the gown.

'You look lovely,' she said, smiling sarcastically.

'You can take your coat off if you're staying.'

'Not really. I used my shirt to staunch your blood.'

'I know.'

He smiled mischievously and she thumped his leg. He yawned and then apologised.

'Sorry. I'm exhausted. What time is it?'

'Half eight in the evening. It's still Saturday. They might kick me out soon.'

'Have you got anywhere to go?' he said, frowning.

'I could go home. Or maybe I'll just crash in the chapel here.'

'I would never have pegged you as religious,' he said, shuffling to sit up better.

'Oh I'm not. But they won't kick me out from there. And I might offer up some thanks while I'm in there. Just in case. I wouldn't want to seem ungrateful.'

He smiled, his fingers seeking hers on the bedcover.

'You rub me up the wrong way and drive me completely mad,' he murmured. 'But dear God I am pleased to see you.'

He lifted her hand to his lips and kissed her fingertips. She laughed.

'Ditto.'

She stood and leaned over to kiss him on the mouth, lingering there.

'But you're a bloody idiot, colliding with a knife like that!' she said as she sat down.

He squeezed her hands, watching the tears brighten her eyes.

'Easy target. I'm six foot three. You can't bloody miss me,' he said, keeping his voice low and tender.

She smiled.

'So, tell me what's happened?' he said quickly. 'I remember going into surgery but I've skipped a few hours since then.'

'Patrick's been taken into intensive care. He's got septicaemia and multiple fractures, including some skull fractures, according to the nurses I spoke to. He's not allowed any visitors. He's critical. Apparently you can look like you're getting better, but then take a turn for the worse a few days later so they're keeping a close eye on him.'

LB nodded. He'd seen the rash that covered Patrick and hoped they'd reached him in time.

'Do you know how he got septicaemia?' he asked, though he assumed that any one of the myriad contusions could have been the cause.

'His ankles. There are deep cuts around them. Where he'd been tied.'

Her voice wavered and LB hurried to move her on to a new topic.

'And Tolland?'

'Arrested. Spilling the beans I think. They wouldn't really tell me but they looked smug.'

Summer fell silent, fiddling with his fingers.

'Oh. Kate Hampton's out of intensive care,' she added. 'It was on the news earlier. She's still in hospital, but out of any danger. Paul *was* by her side, but one of the coppers said he'd been taken in for questioning. I'm not sure he was meant to have told me. She's saying it was a cry for help and they're appealing for some privacy.'

'Fat chance,' said LB, shaking his head. 'For a start, Lothian will need to talk to them about Bruce Macdonald retrieving those letters and trashing the place. And Tolland and Patrick. Tolland didn't do that of his own volition. They'll want to know who was giving the orders; Macdonald or Hampton himself.'

Summer nodded. LB shifted in the bed and gazed at her.

'And you?' he asked. 'How about you?'

'Me? I'm fine. No cuts, no bruises. I'm fine.'

He carried on staring at her, waiting for the truth.

'Well, mostly fine. I'm a bit shaken up. I've never lamped anyone like that before!'

He laughed.

'I'm glad you did.'

'Hmm. You told me to stay in the car or you'd knock me down yourself. Good job I don't pay much attention to you.'

'Mmm. Your inability to do as you're told was *most* welcome today.'

She scowled good-naturedly at him.

'I gave the police my statement while you were being stitched back together.'

'That probably took a while. Did it go okay?'

'Why wouldn't it?' she asked, her face sharp.

'Because you're prickly as a hedgehog?' he said, smiling. She poked her tongue out at him.

'It went fine. They said they'd talk to you and get your statement once you were fit enough to give it. Probably tomorrow morning.'

He nodded. It was all pretty open and shut since they'd found Patrick with Tolland, and if Tolland was talking it would be a straightforward series of arrests and trials. It was also unlikely now that Summer having trampled all over the scene of the abduction would be a problem, something that had been troubling LB for days and which he was eminently relieved about.

'Have you had any news about your friend in Malawi?' he said. 'I can't remember his name. The guy who was beaten up yesterday.'

'Moyenda? Yes! I texted him to ask him how he was and to say that we'd found Patrick. I didn't say anything about what had happened to him. Anyway, he texted back to say he's out of hospital. He also said to stop worrying about things as it would all be fixed in a week. He didn't explain what he meant though.'

LB's brow crinkled.

'Maybe he'll explain in a week. I'm glad he's okay.'

His fingers drew patterns on her hand.

'Summer, can I ask you something?'

She looked up.

'You sound nervous,' she laughed.

He smiled at her and shrugged, wincing as he did so.

'I've got some sick leave to take and you and I have had a pretty shocking few days. Would you like to spend a few days with me? In the Highlands, maybe? You could take lots of pictures if you wanted,' he added hurriedly, watching her face. 'Make it a working holiday perhaps?'

Summer settled back in her chair, studying him thoughtfully.

'I don't think so,' she said after a moment.

His heart sank but he managed to maintain a smudge of composure.

'The clouds are all wrong,' she added. 'I'll leave my camera behind and we can just have the holiday.'

ABOUT THE AUTHOR

Amanda Fleet is a physiologist by training and a writer at heart. She spent 18 years teaching science and medicine undergraduates at St Andrews University, but now uses her knowledge to work out how to kill people (in her books). During her time at St Andrews, she was involved with two Scottish Government funded projects, working with the College of Medicine in Blantyre, Malawi. While in Malawi, she learned about the plight of the many street children there and helped to set up a Community Based Organisation that works with homeless Malawian children to support them through education and training – Chimwemwe Children's Centre.

Amanda lives in Scotland with her husband, where she can be found writing, walking and running. *The Wrong Kind of Clouds* is her debut novel.

ACKNOWLEDGEMENTS

I would like to thank my husband, Colin Nicol, for his undying support in my life. Without his encouragement and belief in me, I would never have got to this point. I also want to thank Dea Parkin at Fiction Feedback who did such a fantastic job of editing this and from whom I learned a lot. My thanks also to my beta readers, especially Gerard McCabe and Liz Surtees, who both gave incredibly useful feedback on early drafts. A big thank you to Macdonald Nkhutabasa, who kept me right with the Chichewa and who does such fantastic work with the children in Chimwemwe Children's Centre. My thanks also to Graeme Bain and PC Tulloch from Police Scotland who helped me with the wording of the arrest. And last, but not least, to all those friends and relatives who believed I could do this. Thank you all.

If you want to keep up to date with all of the latest news, go to
www.amandafleet.co.uk

Find Amanda on Facebook
https://www.facebook.com/AmandaFleetWriter/

Follow Amanda on Twitter
@amanda_fleet1

Join the conversation
#TheWrongKindofClouds